THE
LAST
REDWOOD
CIRCUS

THE
LAST
REDWOOD
CIRCUS

A Novel

THOMAS HENRY POPE

SHIRES❦PRESS

Manchester Center, VT 05255

Name: Pope, Thomas Henry
Title: The Last Redwood Circus : a novel
Description: First Edition | Shires Press 2023
Library of Congress Control Number: 2023905143
ISBN: 978-1-60571-587-2 (Hardcover)
ISBN: 978-1-60571-588-9 (Paperback)

Cover by Dissect Designs

Printed in the United States of America

For Sierra and Eden

Acknowledgements

Year after year, the writing of this simple story surprised me both in its complexity and in the risks required to proceed. This resulted from including three protagonists from different cultures, each embodying a unique grasp of life.

I am grateful to the many people who offered access to resources and information on which this story is built. For the town of Greenley, I thank the community of the Anderson Valley and in particular, reporter Bruce McEwan of the Anderson Valley Advertiser. Mendocino County Sheriff Tom Allman gave me an extensive interview. For his patient explanations of logging, I am grateful to Ernie Pardini. John Andersen and Liz Gorbocci of the Mendocino Lumber Company generously gave me tours of their timberland and lumber mills.

I bow to the members of the Pomo bands of Redwood Valley, Potter Valley, Round Valley, Pinoleville, Manchester, Dry Creek, Coyote Valley, Hopland, and Cloverdale as they pursue dignity and justice.

Holly Newstead and Seasha Robb entered me into the worlds of circus life and gymnastics.

For temple builder, Tadao Kitamura, I relied on my travels to Asia, Buddhist teachers and fellow students, and on my years of designing and building timber frame houses and barns.

Over the long haul, my readers directed this journey: Thank you all for taking time on a work in progress: Jan Wax, Mimi Rich, Xenia King, John Hadden, Cindy Wilder, Barb Goodell, Tina Walter, Valerie Smith, Tom Joyce, and Marcia Bowman. Special thanks to Thom Elkjer.

The struggles of this work brought me to the good eyes, ears, and hands of several editors. Bryon Quertermous, Zoe Quinton, Conor Mintzer, and the incomparable Clair Lamb. I am fortunate for your skill.

Also by Thomas Henry Pope

Imperfect Burials
The Trouble With Wisdom

Author Links

https://thomashenrypope.com
tom@thomashenrypope.com
https://www.facebook.com/thomashenry.pope
Twitter: @thomashenrypope

This edition includes a **Discussion Guide** on the last pages.

A Note about Race and Names

At the time of publication, there are multiple ways to indicate descendants of the original people of this continent. Because of the fraught history between these peoples—whose tribes number close to six hundred—and the waves of immigrants who came after 1491, each name comes with cultural baggage.

Thinking he had arrived in the country of India, the early global traveler, Christopher Columbus, called the inhabitants "Indians." The name stuck—often as a racial slur to indicate members of an inferior race—until the second half of the 20th century, when descendants of the original inhabitants rose up seeking agency to claim their proper place in history and as stewards of their home lands.

They experimented with many names. In no particular order, they selected Amerindian, Native people, Indigenous people(s), Indigenous American, American Indian, First People(s), and the name of the tribe followed by Nation, EG Cherokee Nation. The umbrella term "Native Americans" faltered because it didn't include indigenous peoples of Canada or Central and South America. Interestingly, some tribes have reverted to calling themselves Indians. In the end, whatever name they come to remains a regional and tribal choice.

The result for the author is that no name is free and clear. The literary and linguistic ground is shifty and shifting. I have therefore made an effort to have each character use the names that would come naturally to them. There is no unanimity in their selection, and this mirrors where the culture stands today. Ishi Darkhorse calls himself several things, but he is a member of the fictitious Dead Creek band of the Pomo Nation of northern California.

Due to my white heritage, some may accuse me of cultural arrogance, or worse, for veering out of my "white" lane. As a storyteller, my commitment to the elements and themes of this story overrides this claim. Ishi Darkhorse's passion stands for more than a tribe or a race. He is a man dedicated to righting injustice to people and to the Earth. In this, Delicia Fortunado joins him fully.

One

Greenley, California

ISHI DARKHORSE SWITCHED off his kitchen light and went outside to be with the moon. A few days before full, it had just risen behind the decrepit trailer that came with his job at the newspaper.

Settled on the stoop, he marveled at how the light softened the remains of the burned-out house across the road. How, in the middle view, it cast long shadows of live oak trees onto the dead grass of the valley floor. And beyond, how it cast a golden tinge on the third-growth Douglas fir and redwoods that climbed the coastal hills.

An onshore wind from the Pacific rattled the leaves of the yard's huge eucalyptus tree. Like everything in the valley, the tree was fighting to stay alive in that fifth year of drought. The rainy season had offered only the ghost of a storm, and that had been back in December. This late in the winter, odds were against any more coming.

A month before, Ishi had stood five miles further west, on the cliffs of Northern California's rugged coast, hoping to salve the worst of his wounds from his time halfway around the world. Over and over, that moon had shot horizontal bolts of platinum into the curls of waves breaking after traveling all the way from Japan. Now, as he remembered that night, his subconscious added deformed seal pups tumbling out of that surf and flopping helplessly on the sand. In a flash, he saw the story that would keep him up most of the night.

THE NEXT MORNING, Ishi trotted up the redwood slab stairs to the office of the *Post-Ethical Times*. Though it was early, Efan Brodie's enormous back greeted him. Brodie's fingers were flying over his keyboard. His desktop screen was loaded with text. No steam rose from his coffee cup.

Ishi couldn't figure out what drove his boss to spend most of his waking hours in a room that hadn't been upgraded since the 1960s. Flat, hollow core doors. Wooden desks. Linoleum. Stacks of old newspapers impersonating indoor ornamental trees.

"Good afternoon, Mr. Darkhorse." Brodie's voice was cheery. His typing rolled on.

Four months in, Ishi was getting used to the old man. "I'm an optimist," Ishi said, settling at his corner desk. "Someday I'll be like you, successful in not having a life."

Brodie chortled, still typing. "I have faith in you. Funny, isn't it? Readers consider exposing the misdeeds of others to be romantic. Living with purpose. If that were so, I'd be living several lives concurrently." He raised his hands like a concert pianist at the end of a piece, and joined his palms over his heart. "God rest my fractured little soul. I wonder which one of me would die first." Nothing about Brodie qualified as little—his body, his confidence, his voice. Least of all his vision.

Ishi opened his laptop and turned his chair toward Brodie's. "You said it would happen someday. I'm here to report." He waited a beat. "I finally have a great idea."

Brodie turned, eyebrows raised.

"Not even a year after the nuclear meltdown in Japan, it's already fallen off the radar. And I figured out why. People aren't dying, at least not dramatically."

Brodie jutted his chin. "I grant you, Fukushima *is* a disaster. But it's five thousand miles away." He turned back to his work. "We have to sell papers here."

"Hold on," Ishi said. "Tokyo Electric Power is lying. They say everything at the site is under control. But they're releasing radioactive cooling water into the ocean. And I researched it last night. Only one international outfit still has a dedicated team there—*De Volkskrant*."

Brodie harrumphed. "Of course, the Dutch."

Ishi's enthusiasm would not be crushed. "They've done great work. They've reported on internal refugees, public anxiety, radiation, and the thousands of very polite fishermen unable to even give their catch away."

Brodie stopped typing and looked at the ceiling. "You're not telling me anything I haven't read."

Ishi rapped his index finger on his desk. "*Here's* the story. No one's asking if the ocean can handle the radioactivity, and if it *can't*, how much of it will reach California—which is where our readers live . . . and fish."

Brodie's look told Ishi what was coming. "If and when scientists tell us radiation is getting close, we'll nail that story."

"But no one here is studying it. We need to sound the alarm. Which is exactly what this little paper of yours is famous for." He glanced at the banner a devotee had sent Brodie years ago: *America's Last Real Newspaper*. Brodie had quickly adopted it for the subscript on the paper's masthead.

Brodie's tongue swelled his bottom lip. He tapped the "Save" key on his document, turned toward Ishi, and rested his forearms on his thighs. "Not bad. Keep it in a drawer somewhere. For now we've got to report in present time. The real threat to us this year is fire.

"I can't think of another local newspaper that has subscribers from Mississippi to Alaska. What draws them are local stories composed with absolute authenticity. The way we tackle state politics rings with global sensibility. Your talent is going to make you a great fit here. Your pieces on the night raids in Afghanistan were amazing. 'Native in a Strange Land' is brilliant. It has insight, emotion, and not a whiff of judgment."

One-handed, Brodie rooted in his briefcase. He pulled out a letter-sized sheet and laid it on his desk. "Here's today's work. My snitch in the county planning office faxed it over last night. She figured I'd want to find out why a shiny-shoed lawyer bought a landlocked piece of dirt up behind state land. My old knees aren't up to a walk in the woods. I need you to take a look."

The document was a detail of a US Geological Survey map. Brodie fingered a hand-drawn square in the middle, where topographic lines pinched tight on an already steep slope.

"You're free to call him, aren't you?" Ishi asked.

"And he's free to say nothing. It might help to get your eyes on it first."

"Who's the seller?"

"The county's largest landowner, Hanover Timber Company. Just over an acre. A steep one at that. The sale closed for $475,000. An ungodly price! What it would go for if it were in downtown Sacramento, next to Hanover's main offices. . . . I'm counting on you."

Ishi sighed at the wreckage of his plans. "Okay, but for the record, I'm telling you there's a Japanese invasion on its way."

Brodie tossed a casual salute. "Duly noted. As for the mission here, I suggest you take your gun."

Two

Yamagata, Japan

T HE HUMBLE ORPHAN Tadao Kitamura was still adjusting to the opportunity of a lifetime. Through the dedicated grace of his master Sensei Watanabe, Tadao had risen through the ranks of Watanabe and Son Temple Builders to become the designer of the most important new temple to be built in Japan since the war. Emperor Akihito himself had commissioned the project and shortly thereafter had plucked its name from a dream: The Temple of Listening.

Its placement on the main island's easternmost point was to honor the victims of the 2011 tsunami, whose first waves had barreled forth from a huge undersea earthquake to crash near the city of Miyako.

Tadao's most difficult challenge was to create a shrine that would pacify the celestial forces that had unleashed the suffering. First, he had to rule out the possibility that crucial mistakes made by past temple builders might have contributed to the tsunami from the Tohōku Quake that leveled the power plant at Fukushima. For this, he pored over fifteenth-century hand-printed manuscripts that measured almost a meter on a side. Laid out on those pages, Tadao found the development of the principles all modern temple builders took as gospel. The well-being of Japan's future lay in the balance of his reaffirming authentic access to the spiritual realm.

The other design pressure was the emperor's decree that the buildings stand for a thousand years without the need for repairs. Fortunately, over the centuries, Japanese laborers had planted extraordinary tracts of Hinoki cypress, the supreme native wood for temples, and those plantations had been meticulously maintained. Still, Tadao intuited the need for a revolution in design.

The oldest volumes contained prolific notes and drawings that addressed the art of seducing and pacifying these celestial beings, known as *kami*. Reviewing them, Tadao began to grasp how the designers' profound devotion to place, energy, and simplicity imbued their buildings with freshness that allowed humans and *kami* to commingle in peace.

He worked for weeks on this new paradigm, but every design faced the same problem: Hinoki cypress would not resist wind and moisture for a thousand years. Perplexed, Tadao arranged a meeting with Sensei at the master's house.

At the appointed hour, he found his old master napping in his bed. Gently, Tadao roused him.

Sensei rubbed his face and sat up, beaming. "Do you remember the day we met?"

"Of course. My life began that day."

Contentment radiated from Sensei's face.

"As was usual when adults came to the orphanage looking for children," Tadao said, "I distracted the boys who were crippled or too old to be selected."

"Yes," Sensei said. "I felt your kindness from across the courtyard. And what were you doing?"

"Building kites. But I didn't have proper pieces of wood, so I carved the little scraps we had to fit together to make bigger ones."

Sensei laughed, hiding his mouth behind his hand.

"Then you joined us and asked to borrow my knife, which was the only tool I had. You made what I was trying to do look so easy. All the boys wanted one of yours."

"I made three," Sensei said. "The last one was best." He shook his head. "May I tell you a secret? It was you who inspired me to make a kite that way. It would never have occurred to me. I'm a solid traditionalist. You were *my* teacher at that moment."

With a soft hand, Sensei eased Tadao's jaw back into place. "It takes time for a man to find his way in life, Tadao-san."

Though Sensei's legs were stiff from lying down, he took Tadao's arm and led him to the porch. There, he bade Tadao to sit in the chair next to his, usually reserved for the memory of his wife.

Tadao sat cautiously and took in the grounds. After the war, Sensei had resisted the cultural fascination with Western design. Instead, he'd stayed faithful to the ancient style. He'd made every cut with hand tools. Below wide granite stairs, a flagstone walkway meandered through a garden of perennials, ornamental boulders, and trees. Overhead, the house's thatch roof paid homage to centuries gone by.

Sensei gestured at the work. "I made the mistake of thinking that change was punishment for laziness. I thought if I was disciplined enough and never quit, things would always stay the same." He burst into laughter.

Tadao wondered what was so funny. His teacher had never admitted making a mistake.

At last, Sensei recovered. "But *I've* changed." He laughed again.

Lacking confidence to laugh with his teacher, Tadao spluttered.

"You are probably too young to understand," Sensei said, almost laying his hand on Tadao's knee. "But it's funny when you see that your whole life has been based on narrow views. Because of my nature, I chose a career that held onto the past." He tossed his head toward the building where the Watanabe woodworking crews were at work.

Sensei was talking like an earthquake. Nothing was stable. The immaculate garden could not keep Tadao's mind in the present.

"Mrs. Watanabe and I had both dreamed we would have two sons." He squinted, looking at the past. "But after Satoru, no other child came. Finally, Mrs. Watanabe said to me, 'Go to the British orphanage. It could be smart someday to have a Japanese son who speaks English.'" Sensei pointed at Tadao's breastbone. "There *you* found *me*." He placed his palms together over his heart and bowed.

Tadao worried that the water in his teacher's eyes might become tears. That would be a tragedy that could never be taken back.

"I have decided to make you the person to lead Watanabe into this new and strange century."

Tadao finally found his breath. "But Satoru is—"

Sensei held up his hand. "I have already spoken to him. He will be a solid right hand to you."

"But, Sensei, you know about my—" Tadao raked his hands in front of his body. "My family disease. The radiation. I won't live long. What will happen to Watanabe then?" He lowered his eyes at Sensei's intense look.

"Who can tell us when we are going to die?"

Tadao could not answer.

"I had beliefs about my life and the world, Tadao-san. Now I see they were, if not wrong, not correct, either. Don't make the same mistake. Help the world wake up, and however long you walk this earth, it will be a life well-lived."

"Do I have permission to say no?"

Sensei laughed again. "We can't say no to our nature. Now why did you wake me?"

Three

A T THE FIRST hint of daylight, Delicia jumped into her bush clothes and slipped her camera bag over one shoulder. Before leaving her room, she patted her pocket to confirm she had the keys.

Someone listening to her footsteps on the compound's main house stair would have sensed she'd settled on a midway point between expressing her fury and trying to not wake Joseph and that woman he was with. After a fitful night, the only cure for her anxiety was a destination far from people.

The jeep's tires rattled over the cattle guard beyond the holding pens, and she headed east across the savannah. She had no question where she would first go to look for them: the watering hole by Tragic Rocks. Over the last twenty months, she had taken at least 200 great photos from a concealed spot there.

At the watering hole, her heart sank. The site was deserted. She combed the ground and concluded they hadn't been there since the previous morning. She tracked them north, thinking she might find them in the Sammundo Basin. But as the sun broke the horizon, her binoculars revealed only wildebeests and a small herd of impalas.

The elephants had no need for *her* that morning, she realized. And being alone was already working the magic she needed. With less ambition, she drove toward the big mountain. For reasons even Joseph couldn't explain, they often ventured there if one of the elephant cows was to give birth.

In this more open location, she parked a mile from where she had seen them some weeks before. At the last minute, she grabbed the 30.06 in case a predator cat showed up. She wasn't a hunter—far from it—and Robbie had warned her it was too small a gun for a lion. Still, she hoped that if she needed it, it could give her time to get back to the jeep. Her mood that morning didn't include a death wish—at least for herself. She chose a route concealed in shoulder-high shrubs, pausing often to listen and to check behind her.

She heard them before they came into view. The concern she had upon waking that morning turned to worry. Many were trumpeting in a pitch new to her.

Bending low, she pushed forward. They were standing, bunched, facing a pair of trees across the savannah—their trunks raised, bellowing, feet stamping, bodies rocking, ears spread and waving. The calves were sheltered behind them.

Delicia followed their gaze. Sure enough, a trio of lions, brazen, assessed their options from raised ground a hundred yards away. Watching from on high, vultures circled.

The bastards!

Thinking to scatter the lions, she aimed her rifle over their heads and pulled the trigger.

Inga, the second matriarch, wheeled and made a symbolic charge not toward the lions but toward Delicia. Her movement exposed a downed elephant. Half her head had been hacked off. Her tusks had been taken.

In her horror Delicia scanned the herd through her binoculars, counting. The one not standing—so the one down—was Maya, the one she loved the most, the matriarch of the herd.

Four

ISHI RETURNED TO his trailer and emerged in his camo gear. His travel camera and Sig Sauer M18 rode on his belt. There was no need for conversation about the wisdom of taking the gun. Greenley sat square in the Golden Triangle, media-speak for the three outlaw counties whose thick forests were home to illegal marijuana growers. The vast tracts of forest allowed scrappy locals and foreign cartels to stay ahead of law enforcement in a shifting game of Whack-a-Mole. The high murder rate in the triangle was surely an undercount. Growers, dealers, transporters, and simple thieves were constantly encroaching on each other's operations.

Ishi confirmed that his machete was behind the seat of his truck and pulled out of that residential canker sore, passing the hovels of his neighbors, mostly the families of illegals who worked the vineyards. Tethered mongrel dogs bayed at him.

He drove north on Main Street, the only road through town, past the *Post-Ethical Times* office, up the two-lane highway, past the grammar and high schools and the old-timey museum that offered a lackluster tribute to the early days of logging; past expansive vineyards on both sides of the road, each marked by a tasting room that, in season, catered to tourists from the Bay Area; past the lane to the resort for at-risk children who were sent up from that same Bay Area; and through a cluster of buildings too small to be called a village, with its Catholic church, modest grocery store, and its little hotel shuttered tight, waiting for spring.

He drove on, passing ten more vineyards, the pottery studio, and a lumber yard that stood in the middle of nowhere. At last, he turned left on the road that would take him west across the Greenley River and up to the top of the coastal hills.

Heading down to the river, he noticed that the sign marking the right-hand driveway into Minkle's Orchard looked the worse for wear. Surprising, since it was a prime piece of the valley's agricultural wealth. But tastes had changed. The assault of wine money had left Minkle's the last orchard standing in a valley that used to have nothing else.

The property had an extraordinary neighbor to the west. A great swath of virgin redwoods on the hillside ran right down to the river. No local could remember what magical force had compelled the nineteenth-century loggers to stop clearcutting those giants when they came to that section of the Greenley. In the 1940s, the state had rescued that stand from the Beckett family, which had held it since the loggers moved north. They'd created Beckett State Forest to protect forever some of the best old-growth coastal redwood groves in California.

Ishi had met those 1,500-year-old trees during a sixth grade field trip. When he'd returned from overseas, he was sad to learn the state had closed the park to balance the budget. Wine enthusiasts just weren't interested enough in trees to pay foresters to live and work there.

The bridge that crossed the river was from an earlier time—one lane, arching long and gracefully over what had been an important spawning stream for salmon and steelhead. The drought was driving a final nail into the species that had called Greenley home since before humans arrived.

Had Beckett been open, the shortest route to the acre Ishi sought would have been hiking up from Beckett's main campground and crossing into Hanover Timber's holdings, which stretched over the hills all the way to the coastal highway. As it was, he drove uphill past the Beckett sign, now overgrown, and through long switchbacks to the height of land. To keep people from going through his truck, he pulled deep into the Forest Service fire access road. He estimated he had a three-and-a-half mile walk ahead of him.

The Hanover land was rebounding after a second-growth cut some eighty years earlier. Poison oak and invasive plants narrowed the fire roadway. Between enormous redwood stumps, still resisting decay from the *first* clear-cut in the late 1860s, Douglas fir was growing strong. Drought had made the land crisp.

As the military had trained him, Ishi hushed the sound of his boots.

Two miles in, fresh four-wheeler tracks coming up from the ocean side warned him of drug growers. He heard no motors but to be smart, he walked a course parallel to the road fifty feet downslope.

When he gauged he'd traveled three miles, he took an azimuth northeast descending toward the acre Brodie's snitch had marked. Before long he came upon two parallel courses of orange plastic tape on branches and on stakes driven into the ground. Signs of surveying. The lines wound their way downhill in what was clearly a layout for a two-lane road with turns sweeping wide enough for large trucks. A mile on, yellow ground stakes marked the uphill boundary of the acre. Beyond them, the land fell away sharply into a chasm.

Hearing water, Ishi circled around and down the slope and came to a frothy blue spring, gushing fiercely enough to keep the pool below it flushed clean. Why had he never heard of this cascade of water several miles above the state forest? It was a blessed sight. And an even more blessed sound.

Someone with deep pockets was planning a road across vicious terrain to get to it. Perhaps a savvy dope grower was preparing to go legit in anticipation of marijuana becoming legal. The purity of the water suggested a water bottling plant. That would explain the width of the road. Or perhaps some hedge fund type was going to drop in a private retreat. Ishi's lips curled at the sacrilege.

The chasm above the spring climbed steeply. Through a break in the trees, a column of light lit the pool. As chilly as the day was, Ishi stripped and dove in.

The cold of the water stunned his system. Feeling himself sink, Ishi swam hard back and forth. He had never been in water so clean. He emerged lighter, as if the water had ripped away some emotional layer. Perhaps to avoid the shadow of other emotions, he quickly labeled it as guilt.

With new-found energy, he decided to follow the water down to the river, use Greenley's riverbed as a trail out, and catch a ride up the mountain to his truck.

THE SHIFT OF the trees from sixty-year-old Douglas fir to old-growth redwoods reminded him of the time he'd walked off San Francisco's Grove Street into the grandeur of Symphony Hall. The feeling was akin to heartbreak. This tiny pocket of glory didn't do justice, *couldn't* do justice, to all that had been lost at the hands of those who had so thoroughly "discovered" California. Adding insult to injury, no one was coming to experience the power and chaos pulsing through this primeval land.

Time was getting on. Walking around fallen behemoths was slowing him down. Brodie wanted two articles from him that afternoon. Vowing to return some day, Ishi left the water course and made a beeline for where he thought the Beckett campground was. When he reached groomed trails, he was happy to find nature reclaiming them. They led him to the complex of buildings. From there, he trotted out to the main road and stuck out his thumb.

He had lived for so long with one foot in the white world, he was a little surprised at how many cars passed him by. But Greenley was still firmly in the grip of 1950s America, which was why Brodie hiring him had been a stroke of grace.

As soon as he turned to climb the grade, a yellow Ford truck with peeling paint pulled over for him. He never expected a woman to bother giving him a ride, let alone two. They were as opposite as first glances could make them. As the passenger moved over to make room for him, he saw smooth skin and a fit body packed into jeans. Her hair, straight and dark, made him think indigenous, like him, but when she sat up, her features said European. Late twenties. The driver was a generation or more older, tough and wrinkled. Freckles on her arms.

She turned to him. "Did you fall off the troop truck?"

Her breath smelled of cigarettes. Her eyes blazed humor. She looked at him a little longer than most people did, especially when she should have been paying more attention to pulling back onto the road.

He'd forgotten he was in his army camo gear. Maybe she hadn't seen he had a sidearm holster until it was too late. When he laughed, the woman beside him relaxed a little. She had pulled her body over enough so that they wouldn't touch. She gave him a quick glance. Dark eyes that saw a lot. An arresting face.

"Thanks for saving me a hard hike."

"I figured you'd die trudging up this grade in those boots," the driver said. "Are you a Pomo?"

He liked her a lot. "Yes, ma'am."

"I'm planning to never be old enough to be called ma'am," she said. "I'm Stephanie Lugano. I live in the village on Elkjer Lane."

"I'm Ishi. Ishi Darkhorse. I appreciate the lift."

"Ishi. Is that some kind of Japanese name?"

"No, ma'am . . . Sorry. No. It's the name of the last wild Indian in California. He was the only survivor of the ambush of his tribe."

"Oh, Darkhorse. You're the fellow Efan Brodie hired after his partner got sick. I've been reading your articles." She addressed her passenger. "We've got the coolest little paper you've ever seen right here in Greenley. This is my niece, Delicia Fortunado. Have you heard of her?"

Ishi shook his head. "Should I have?" He felt rude for talking as if Delicia weren't there, so he looked at her. "Don't take it hard. I've been away."

"Afghanistan, right?" Stephanie caught Ishi's look and shrugged. "It's a small town. We don't have anything to do here except talk."

"Maybe I should get my news from you," he said.

Stephanie laughed and elbowed the young woman. "Today's news should announce that my niece is in town. Not a big story . . . until you find out who she is. Delicia's the one you want to talk to."

Delicia stiffened.

"She's famous. She's—"

"Stephanie, please."

"It's going to come out eventually, honey. If you talk to him first, you can—what do they call that? Control the narrative."

With Delicia turned away from him, Ishi looked at her again. She was in amazing shape. Upright posture. The muscles in her forearms had definition. Her hands were used to work, nails cut short.

"May I ask what you do?"

Delicia sighed. "I was an aerialist."

While he was trying to remember what that was, Stephanie said, "High wire. One of the world's best. And she will be again. The only one to ever do the moonwalk on the wire."

Delicia seemed caught between embarrassment, irritation, and pride. Not a place Ishi would have expected anyone described as world-famous to find herself.

"Can we talk about something else, please?"

They sat in silence as Stephanie hauled around several uphill 180-degree turns.

"How long are you here for?" Ishi asked.

"Not very long if she keeps embarrassing me."

"I'm sorry, honey. I don't get out much. I am so happy you came to see me." Stephanie changed her voice to get Ishi's attention. "She just flew in from Africa." And with more warmth again to Delicia, "We're going to get you back in shape and turn you loose on the world better than ever."

Ishi waited a few beats. "It's good you have a champion on your side."

His words made him lonely. Maybe it was time to call his adoptive parents.

He thanked Stephanie when she dropped him at the top of the grade. To Delicia he said, "If you ever care to tell your story, I'll be faithful in presenting it."

Five

BRODIE PRINTED OUT Ishi's best picture of the spring and pinned it to the wall they used to map out their more complicated stories. He and Ishi both sensed this one-acre sale was the cherry on top of a cake they couldn't see.

The break came two days later, when the snitch from the county records department sent a closing statement for another deed signed by the same straw-buyer lawyer. Judging from the sales tax, Hanover Timber Company had, for a pittance, granted the rights to the water course from the spring down to the back border of Beckett State Forest in a fifty-foot right-of-way.

The document rattled Brodie. He pinned it up alongside the US Geological Survey section that had come with the deed for the spring. Then he went quiet awhile, staring at that wall and occasionally writing a note.

To break the mood, Ishi said, "Same seller, same buyer, ostensibly the same project. What's the possible reason for these two sales closing on different days?"

Brodie nodded. "A lawyer padding his account? Possible." His tone said that wasn't it. "Technically, the same lawyer doesn't mean the same buyer. In any case, my gut says 'obfuscation.' Small sales draw less attention than large ones. There's a lot of money behind it, and now it's knocking on the door of state land. It's no secret I wouldn't trust our governor to take the family car to Tastee Ice Cream. The water from the spring already runs through the state land, so whoever needs that water ain't the state."

"Could the state be planning to reopen the park?"

"Haven't heard a peep about that. But, like I say, they've already got the water."

"Could the buyer be *working* for the state? Maybe the state's going to build a reservoir in the forest."

"From what you say, the water from the spring is about all that is feeding the river anymore. If the state dams it up, it's bye, bye, Greenley River. The vineyard owners wouldn't stand for that. They're on the edge as it is."

After they completed their articles for the day, Brodie set Ishi to compile a list of surveyors between Mendocino and Sacramento. "Call each one. We're looking for a loose pair of lips that'll tell us if they've done work for Hanover—and if we get lucky, who the buyer is. Use your Pomo charm."

Ishi went to work, wondering what if anything characterized Pomo charm.

Brodie was poring over the declaration list of donations to Governor Murphy's campaign, looking for a hidden quid pro quo from Hanover or a group of its principal officers. He swore.

"What'd you find?"

"No." Brodie ignored Ishi's question. Then louder, "No! I should have known. You ever heard of De Boulette?"

Ishi shook his head.

Brodie raised his eyebrows and pointed to Ishi's desk. "Google them and let's talk."

Champagne producer Domain De Boulette announced itself as the *world's number two purveyor of fine Champagnes and wines*. Ishi's service in the mountains of a foreign land had kept him in the dark about the fact that De Boulette Champagne was fast becoming the drink of the world's elite. *Celebrating dignity and love*, its tagline said. Backed by ocean views, models in white silk gowns held glistening flutes and eyed square-jawed leading men, who posed in studied indifference.

"That starts at about sixty-five dollars a bottle," Brodie said, looking over Ishi's shoulder, "for the bad harvests. De Boulette has wanted a place in this valley for the last fifteen years. One prize property after another has been denied them through serendipitous misfortune—read: local manipulation. The vineyards don't want De Boulette's cutthroat competition here. I just found their donations to Murphy's campaign sky-rocketed three years ago."

He looked at his watch. It was almost quitting time. "We've got to see Josh Minkle right now. This time of year, he'll be working late."

BRODIE DROVE THEM north out of town. He turned west on the road to the coast, and right into the main entrance of Minkle's public compound. Perhaps for aesthetic considerations, some owner decades before had chosen to keep the apple processing and equipment barns back from the road. The driveway snaked up pleasing curves through five acres of mature apple trees. At the Y, Brodie followed the sign for the barns.

Business must have been good once to necessitate such a sizable parking lot. Both barns had the Ackerman County roofline design, a large main gable flanked by flatter pitched additions. Ishi had seen a touched-up photo of them on the jugs of Minkle Cider in stores as far away as Sacramento and Eureka. In real life, their metal roofs were brown with rust. Their siding needed paint. An antique wagon with wooden spoked wheels sat in a grassy area in need of trimming.

Last fall's harvest was long gone. The sliding doors to the storage and pressing barn were open. The earth inside and out was a fine red powder.

"Go give a holler for Josh," Brodie said.

Ishi got out and did, but an empty building has a certain feel. He made a tour of the equipment barn. Machinery of different decades and in various states of disrepair filled the open bays under the additions. He returned to the car and told Brodie he heard a tractor motor idling somewhere to the north.

Minkle's property sat between the valley's two-lane highway on the east and the river and Beckett's redwoods on the west. A gentle north-south ridge ran the length of the property like a spine. It shed early and late frosts. Excellent for apples.

Brodie drove his Mercedes through a section of some of the oldest apple trees Ishi had ever seen. He knew the farm roads and stopped beside a rough metal building that had its door pulled back. At the sound of the car, a wiry man in his late fifties lifted up from his task at the work-bench.

They met in the worn ground outside the shop. The man's face was kind, weathered, framed in grey curls and long sideburns. He showed his grease-covered hands as a reason to not offer a handshake.

"It's rarely good news when you come to see me, Efan." He scanned Ishi. "But if you've brought me a pruner, I'll be grateful."

"This is my new man, Ishi Darkhorse. And you're right. I have bad news."

"Josh Minkle," the man said to Ishi. "What's up now?"

Brodie pointed up the slope. "We have articles soon to come out about a couple of land sales above you."

"Hanover?"

"It was news to me, but you've got a spring on the mountain above you."

"So I've heard, but I've never been there. Too busy. But without the water coming through Beckett, this valley wouldn't have much of a river anymore."

"I went up there two days ago," Ishi said. "It's quite a spring."

"And somebody's bought it," Brodie added.

"Bought it? On Hanover land? That's wild woods up there, isn't it? Who bought it?"

"We came to ask if De Boulette has been back around lately."

"Jesus!" Minkle went into the shop and returned rubbing his hands on a grease rag. "Those bastards!"

"It's a straw purchase, Josh. So we don't know the buyer yet. We're working to crack the case. Have you seen any of their people lately?"

"Yeah, that Olympic prick Baskin came by in late December with a couple of goons. Found them kicking around my main barns as if they'd never been here before. They were indirect. Which made me worry. Baskin said they'd just come by to say hello. Like we were old friends." He turned to Ishi. "They made me miserable a couple years back. Of-fered me different deals to buy me out. Money nobody would sniff at. I told them it's not for sale. They'd rip out all my trees and put in a vineyard for a tax write-off. What the hell would they be going to do with the spring?"

"I was hoping you could tell us. There is another piece that worries me more. Same straw buyer bought a right-of-way for the course of the water from the spring down to Beckett's uphill boundary. We'll keep you informed and—"

"You do that."

Brodie's irritation seemed to tip toward agitation. "I can't imagine things have changed since the last time we talked about it, but have you got plans for that 350-acre piece on the north end?"

"Not with the drought. As you know, I'd love to expand up there, but in this climate young apples need a lot of water."

"Would you mind if I take Mr. Darkhorse up there to see it?"

"Any time."

Six

EVEN THOUGH DAYLIGHT was fading fast, "any time" turned out to be right then. Brodie made his way back to the valley's main road and headed north. In a section rendered nondescript by roadside brush, he eased left across the southbound lane and into a narrow pull-off Ishi had never noticed.

Brodie got out, leaving his door open. Concealed in the undergrowth, moss grew thick on a split rail that hung between two rotting posts. It broke when Brodie lifted it, and he threw the pieces aside. Beyond was a dirt track with grass between the ruts. He drove, oblivious to scraping his undercarriage—which, considering it was his wife Dori's car, underlined his impatience.

On Brodie's side, a little house with a collapsed porch pressed close. Leafless vines of poison oak snaked over and under the clapboards.

The road climbed through switchbacks. Brodie's tires spun in loose gravel. At last, they came to a vast open area, at least two hundred acres, level like the valley floor. Brodie drove halfway along the northern edge, swung the wheel, parked heading down the valley, and killed the motor. Ahead of them, the craggy stumps of a vineyard gone by stood askew in their rows like headstones in an eighteenth-century cemetery. A hundred yards to their right, a wall of mammoth redwoods bordered the vineyard. The top arc of the full moon had just broken the line of the eastern hills.

Brodie hitched his right knee onto the console and exhaled loudly through his nose. "I think it's time I get something off my chest."

"Up here?"

"Just listen. Can you just listen?"

Ishi couldn't read the look Brodie gave him.

"When Dori heard you were a Pomo, she told me to hire you. She thought it would help."

Ishi felt slammed on the sternum. He'd dealt with every kind of weirdness about his heritage, but he'd never suspected Brodie would be so condescending. "I don't need any help." He flashed on the bitterness that ate at him in his first year in the elite boarding school to which his adoptive parents had sent him.

Brodie hammered his thigh with a fist. "No. She thought it would help *me*." He studied the redwoods.

Ishi sat bewildered.

"A couple years ago, I came into possession of a trove of papers going back 160 years. I thought it was a journalist's dream . . . until I started going through them. Turns out they were papers of the surviving brother of a pair from Ohio, named Samuel and Charles Gervin. They came looking for gold.

"I never knew that, in the beginning, Indians worked claims, too, right alongside the whites." He put his hands on the steering wheel as if to keep his emotions in check. "But late-coming miners saw them as competitors for 'their' claims. Charles tells how they killed Indian miners and stole their gold right off their bodies. That first year, though, one of Samuel's victims wasn't quite dead. He reached up and cut Samuel's throat."

Ishi revealed none of the joy that flashed through him hearing how justice had been served.

"His death inspired Charles to what you might call missionary zeal. He signed up with a state-sponsored militia to"—he waited a second—"kill Indians for five dollars a head."

The balance of discomfort shifted to Ishi.

"After they wiped out the Nisenan, Charles joined the militia heading north." Long pause. "Do you know Bloody Island?"

Ishi nodded with gritted teeth. Every Pomo knew Bloody Island.

Brodie opened his door. "Let's get out."

A minute later, they leaned against the front fender of the Mercedes and faced the trees. "Charles Gervin aspired to literary fame. His account of Bloody Island in the *Daily Alta California* would have made John Wayne puke. Over twelve years, he led five campaigns: two against the Tolowa, and one each against Sinkyone, Yuki, and Wailaki. He died in Arcata a very wealthy man."

Brodie knowing tribal names was a surprise. Still, Ishi wanted to kill the messenger.

"Come," Brodie said. He walked slowly and talked to the ground. "As you know, I am a dedicated cynic. And I've had to cut through a thick layer of American jingoistic narrative to get some semblance of reality about all this. Whites who failed in the gold fields took tribal hunting grounds to graze their cattle and horses. Forced into privation, Natives killed cows to survive. In 'retaliation,' militias tracked bands at night by their fires, surrounded them, and slaughtered them at first light. Ethnic cleansing under the guise of justice."

As usual, Brodie had done his homework.

The full moon began to rise. Halfway to the redwoods, Brodie stopped and pointed. "Amazing specimens, aren't they? The hill offers protection from coastal storms." He extended both arms, and turned a full 360 degrees. "It's a beautiful valley. Pastoral, serene, rich. People come every year by the thousands to glimpse hope and drink the wine from this soil." He kicked the dead stump of a vine. It broke clean off.

"I've always been amazed there's no history of Indians ever being here. Probably the only valley in this part of the state that didn't have any. But just look at it.

"Eighteen months ago, in the last box of Gervin's papers, I found a typewritten sheet. He wrote it late in life, and it was like a story he could no longer keep to himself. The account describes this place to a T." He motioned to the redwoods and the cliff across the valley, eroded to look like a pipe organ.

"I believe he found a Pomo village on this spot. A big one." He turned to Ishi. "As far as I can figure, he never published this story." He stopped, as if begging for something. "Dori's been pushing me to stop keeping this news to myself."

Ishi felt Brodie's mix of fear and grief as precursors to assault. He freed his hands for anything. "You better have a good reason for telling me this."

Brodie held a breath and let it out with a blast. "I'm sorry the timing is all wrong. I'd thought I'd let a year or more go by before bringing you here. But my gut tells me De Boulette is up to no good again. It's always been my intention to make this detail of history right. I want you to break this story, Ishi. If you're willing, I'll give you a copy of Charles's account."

AT THE OFFICE, Brodie handed Ishi a two-page article. Attached was a sticky note: *August 1856.*

An Action Against the Pomo at Singing River

Proceeding from our victory over the Wintu on the 21st, we rode south and then inland from the ocean town of Mendocino keeping to the ridges, so we could observe two valleys at once. At about four o'clock on the 30th, our scouts saw signs of a village on the eastern side of the coastal range about three miles ahead and perhaps a thousand feet lower. Tired as we all were from forty days on our mission to pacify California, I was proud of how quietly my men moved and how we reached the valley before the last of the daylight. We secured our mounts, leaving them with our Indian scouts, two Tolowa that were indentured to me and a Karok volunteer. After midnight we climbed a slope and found the village on a large open piece of land using a stand of massive redwoods and a coastal hill as protection from the weather. Next to a good river, it was a perfect site for a cattle ranch. To find the place again, I made note of a peak to the east where elements had etched a cliff to look like the pipes of a church organ.

With exceeding care, we surrounded them and waited for dawn with our rifles at the ready. I announced the attack by firing my Sharps into the wikiup where I presumed the chief slept. Our guns rolled like thunder and we shot as fast as we could reload. Under the rain of lead, some of the wikiups collapsed before anyone could come out. As we'd seen many times, male savages made to defend their families by sprinting out with arrows notched. Most were cut down before they could string a second one. Women emerged, dragging their children in the direction of the river. Because savages can disappear like snakes, we did everything we could to keep them in the open ground. The air was blue with gun smoke and the blessed sound of Indians dying. At my signal, we charged and chastised them with swords, hatchets and knives as efficient as any army unit. With the exception of two squaws that we held for their beauty, we spared no one. Not even babies, because nits make lice. Before the sun had crested the eastern hills, the valley was at peace.

We took one hundred and eighty-seven scalps, which was a record for my command and the most of any engagement I witnessed except for Bloody Island.

To burn the bodies, we built a pyre with the wikiup materials and threw on their foodstuffs, tools, and baskets in case another tribe on the run happened to find the place. All that day and into the night, my men relieved themselves of their well-earned loneliness with the two squaws until they passed away. I did not join in their pleasure, because of my sanctified love for Jenny and because of the disease all squaws have. We lost one man, a Daniel Fitzgerald from Crescent City, who took an arrow in the neck when he was reloading. He died the next day and we gave him a Christian burial. It was a sorrowful journey leading his horse home to his family.

IT WAS LATE. The bed in Ishi's trailer called to him. Instead, he drove over the hills that held the headwaters of the Greenley River. The road descended into a smaller watershed that in good years would see sixty inches of rain, rugged land that backed up into the inland slope of the King Range. The ocean side of those hills was so rugged it had long ago earned the name The Lost Coast, because it had defied attempts to carve a road along it. It stood as the last, proud stretch of California's pre-white past.

The sign announcing the Dead Creek Rancheria had collapsed during Ishi's service abroad. Anticipating the event, some mischievous Pomo had set up a pool of money to be awarded to the person who guessed closest to the date that the sign would fall. Everyone agreed it was better use of funds than putting up a new sign.

In the late 1950s, the logging company that had leased the land from the state clear-cut it and left it looking as if it had been bombed. State foresters predicted the redwoods and Douglas fir would be slow to regenerate on account of the poor quality of the soil. Broad swaths of the land grew up in manzanita, willow, and live oak, all generously veiled in poison oak.

Ishi's band of Pomo had never been granted a viable home. It shuffled from pillar to post while its petitions for recognition were ignored. Finally, in its parsimonious wisdom, the state had carved out this 428-acre plot to become their Rancheria.

It was close to midnight when Ishi passed the Grandma oak, a colossal mushroom-shaped specimen with twisted limbs that was the Rancheria's central landmark. Every Dead Creek Pomo event took place under its huge crown. Being useless for timber, the clear-cutters had left it. A circle of road enclosed it and the grassy area it stood in. Like spokes on a wheel, five roads ran off from the circle to houses and trailers spread across the land.

Even at that hour, several people stood by the dregs of a fire in the outdoor grill. Ishi wound his way along the dirt track north and parked behind Amber's weather-beaten sedan. To defend against being shot, he made no effort to mute his arrival. Not that Amber was quick to draw—she didn't have a gun—but if her brother, Marco, were with her and his 16-year-old testosterone had driven him to get one, Ishi made sure to announce himself. He slammed his driver's door and let his boots resonate on her little wood porch.

A dim glow shone from inside the house, which had started out as an old Airstream trailer. It had been put up on blocks and had two wood extensions added. Amber's father had left it for her a couple years before, as part of his galloping off with a redheaded redneck he met at the Gunner Casino outside Santa Rosa.

Ishi rapped, then rapped a second time.

Marco appeared disheveled and sleepy, not at all the defender of the home. He perked up the minute he saw Ishi.

"Ho, Ishi. Good to see you. What's the news? Got any beer? Want to hang?"

Ishi patted Marco's shoulder. "Not tonight. We will, though. I promise. Maybe we'll go diving for abalone when the season opens. Came here to see your sister."

Marco snorted. "I knew that. I'm not stupid. But she ain't here. She went to Healdsburg with Bernice. Don't know if she'll be back tonight." Marco waved toward the back room. "But she won't mind."

Ishi was too tired to strategize another plan. Saying thanks, he made his way through the nine-by-nine living room, where the TV was on low, and down the little hall to Amber's room. She kept it clean. The bed was made, which always made Ishi pleased and uncomfortable. He knew how to pass muster, of course, but if no one was checking, he'd let things slide. He slipped off his rough clothes and was asleep in a minute.

He was awakened by an emotional wind zipping into the room in the form of Amber, who was undressing as if trying to win a contest for doing it. Her cool skin joined him under the covers, and her hands ripped off his underwear.

"You wouldn't believe how pissed I was coming home," she said. "I had Bernice drive me out to your place on the way through Greenley. And when you weren't there, I was gonna kill you." She kissed him as if it were second best to inhaling him.

No one on any continent had ever kissed him as good as Amber did. Right from the first time under the Grandma Oak, when he was thirteen and she was twelve. She was at least half the reason he'd found his way back to the Rancheria after his service.

IN THE MORNING, before they were awake enough for words to come, they made love again. After, still sitting astride him, she wound her long hair back and up.

"You being here was the nicest surprise."

He ran his hands down her breasts and cupped her hips. "It's always like coming home, babe. Sorry it's been so long."

She cocked an eyebrow. "If you tease me about home, I'll tie you up right now and call it done." She lifted her hips, letting him slide out of her, and lay beside him.

She was right. His push-pull about settling down and even about where he belonged on the planet had stirred every emotion between them that men and women could have. "Are you losing a little weight?"

Her exhale signaled relief at the change of subject. "Might be. I'm doing a lot of dancing. Mama Lupine says she's gonna die soon. She wants us to learn all she knows before she does. She works us pretty hard." She nuzzled his neck. "Come dance with me. Eli says you were really good when you were a kid."

"I don't think he ever saw me dance," Ishi said. "If he did, he was probably so drunk even a possum looked like a good dancer."

Ishi's memories of dancing were tucked behind those of his mother's illness. His father, Eli, and Uncle Zack had been shipped off to San Quentin—three to five, for driving someone else's Mercedes. The tragedy was, they'd had no particular destination in mind. At twelve, Ishi was man of the house. His mother said his going to school was the only thing that could please her. So he went and did well. His dearest boyhood memories were those few smiles she gave him that weren't masking her pain. Shortly after her death, the Studebaakers came looking for an Indian boy to raise.

"Old history, Ishi. Now he's telling us all to stop drinking. I'm worried about Marco. He's started, you know. I think I should quit, for his sake."

He looked at her with more consternation.

"It pulls at me sometimes." She shook her head. "Like it wants to swallow me up."

He cradled her jaw until her worry eased. "He *is* sixteen," he said.

"But he acts younger."

"As long as he's not doing meth."

"I don't think he is. I warned him he'd have to move out."

"Is he still skipping school?"

"Can't make him go. Maybe he'll listen to you. He's got that picture of you in his clothes box. The one in your dress uniform you sent me before you shipped out. I stared at it so much the color faded."

"I'd hate to disappoint him, but I don't think he's Marine material."

BEING PART LATINA, Amber whipped them up a plate of chilaquiles. They shared it standing near the warmth of the stove. Then they took Ishi's truck down the road to Eli's house. Ishi still had his choice of bridges to rebuild with his father.

Seven

ON DELICIA'S FOURTH day in Greenley, her jet lag headache was fading. Her visual sense was more reliable. Her body, long accustomed to hard exertion, was rebelling against the forced inactivity of airports and airplanes and against her disrupted sleep. Her aunt Stephanie offered her little beyond fresh eggs, constant chatter, and a chair in the sun.

Stephanie had left early for her twelve-hour shift at the hospital in the county seat. With her gone, the quiet and the lack of familiar reference points allowed Delicia's doubts about how suddenly she had left Africa to flood in.

In the hope of banishing them, she headed out the door to explore the village they had driven through several times. The daylight hours on the north side of the equator were different. She was surprised to discover it was already late morning.

The town was a world apart from those in Zimbabwe. Dr. "Joseph" Waluco Massuma had invited her to live on his wild animal preserve to continue her rehab from her career-ending—or as he said in the early days, her career-*interrupting*—fall in Moscow. Missing here in Greenley was the casual warmth of people whose outer lives were inseparable from the reality of surviving what the climate and soil delivered through the seasons. Missing were the spontaneous eruptions of laughter and joy that accompanied the meeting of neighbors. Missing were barefoot children who followed their mothers like ducklings heading to water. That easy pace had no analogy among the hard-driving and well-dressed people she encountered on her walk along Greenley's main street.

The quality of California's heat was different, too. Drier, less debilitating. There were no clouds, much less any portent of afternoon thunder and rain. Already she missed that drama in her daily rhythm. And, of course, all of Greenley's streets were paved. The stores were fancy, carrying things Zimbabweans had no use for.

A handful of café tables under umbrellas clustered on the sidewalk. She smelled the coffee and sugar before she could see cups and plates. She quickened her step and took her place in the short line. In Zimbabwe, visits to town were rare. Outside trips were Joseph's routine. But when she did go, coffee was *coffee*. One choice. Here, a long list on a blackboard disoriented her so much that she annoyed those behind her, trying to decide what to get. At last, though, she gathered a cup and a plate and looked for a table in the sun.

In their constant vigilance for the humanity around them, Zimbabweans would have squeezed their children in closer to give her a seat. Patrons here were absorbed in their cell phones.

The posture of one fellow stood out, though he, too, was working at a screen, typing away on a laptop. His thick ponytail identified him as the man Stephanie had picked up on their way to see the Pacific two days before. He had seemed nice enough.

Delicia walked to his table and asked if he would mind letting her use the spare chair.

His eyes stayed on the screen. He kept typing. "Of course."

She should have been more grateful, but his one-pointedness felt like a wall. She sipped and nibbled. Cast her eye around the patrons. A number of them were looking at her. When she returned the looks of the men, their eyes darted away. This, too, was something she hadn't had to deal with for a while, at least not like this. It had been a double-edged sword. Singled out for her looks, and yet singled out only for her looks.

When she turned back to her food, her tablemate was looking square at her.

She came right out with her ignorance. "I'm sorry. I've forgotten your name."

"Good morning." He looked at his watch as if to verify that it still was morning. "It's Ishi. And yours?"

His smile seemed forced, which knocked him down a few notches in her estimation. "Delicia. Sorry to interrupt your work."

"If you can stay a little," he said, "I'd be happy to hear Delicia's Chapter Two. I need a few more minutes to slap this piece out."

She was pleased at the prospect of having someone to talk to without a language barrier. She waited, considering whether their truck ride conversation had been worthy of being Chapter One. Maybe everything in his life had the structure of a book. His not remembering her name meant he hadn't Googled her, as Stephanie had prompted him. She was glad of that. Whatever conversation they had would be equal in give and take.

For much of her performing life, most strangers she'd talked with wore press IDs around their necks. They'd arrived knowing altogether too much about her, including the list of her sexual partners.

For the third time since she'd sat, a lumber truck loaded high with long, skinny logs rolled along the main street. Their diesel fumes and the sound of their gears demanded attention.

At length, Ishi closed his laptop. The bread of his half-eaten sandwich had curled from sitting in the dry air. He finished it off and wiped his lips with a knuckle. "I hope it's okay that I'm not in a 'jolly reporter mood' today. Trying to figure out if I'm even chatty. So we can keep it light."

This lack of invitation from a man intrigued her. "From looking around, I'd say you're an outsider here. Must be interesting for you to be so deep *inside*."

He looked her in the eye a moment, then said, "Or, if you don't want to be light, you can make profound statements about me that happen to be true." Someone else would smirk saying such a thing, but Ishi seemed helpless, like a beetle caught on his back.

"I assume you're passing through town. There isn't much for work here unless you want to prune a hundred miles of grape vines."

"I'm a logger," she said, shocking herself.

"That's too bad." He didn't skip a beat. "I'm about to take a walk in the redwoods. Meeting you is ruining it for me."

She toyed with the last of her muffin. "I'm lying. I've never even seen redwoods. My aunt tells me there big ones around here. I understand if you want to be alone. But if you have room, I'd love to see them."

MOMENTS LATER, SHE was in his truck heading through the valley. "You're right," she said. "I won't be around long. I needed a breather from Africa."

"That's your home? What part?"

"Zimbabwe. Have you ever been there?"

"Never. What took you there? Were you following a dream?"

She let a breath cycle through. "If I was, it's not there anymore."

She expected *some* kind of response.

"I lost a dear friend two weeks ago."

He looked over, but still didn't speak.

"An animal friend."

"You mean died? Are you an animal trainer?"

"What makes you say that?"

"Your aunt said high wire. I guess I put you in the circus. Does Africa have circuses?"

"No, I went there to heal." All of a sudden, she seemed full of things to say. "I fell during a performance in Moscow."

"*Fell?* From a *wire?*" He scanned her body. "Did you miss the net or something?"

"There *was* no net. That was part of the draw."

His forehead wrinkled in projection. "How far did you fall?"

"Thirty-seven feet."

"You're lucky to be alive."

"It's true. And I had the best surgeons in the world. I have a fistful of titanium screws in me." As Exhibit A, she lifted her left foot and wiggled it. "Also in my pelvis. And this femur." She rubbed her right thigh.

"Pain?"

She liked how his mind moved. "Sometimes. In certain positions. But I'm mostly healed."

"No fear?"

"You mean of falling? No." She reviewed pleasant memories in Africa. "The men at the wild animal preserve where I worked hung a slack line for me. I've been up a lot this last year. It's a different skill than the high wire. Different balance. Different strength. My workouts entertained them. Got me over the hump. The emotional one. Got me itching to get back on the wire."

He gave her a longer look as they slowed for the little village half-way up the valley, then shook his head in disbelief. "I'm not afraid of heights, but there's no way you could get me out on a wire."

"I started young. It became like walking down a sidewalk."

"Your aunt said you do some kind of walk up there?"

"You ever hear of the moonwalk? Michael Jackson?"

He squinted, looked at her again. "And you really want to get back up there?"

"It's a long shot. My fall will probably keep me from being hired. Circuses don't want to take a chance on damaged goods."

The silence was short, but she filled it with painful thoughts. "Let's change the subject. Maybe the redwoods will lift my spirits."

"I'll get you started, but I'm going to do a little digging nearby."

"For what?"

"A needle in the haystack of history."

This time her silence made him fill it.

"For remnants of a village."

"Really? What happened to it?"

"A massacre. A hundred and eighty-seven people."

"Jesus. I don't remember hearing about it."

"It was over a hundred and fifty years ago."

Delicia must have missed that part of history. "Who killed who?"

He seemed hesitant. "I suppose I should have told you before we left. *If* it happened, a white militia slaughtered an entire village of Pomo people."

She'd spent two weeks swamped by thoughts that Maya's death was the worst possible thing she could imagine. Emotions had been weighing her down. The partial list was anger, horror, guilt, grief, and emptiness. Ishi's story was a major course correction. "Is Pomo a tribe? I've never heard of them."

"It is. Tribes that didn't fight back got forgotten." He pursed his lips. "This climate is easy, and there was lots of food. Tribes here were peaceful. They hardly knew how to fight."

When Stephanie had picked Ishi up, he'd been wearing what looked like official armed forces camo gear. Which seemed at odds with his statement. "When my aunt asked if you were Pomo, I didn't know what that was. This massacre is personal for you, isn't it?"

Out his window, a deep green band of color sat above a hill covered with leafless apple trees. See those? They're the tops of the redwoods we're going to see. You won't be sorry."

Ishi pulled the truck left off the road and drove up a gravel track. On top, they came to a bright world, an abandoned field. At the far end, a battalion of redwoods soared along the base of the slope that formed this side of the valley.

"Have you been here a lot?"

He seemed too absorbed to reply. He looked the land over, then drove most of the way along the northern edge of the field, where without a word, he pulled the key and got out. She followed. He lifted a shiny shovel from the truck bed and ripped off its price tag. "All I have to do is dig up this vineyard. That'll take a good part of the afternoon. I'll get you home by dinner, though."

He said it flat, but she knew he was kidding. Still, some part of him seemed capable of the proposition.

He pulled two bottles of drinking water from behind his seat. Taking them from him, she followed him on the track of dead grass that farm vehicles had made long ago.

From her work in Africa, she knew ground. This soil had been baked so hard his shovel would be useless. "What do you hope to find?"

"I don't know. Something out of the ordinary."

Considering people might have died brutally there heightened Delicia's attention to details. As if past and present had no real boundary. And in their own way, the size of the trees bordering the field messed with the concept of time. Except for color and texture, Delicia could think of no adjectives to capture what she saw or how she felt, except insignificant and drawn to them.

"Was there a date for the massacre?"

"August 30th, 1856. At dawn."

The intensity of his answer shut her down.

He walked with no hurry, stopping occasionally and looking around. She liked his eyes, the perch of his head, and the sheen of his hair. His ponytail was as thick as a baseball bat.

In front of the trees, the land dropped off. It was a stream bed—no, a riverbed with the farm road running parallel to it. On the river side the lower redwood branches stretched across the water, shading it. But the water was low. Boulders with their tops worn smooth from the passage of water stood high and dry.

"How's your balance? I mean with your foot and all. Can you leap rock to rock?"

The shackles of her past broke free. Holding a bottle in each hand, she whooped in celebration and pranced across the bed without a misstep. She turned back. "Feels okay to me."

Ishi tried to plant his shovel into the dirt. As Delicia had suspected, it wouldn't go in at all. He threw it down. "I can't compete with you," he said. "Turn around so I don't make a fool of myself."

She didn't, and he needn't have been modest about his abilities.

In the grove, language immediately proved pathetic. To catch the majesty, she relied on her senses: the endless earth tones of the bark, and the fissures in it, big enough to swallow her forearm; roots bigger than many of Zimbabwe's most impressive trees; burn scars, some big enough to walk into. And still the trees flourished. Trunks like buildings, climbing straight in ways that would impress the ancient Greeks. First branches high enough that she had to crane her neck to see them. Nothing could be their equal, nothing could take them down. And under the canopy, only rare rays of sunlight broke through. The air green, cool, moist, so different from the field that was right there. And the ground. Was it ground at all? The deep covering of needles that were the diameter of pencil lead made each step feel like walking on a cloud.

Eight

DELICIA ASSURED ISHI she had a good sense of direction. After entering his number into her phone, just in case, he left her to wander in the groves as she pleased.

He crossed the riverbed again, this time with no pressure to perform. The low water reminded him it was time for a follow-up article with environmental scientists to find out whether salmon were still spawning in the Greenley River. Was the spring up the mountain their last lifeline? Or were they already something of the past?

He took his shovel to the middle of the vineyard, turned, and imagined various configurations where the Pomo would have placed their wikiups. Close to the water's edge would have been ideal for so many processes of subsistence living. But if the heaviest rainy seasons flooded the river over its banks, they would have known to construct them further back.

Then again, their *exact* placement wasn't the issue. Where would the militia have made their funeral pyre? If they'd built it back from the water, the few things that wouldn't burn, the artifacts he hoped to find—arrowheads, stone ax heads and perhaps some shells—would have been scattered when the ground was plowed.

The massacre day was in August, so the land would have been parched. Surely the militia was aware of the fire danger. He guessed they would likely have set the pyre near the river in case the flames got out of control.

Before going there, he tried his shovel where he stood. Years of dead grass had formed thick layers on top of the clay soil. He scraped back the vegetation, tipped the shovel point down, and jumped hard with both feet on the shoulders of the blade. The handle almost ripped out of his hands from how hard the soil was. He had the wrong tool.

At the water's edge, plant growth still had hints of green in it. Digging there, he was able to make a little divot. Still, breaking that ground could take days.

He walked north to the end of the vineyard for another vantage point on what history had hidden.

Wheeling, he walked back in the riverbed itself. The banks of rivers also held stories—in the gravel, in the stones and boulders marching slowly toward the ocean, and in the ledges that time and water had carved smooth. If they'd put the pyre near the riverbank, erosion might occasionally have exposed some relic before a later year's high water washed it toward the sea.

The bank was relatively soft, clay mixed with gravel. As he went, he turned over the vegetation and scraped the soil. But even that operation along the whole length of the bank would take him a number of hours. Instead, he made his way downstream, digging here and there.

When the vineyard ended in the swale that separated it from Minkle's main property, where the apples grew, he headed upstream again, this time dragging the blade of the shovel over the grass along the edge of the riverbank. When the metal pinged against stones, he exposed them. He found some unusual ones, chunks of quartz.

Two hundred feet from the northern end of the vineyard, his shovel made a brassier click. Kneeling, he ran his hand through the area and found a small, two-inch curved piece of metal sticking slightly out of the soil. Perhaps a farmer's broken tool. He dug carefully, freed it, and carried it to the water to wash it.

His heartbeat quickened as he realized it was part of a larger cast piece—the lever mechanism of an early repeating rifle. Excited and more carefully, he excavated a ten-foot section along the bank and was rewarded with a breechblock and a rifle barrel. Corroded, but he had no doubt what it was. If he could ascertain it had been cast before 1856 . . .

No sign of its wooden stock remained.

Eager to get back to town, he left the shovel, lever mechanism, and the gun barrel on the bank, palmed the breechblock, and went looking in the groves for Delicia.

The land hadn't been walked in a long time, and her trail was easy to see. It was no surprise to him that her track wandered around the bases of the giants like that of an intoxicated soul. Twice, it looked as though she had sat down.

He caught sight of her blue top in the distance, sitting by another behemoth, leaning back into the trunk between two large roots. He was reluctant to disturb her, but his urgency pushed him forward. As a compromise, he approached respectfully. When she saw him, she drew her sleeve across her eyes.

"Looks like you've found something," she said.

He turned his palm up to show her.

"What is—"

"The guts from an old rifle. The breechblock." He squatted. "Are you all right?"

She nodded. "This place pokes me deep."

He let her words hang.

She turned her attention to her thumb working in her opposite palm. "It reminds me of Zimbabwe," she said at last. "I didn't tell you. The animal I lost was an elephant. Maya. The matriarch of the herd. Poachers killed her for her tusks. She was my queen. See, I rode elephants my first years in the circus, did tricks on them, cared for them. That's why Joseph —err, Dr. Massama—hauled me to his animal preserve. He thought I might heal there."

She shook both hands as if to free them from something unpleasant, then looked at him. "I don't expect you to understand, but I feel responsible."

"For the poachers?"

"Yes. If I'd never gone there, it wouldn't have happened."

It was a dumb argument. Counterfactual. One that military trainers made sure to cut off at the root. Delicia would have to work this out on her own. He said nothing.

"Being here," she said, "I feel like the trees are hearing me. That's what I need. To be heard and forgiven."

In the distance, movement among the giants caught Ishi's eye. Three men were headed their way, walking through the trees close to the river. From their dress and their gait, it was clear they weren't tourists. They smacked of officialdom.

He put his finger to his lips. She turned to see, but he motioned to her to stay put. "Please." He handed her the breechblock. "And don't lose this. I'll come back for you."

When she nodded, Ishi identified a tree closer to the river that would afford him a place to hide near their route and scope them out. Drawing on his Marine skills, he moved quickly, quietly, low to the ground, and then hunkered in the roots of the tree. Instinctively, he patted the several places where he would normally park his weapons. He didn't have any.

Male voices: three, incautious, interrupting each other. Less than a hundred yards away.

Ishi laid a pancake-sized swatch of moss from the dark side of a root on his head, then rolled to observe. One at a time they appeared from behind a distant redwood pillar a hundred feet from the stream. Middle-aged. Two were comfortable being outdoors. The third wore a wide-brimmed sun hat and was a little on the doughy side. He was doing much of the talking. And Ishi had miscounted. A fourth person followed them, a woman in uniform, a few steps behind. The green, the cut, and the in-signia said California State Forester.

The burly man in the lead walked like a warrior of the woods. A ball cap. Wool jacket. He scanned the trunks up to their first branches. His speech was short phrases. Behind him came a younger, Iron Man-contes-tant type, but well dressed. His eyes scanned the forest at head height.

Ishi wondered again if the state was going to reopen Beckett Park to the public, though this part of the land was beyond where tourists visited.

When they had cut the distance to Ishi in half, Iron Man stopped and gestured across the stream at a large stand of apples on Minkle's hillside. Their first green leaves were popping out.

"Minkle's an idiot, if you ask me. He turned down enough money to buy and sail a yacht of his choosing until the day he dies. He says his mission on earth is to tend those ugly sticks. He says they're like family."

Burly Man laughed.

Sun Hat said, "Talk about being a glutton for punishment. The guy's dumb as a post. He could have bought a *fleet* of yachts. Maybe a marina."

Though the woman forester glanced often at the trees, Ishi couldn't read her. This was her bailiwick, but her power among them seemed like that of a trailer being towed behind a vehicle.

Coming abreast of him not thirty feet away, they stopped for a confab. The forester had her back toward him.

"That land there," Sun Hat said, pointing to the apples, "the way it slopes just begs to be in late-harvest cabernet."

The comment swatted down Ishi's first idea of their mission. These were wine people. And walking the neighboring piece was their way to assess Minkle's without trespassing.

Were they De Boulette?

"The next piece up is perfect chardonnay ground. The Italians that planted it used an old variety they'd brought from home. But the root stock they chose didn't go deep enough to thrive in California's dry years. Design is itching to put the tasting room and visitor center right by the water."

Dammit! You had to get up early to think faster than Brodie. He'd been absolutely right to warn Minkle about De Boulette's donations to the governor's reelection. Ishi wondered if he'd also definitively linked them to sale of the right-of-way down from the spring.

The forester swept her left arm toward the trees. "What kind of grapes are you planning for here?"

In the context of the little Ishi had heard, this seemed like a logical question . . . for about two seconds. His mind kicked into overdrive.

Grapes here? This was state land. And *no* one took old-growth groves down anymore. He saw the trees felled, all facing north, waiting to be bucked up for transport to the mills. A painful image. Had the state made a deal to *lease* state land to De Boulette? Could it even do that? With De Boulette controlling both Beckett and Minkle's, every vineyard in the valley would be stressed.

"The analysis," Sun Hat said, "is this will become the best ground for Merlot. Cutting out the land that's too steep, we're looking at almost six hundred acres . . . with water. It will be the acquisition of the century."

Ishi's shock gave way to remembering his job. With his phone, he took pictures. He got closeups of the men's faces and caught the forester when she turned almost toward him.

He was pushing his luck. But what were the downsides of being discovered? Perhaps he should simply walk over and introduce himself to see what their reaction would be. This was news . . . because they had said aloud what neither the state nor De Boulette had announced publicly. He was in their board room while collusion was underway.

Iron Man pointed up the hill. "That spring will give us gravity feed irrigation forever . . . unless you believe climate change nonsense." He laughed derisively.

The other men joined in.

They continued north. While tagging along behind them made it difficult for Ishi to catch everything, he heard nothing that contradicted what he had already grasped.

Burly Man responded to questions about dropping the trees and the logistics of erecting a derrick to swing the logs directly onto trucks sitting on Minkle's land, "because there is more gravel over there to set up on."

They eventually came to the grove across from the old vineyard. The forester said it would be hard to take those trees down, not because of their location but because they were some of the oldest trees standing on the coast.

"If they were on any other public land and Governor Murphy allowed these to come down, he wouldn't stand a chance at getting reelected. I hate to say it, but my advice is to drop these in the first days after the sale goes through, even if you can't transport them right away. Before any public outcry can be made."

They clambered down the forest side bank of the river—Burly Man doing so gingerly—and crossed in nearly the same path Ishi had taken coming over. The first thing they found was his shovel. Iron Man picked up the rifle barrel and continued into the vineyard.

At that, Ishi pranced across the stones in the river and hustled after them.

They stiffened as a unit when Ishi called, "Are you lost?"

They knew they were trespassing.

"No," Iron Man said. "We were just walking the woods and came here to get a better view of them. Hard to find any place to stand near a redwood and take it in." He held out his hand. "I'm Stephen R. Baskin, with—" and he rattled off some corporate word salad that ended in "Acquisitions," but avoided the company name. His grip announced that giving an inch was not his MO. He had heavy black eyebrows and a long vertical scar down his left cheek.

Ishi looked at the forester.

"Nancy Gilman, California Department of Forestry and Fire Protection." She was pretty, though far from dainty. Late thirties, he guessed. She had perfect teeth.

"You mean, CALFIRE," Ishi said.

Some part of their condescending air broke.

Ishi addressed Burly Man. "What are you acquiring?"

Burly Man hoisted his palms surrender-style. "Just along for a nice walk in the woods."

Ishi looked around the vineyard, showing the chip on his shoulder. "There are no woods here." Neither his Pomo roots nor his time living with the Studebaakers had trained him in toying with people. But in that instant, he thought he might like to get good at it.

"We crossed over from Beckett," Sun Hat said. His field shirt tag said "Caldwell." "I'm an agricultural consultant. Soils. Just was curious what this meadow is."

"The property belongs to a Mr. Minkle. I'm sure you can get permission from him if he wants to give it." Time for a curve ball. "Is the state gonna reopen the forest?"

One way or another, if they answered, they were going to hang themselves. He took delight in imagining them strung up from high branches in the redwoods.

"To be honest," Baskin said, "we're looking at every possibility. We're land people. Stewards of the land. They aren't making any more of it. Can't stand letting it go to waste."

Ishi turned to take in the forest, then back. He waited. "It looks fine to me the way it is."

Nancy Gilman couldn't help herself. "That's a beautiful stand right there. It's only my second time to Beckett. The last time I was in grade school."

Ishi smiled. "That's about a second ago in redwood time." He hoped she took it as a light punch to her gut. Their practiced misdirection was pissing him off. Did they teach that in business school?

"You're a long way from the old visitor center. Are you thinking of expanding the access roads up here?"

"You haven't told us your name, sir," Baskin said.

"Ishi Darkhorse. My people are local."

Baskin seemed not to pick up on Ishi's meaning. "So you work for Mr. Minkle?" Maybe the asshole had never bothered to learn how to tell the difference between Mexicans and Indians.

"I've met him. Do you want me to arrange a meeting for you?" He didn't wait for an answer, but addressed Burly Man. "Do you work for Hanover?"

"I cut on their land sometimes, when the contracts come, but I'm independent. Pinky Grayson."

Ishi could tell they all were wishing this meeting was adjourned.

"If you don't mind, Mr. Baskin, I just dug up that rifle barrel and am planning to take it in for analysis."

That request found the first chink in Baskin's armor. He handed it over without hesitation.

"So are you all working for De Boulette?"

There was clearing of throats. Baskin said, "You seem to know more than you are letting on."

Pinky Grayson broke the oddness, said he needed to be getting back. On that cue, they headed toward the riverbank. They didn't speak again until they were across the river.

Ishi thought that standing to watch them like an offended landowner would be his strongest move. He regretted only that he couldn't hear everything they said next.

As she clambered down the near bank, CALFIRE's Gilman turned to look at him one last time.

Nine

As soon as De Boulette's party was out of sight, Ishi called Brodie. Brodie was remarkably composed; corruption and theft were his life's work. Compared to the redwood tragedy in the offing, Ishi's discovery of the rifle seemed not to interest him.

But when Ishi said he wouldn't be able to return to the office until he collected a woman he'd brought with him, Brodie turned caustic.

"Are you working, Mr. Darkhorse, or on a date?"

"I'm calling it work," Ishi said. "She has a story, but I'm not sure what it is."

While waiting for the De Boulette party to finish its tour and clear out of that end of Beckett, Ishi chewed on the Shakespearian irony of the trees enthralling the very characters who were plotting their demise.

The trees were invincible to everything nature could throw at them. Even fire rarely took them down. And it was the groves that had made the site a viable home for the Pomo. But chainsaws were another order of enemy. He flashed on the wasteland left after they had been hauled away, then on acres of perfectly true lines of grape vines climbing that slope.

Conjuring ways to keep De Boulette out of the valley, he crossed the river to find Delicia. She was asleep under the tree where he'd left her.

He told her the story, but she learned more about it when he stopped at Minkle's.

They found him pruning Gravensteins. The massacre story and the rifle parts made Minkle tender. De Boulette's overarching wickedness made him boil.

"It would be best if we get Mr. Brodie's ideas on how to proceed with De Boulette," Ishi said. "If anybody can trip them up, it's Efan."

Grasping how he and his land could become the center of the news, Minkle raised his fist. He volunteered his parking lot for mobile units of TV stations if the fight got nasty.

"Do you know anyone with a backhoe?" Ishi asked.

"I've got one. For putting in saplings and hauling stumps. Can you drive one?"

"I wouldn't trust me with one."

"See that big guy over there? Miguel. If you pay his wages for a few hours in the morning and a couple of bucks for diesel, he and the machine are yours."

They bumped fists. "I've got to take this woman home and do some research," Ishi said. "If Miguel can be there tomorrow at nine, I'll bring all the hands we need."

Before leaving Minkle's, Ishi called his father on the Dead Creek Rancheria to have him gather a crew of Pomo and soil screens to help with the dig in the morning.

Dropping Delicia off at her aunt's house, he apologized for dragging her through such a painful day.

"Oh, no," she said. "The trees were worth it."

ISHI WALKED IN to a torrent from Brodie.

"I want the whole countryside to howl about the injustice." He had already looked up Baskin and Caldwell. Baskin was "on De Boulette's board. Long Bay Area pedigree. Cal, then Stanford." He read from his notes. "Caldwell . . . Leonard. U of Iowa, Michigan State. Ag positions in a dozen institutions. Thanks to you, we're one step ahead of the criminals. But it won't last long. You gave them your name, right? I have no doubt, they're gonna search you and track you to me, who they *do* know as a long thorn in their groins. So we gotta move. Can you write tonight? I want this whole spread out in the morning. Before you get back here, I'll lean on my old friend Bill Wahling at the *Chronicle* to see if he'll run this in their Special section for tomorrow night. That's going to make people on several continents scramble. I love this game . . . Except when it's for real." His mocking smile turned morose.

It was the adrenaline of finding himself on journalism's main line at last that drove Ishi to agree. "First, I'm going to clean these rifle parts and pin down the make and the year."

In an hour, he had identified the gun as a Sharps model 1852 rifle. The number indicated the year it had been manufactured in Hartford, Connecticut. If Charles Gervin's men carried these, their weapons were state of the art.

To decompress, he stole five minutes to research Delicia Fortunado. Stephanie Lugano was right. Delicia had been a goddess of the high wire.

"As for your main work," Brodie called over from his desk, "it's time you draft your first article on the massacre series. If you find artifacts tomorrow, I want it to come out on Friday—right before the weekend, which always lets news explode or fester, depending on which side it falls. Felling a redwood forest, coupled with an international bully putting up a tasting room on an Indian burial ground could seriously soak De Boulette's reputation. We're lucky on this one. The destruction of beloved symbols is easier for the public to grasp than parsing texts detailing legal crimes.

"This article here," he tapped his computer's screen, "is the first installment on exposing the sexual relationship between the state and De Boulette. What a *naughty* couple we've caught *in flagrante delicto*. Who would have ever thought!" He laid his hands over his heart like a Victorian matron hearing bad news.

"I'll consider the week a success if Governor Murphy's publicity office issues forceful denials on Monday," Brodie said. "Then we'll stick it to them. We'll publish the pictures."

IT WAS CLOSE to ten when Ishi and Brodie left the office. The *Chronicle* editor said he would be happy to help put the screws to De Boulette by publishing the *Post-Ethical Times* article as a special feature.

Ten

TO PERFECT HIS designs for the Temple of Listening, Tadao Kitamura had several times visited the magnificent promontory where the ocean *kami* would come ashore to meet the devoted people of Japan. The level site on that rugged coastal mountain was rare indeed. And the ancient fir trees that clung to the rocky soil and that had grown twisted in the wind gave the place an elemental feel. Tadao saw the wild energy of the place as inseparable from the mission of summoning those forces of nature.

The greatest oddity was the seven-meter tall, black monolith with angular faces that stood smack in the middle in the grove. Its lack of resemblance to any stone on the mountain conjured notions that a dragon had dropped its dagger during some celestial combat.

Because its power demanded attention, Tadao resisted Sensei's son Satoru's opinion that they should remove it. By incorporating that black stone into the sacred interior courtyard, his designs dared do the unthinkable. They abandoned principles of symmetry and, worse, of rectangles that underlay centuries of devotional buildings.

He still had not hit upon the magic that would enable the temple to stand for 1,000 years, but he was working on an idea of adding flexible wooden screens along the eaves that would sing and clack as they deflected wind-driven water away from the critical joinery of the roof.

At the same time, having been named heir to Watanabe and Son Temple builders, Tadao was shouldering a range of new skills. He was required now to speak to and guide journeymen and apprentices alike in ways that would meet what they, in their various stations, saw and believed. For a man used to dealing with the docility of wood, this seemed nigh impossible. He had contracts to negotiate and materials to inspect, purchase, and store under proper conditions so they would be in their optimum state when a project commenced. He had to attend events of commemoration.

After a particularly trying spell of several days, Tadao lay down his drafting pens and set out for the workshop. The sounds of handsaws working through the grain of wood and of mallets driving chisels into mortises comforted him. The smell of Hinoki sawdust eased his stress.

To his chagrin, upon seeing him, his old work comrades stopped what they were doing, cleared space for him to pass, and bowed as he came near as if he were a holy man. Tadao's method of denial was attempting to stay bowed longer than they did—which, given that that was the custom for persons of lower rank, led to some strange interactions.

Finally, he announced to all who could hear, "Thank you. Sensei has been kind to ask me to help Watanabe go forward with this Temple of Listening project, but because he is still very much alive, bowing to me seems disrespectful to him. Please go back to work."

Caught between two formidable logics, the craftsmen made lightning-quick bows to acknowledge tradition, while hoping not to be seen doing so.

Coming to his old work area, Tadao shooed a team cutting hammer beams to another station, donned his work belt, and presented himself to the foreman for the temple project that the shop was building. He demanded the joint specifications for the centermost king post of the building, the beam that supported the ridge and received collars, girts, and complex diagonal bracing for its truss at various points over its length.

The resonant sound that the piece of Hinoki made when laid across the workhorses cleared Tadao's mind. The tree had been one of many felled years before, shortly after Watanabe had accepted the project. Back then, after the trees had been peeled, several venerable craftsmen read the grain of each and directed younger workers to cut them into beams, leaving extra wood in each dimension that would be removed when the frame was constructed. Then, before each beam was placed under the drying roofs for the requisite number of years, its characteristics of strength and beauty were assessed, and it was marked for the exact position it would occupy in the temple. Now thoroughly dried, Tadao's king post had recently been milled to its precise finished dimensions and planed in preparation for fashioning its joinery.

Using his thigh in concert with his hands, he rolled the beam onto its four faces, inspecting it for knots and defects in the grain, keeping in mind where the mortises would fall.

A tree matures uniquely, responding to weather, drought, the influences of neighbors, light, the quality of the soil, the slope of the ground, and its genome's mysterious call for branching. Tadao tested and confirmed the choices made years before about the beauty of the sides the worshippers would see when they gazed overhead. With his marking tools, he laid out the tenon that would lock the king post vertically into the ridge beam.

Then he laid out mortises and shoulder housings for the truss girts, and other mortises to receive the curved bracing that would keep the frame upright and true, earthquake after earthquake. In a country where the ground routinely shook, the beauty of construction-grade wood like Hinoki was its characteristic of flexing to absorb stress without losing any of its vertical integrity or strength.

Over the hours, Tadao bored out the bulk of the mortises, finished them with chisels so that the cross grain shone like the faces of jewelry boxes, tested them with template tenons, and hand-planed the shoulders and recessed faces that would house the girts. The jolt of the mallet in his hand, the chisel blade parting millimeters of wood, and especially, the slicing sound of the plane peeling off translucent and aromatic ribbons that stroked his hands as they fell to the ground repaired him enough to return to his new life as designer and leader.

Eleven

ISHI'S YEARS AWAY from his tribe had forced him to abandon the Pomo sense of time, which sometimes resembled no sense at all. But he was relearning. Which was why he had asked Eli and the diggers to arrive at 8:00 a.m. when the backhoe would be arriving at 9:00. Of course, in case lightning struck on a clear day and the Pomo did honor the God of Greenwich Mean Time, Ishi had to be at the turnoff to Minkle's vineyard land at that earlier hour to lead the way.

Still in a protective mode about the place, he pulled his truck up the road out of view of passing traffic and placed himself on a bank where the Pomo would see him. Already at that time of day, logging trucks passed every five minutes loaded with spaghetti logs, cuts of new-growth redwood forty feet long, though no bigger through than two feet on the butt ends. They were making the three-hour round trip to the mill in the county seat, where the wood would be processed into two-by-fours and lattice. School buses traveled in both directions.

By the non-reaction of the drivers to his presence, Ishi felt he had melted into the landscape. Being an Indian specter put him in better alignment with his mission.

He heard the Rancheria trucks coming down the hill before they pulled around the bend; mufflers were for white people. Eli's truck was in the lead, with its eight-point rack of deer antlers mounted on the cab. That morning several of the points were festooned with white ribbons, as if the Pomo descendants were arriving late to propose a truce for the militia's assault. Had they arrived on that 1856 day at quarter to nine, Eli's mission of mercy would have found the village already leveled, with the fire and rape well under way.

Eli tooted his horn when he saw his son and pulled into the narrow strip alongside the highway. There were two trucks, and as they slowed, several people riding in the pickup beds stood to see where they were. All except Dennis, the communications nerd, had long hair that blew in the breeze.

Ishi went to Eli's open window. He looked a little sleepy, but cheerful. He'd managed to drive with that cast on his leg. Amber sat in the middle, squeezed in by her brother, Marco. Her hand pulled her hair back as if it were a form of greeting. As usual, Marco's eyes sought acknowledgement. Ishi smiled at both of them.

It was testament to Eli's place of respect in the tribe that he had gotten that many people to show up that early.

"Did you bring the gravel screens?"

Eli pointed to Big Wally's truck. "They got 'em."

Ishi greeted Dennis and Crow in the back and waved to the second vehicle. Amber's friend Whammo's purple hair was visible through the windshield. And, good! Big Wally was behind the wheel. Which meant something would get done.

"All right. Use your granny gears on the first part." Ishi modeled it for big Wally, whose upright thumb appeared out the window.

Driving up, Ishi regretted the cloud of dust his truck was laying down for them to drive through. When they broke into the vineyard, he led them along the tractor road on the northern edge of the vineyard, heading for the riverbank. To the right, a downslope was thick with manzanita and live oak.

When they parked back from the river, the roar of a heavy machinery motor was making its way to them from the south. Ishi opened Eli's door out of deference, but knew better than to offer him a hand getting out.

Amber scooted out the driver's side like a greased seal and kissed his neck.

In return, he sniffed her hair. "Ready to get your hands dirty?"

"Pffft!" she said, spitting into her right one and wiping it on the long skirt she always wore when off the Rancheria in case an opportunity to dance presented itself. Laughing, she tugged up the fabric to reveal worn-out jeans underneath.

Big Wally commandeered Marco and Crow to pull the digging tools and screens out of both pickups. They stacked them near where Ishi had found the rifle.

They were all rotating in the space—a little wobbly, it seemed to Ishi, like dreidels in slow motion—lapping up the light, the hills, and the expanse of sky like sugar water. Most every location held a sense of magic their Rancheria didn't have. Which was why most of the Dead Creek Pomo tended to stay put. Depression was easier to endure when not disturbed. At last, they turned to the trees.

Amber raised a hand to her breast. Crow wagged his head in awe.

"Wish we had a stand of those up by us." Big Wally said.

"These are the biggest trees in Beckett," Ishi said. "Funny the state put the campground so far away. Looks to me like people rarely got out here to see them."

"And the river running right along them," Eli said. "Makes no sense the loggers didn't grab them. Easy picking!"

The backhoe had come into view. Its digging arm bounded as it came, like a drunk conductor's baton.

Ishi called the Pomo to him. He explained in a few sentences that they were looking for relics from a Pomo village that might have stood there. He told them about finding the rifle, and apologized for not bringing it.

All eyes were on him when he and Miguel had a conference, speaking over the rumble of the machine. Being his own kind of indigenous, Miguel became excited when he learned what Ishi was looking for.

Miguel dragged the backhoe's bucket sideways a few feet from the stream bed, to scrape away the dead grass. Big Wally and the others opened the tarp eight feet from the machine so it could swing buckets of soil onto it. That way they'd be able to sift through *everything*. Miguel cleared another swath to dump the soil after they'd gone through it.

Eli propped up Dennis's screens on their 2 X 4 frames. With the care of a cat working a litter box, Miguel fished one bucket of soil at a time from the riverbank and dropped it gently on the tarp in front of the screens. With more care, Eli's two men friends shoveled the soil onto the two-inch screen, and the women used small boards to coax the dirt through. Stones that were too big got swatted away. They next sifted the soil through the one-inch screen, where all free hands went through it.

The sun and its heat rose together. The Pomo shed their outer layers. Ishi observed the sifting, and put his hands in the dirt. Beyond looking for objects that might prove this was the home of a vanished tribe, he sought the intangible essence that Pomo footwear had left as they walked to fetch water for cooking and basket work. Many times he made his way back and forth between the sifters and the stream bed. The dirt Miguel scooped was clay on top of gravel, showing the farming hadn't disturbed it.

When an hour's work came up with nothing, Ishi and Miguel walked the riparian length of the vineyard. Ishi didn't tell Miguel all that he'd guessed about the place. And it was clear Miguel couldn't understand some of his sentences, but it seemed he was considering the main point. If people had been here, where might they have constructed their wiki-ups?

Of course, if they had been stretched all along the bank, a likely place for the pyre would have been roughly in the middle. Gervin wrote that he took 187 scalps that day. Ishi figured that could mean at least forty wikiups. If they had been scattered through the open ground, the pyre could have been in the middle, perhaps a hundred yards from the stream. Ishi wished for once that he had the powers of divination his Marine comrades had attributed to him for being born Native .

He walked to the middle of the vineyard. If the pyre had been there, any artifacts would have been scattered by the plows. Would a hard-scrabble rancher even have bothered to notice an unusual item brought to the surface?

As Ishi made his way back toward the water, a beam of sunlight caught him hard in the eye and vanished. He backed up several steps and walked forward again. The phenomenon repeated; a brilliant instant of light not far from where the sifters were doing their work. It glinted like metal or glass. But it was tiny, and he was too far away to pinpoint it in the dead grass.

He signaled to Miguel to kill his motor. Then he asked Marco to walk toward where he was pointing. When the light went out, he told Marco to stay right there until he arrived.

He and Marco bent low, trying to catch that light closer to its source. Marco saw it again, and in a minute tracked it to a place fifteen feet from the river.

He dug out a piece of black rock, thin, narrow, an inch and a half long. Shiny, hard, brittle, and one edge of it was ragged and sharp as a knife.

The name of the stone escaped Ishi, but northern California Indians had used it to make heads for their arrows. He had the sifters bring their gear over and had Miguel dig there. In the first scoop, they found eleven arrowheads. Each seemed to have defects, so perhaps this was an Indian dumping ground. Miguel shifted his bucket farther left each scoop. In the third one, the soil was rich with carbon. As he shook his bucket to free the soil, two large rocks slid down the side of the pile. Flecked and very hard. Ishi turned one over and then the next. They had clearly been one stone once, and when he fit them back together, the surface was a wide smooth depression.

All the Pomo went quiet, as if recognizing a ritual object that resonated in their bones. It was a mortar, the tool tribes had used for countless generations to grind acorns. Amber was particularly excited. Pomo women still used this tool during their gatherings of the tribe.

The boredom and complacency that had developed over two hours of fruitless searching vanished. All of them, and Miguel too, were pawing through the piles of dirt. Marco jumped with the shovel into the hole and dug carefully below where the mortar had been. With a cheer he hoisted the tool that had helped smooth that concave surface, a stone pestle carved to fit the hand.

Their elation gave way to stillness. All of them watched Eli work himself and his cast down onto the ground so he could sit next to the mortar. "I used to watch my mother work one of these," he said. He palmed the pestle and moved it across the surface as if he had done it all his life.

They wondered if they would find bones, but Eli doubted they would. If they had been burned, he said, they would have become very brittle to the elements and to the plow.

They thought some of the clumps of white shell might have been cowrie. But the day changed dramatically when a flattened piece of lead was sifted out on the finer screen. It was the size of a quarter, and looked as if it had melted and cooled.

Before noon, they had sifted six scoops from that spot. The sobering part of their work was a double handful of lead bullets, thirty-two of them, released by the bodies of Pomo as their flesh burned. Three of them had made it through that day's fire and down through the 160 years since in almost perfect shape, with three concentric grooves carved into the barrel of the bullet below the pointed head.

They had come looking for a village, and had found a burial ground.

People working together sometimes know when a stage of work is done. The Pomo signaled they had arrived at that point by hanging aimless. At last, they walked to inspect the river. Miguel's familiarity with Catholic ritual and reverence bade him to back away with devotional bows. He made for his backhoe. When Ishi and Eli went to thank him, his face appeared angelic under sweat, grime, and sun-ravaged skin. He drove back to Minkle's.

Helping Eli negotiate the boulders, Ishi's brothers and sisters walked through the water into the redwood grove. After wandering with their necks craned and their hearts broken in a different way than in the previous hour, they sat cross-legged in a circle on that soft ground and shared food Whammo had brought.

Still on the case, Ishi took closeup photographs of the bullets and spent half an hour locating his archeology professor from Sac State.

Yes, his professor texted, *send me the pictures.*

The professor's analysis came as they were loading tools into the trucks. No one in the department had any doubt. These were bullets designed for early Sharps rifles.

Eli's response to that day would determine what happened in the near term. When Amber said they should figure out a way to give the Pomo victims a proper send-off to the spirit world, Eli wrapped his arms around her. "Yes. Yes."

Amber didn't hide her disappointment when Ishi said he wouldn't be heading north with them. She rubbed his back with an air of stoicism. He held her close and promised he'd see her soon, but he still had a long day ahead. No doubt, before he could get an article out, the story of Pomo massacred in Greenley would travel through the tribal communities up and down the coast. He wondered how long it had been since a tribal nation genocide had been publicly aired in California.

Driving to town, he felt giddy at the heightened kinship with his people. And aligned with Eli in a way he never had been before. As the hours passed, sweet memories from his childhood bubbled up. Times with his family and the Pomo. Yes, they were a broken tribe, living on what amounted to a forest dumping ground. Their human failings were impossible to hide, to the extent that they didn't even bother. Some wore them as ornaments of pride, others as badges of protest. But they were a tribe nonetheless, trying to move forward in a world that had been quite efficient in discounting them.

Twelve

ISHI'S NATIVE HERITAGE left Delicia unsure of how to relate to him. During their visit to the redwoods, she'd tried to hide the swings of her emotions. After returning home, she characterized the day as devastating—devastatingly profound, beautiful, and heart-wrenching.

IT HAD STARTED off innocently enough, sitting at his café table. In the middle, Ishi had rescued her from a bout of depression, a feeling that in coming to Greenley, she had made a terrible decision because the place had nothing for her. Next thing she knew, she was in a small paradise nestled in a grove of some of the oldest trees on earth.

From the moment she saw them, it was clear her old way of viewing the world needed an overhaul. She wrote in her journal that the trees themselves were transforming her psyche, with no more effort from her than simply being among them.

Aunt Stephanie, who was not gifted in picking up on people's moods, noticed enough of a change to mention it as they ate their dinner. As Delicia recounted her activity, Stephanie's brows arched high and her mouth pursed tight.

"Mmm," she said sweetly, as if grasping a message written across the sky: her niece was in love.

Delicia, who *was* gifted in reading subtext, waved her hand, as if trying to stop a truck heading the wrong way on a one-way road. "It's going to be a long time before I love another man. Joseph's errant dick has cured me of that. Anyway, after losing Maya—"

"Sorry, honey. Who's Joseph again?"

"The guy who founded the Tsongumatta Refuge."

"Were you sleeping with him?"

Delicia set her plate in the sink with a clatter. "He came humbly all the way from Zimbabwe to my hospital room—if you can imagine it—to invite me to rehab my injuries there. Turns out that was only part of his plan."

THE NEXT MORNING Delicia drove Stephanie's truck to the closed entrance of Beckett State Forest and concealed it under overhanging brush. She slipped the strap of her pack holding water and snacks over her shoulder and hiked in on the asphalt road. Past the forest service gate and past the visitor center, she came to the park center, with its bathhouses and lecture amphitheater carved into a bank with redwoods all around. A hand pump marked the crossing of trails coming from camping areas. When she raised the pump handle, frigid water from a deep artesian source exploded onto the concrete slab and soaked her boots.

It occurred to her that to get space from Stephanie, she could come and live here undetected for a good while. She went so far as to scheme hanging a slack line between the two redwoods that flanked the amphitheater. Then she could continue her healing as she had been doing in Africa.

She made a theatrical twirl on the "stage," taking this suite of dreams to the next level. Which—if she played it right with the media—would be getting the governor to open the gate someday to let people in to see her "comeback performance."

How perfect that she'd met someone in the media right away.

She was deep in reverie when a dark fantasy interrupted her. Loggers were pouring in and dropping the trees, driven by whip-snapping Machiavellian overlords wearing caps that announced them as De Boulette.

This got her up and moving to her intended goal, which was to tour all the groves she could find. After studying the trail guide that was etched into a huge wooden slab, she set off on the trailhead.

Though the trails needed maintenance, they were easy to follow. At intersections or where trees had fallen across the trail and not been removed, little wooden signs kept tourists from disappearing into the vast reaches of forest.

And the trees *were* marvelous, each unique in color and shape and deformed from when other giants had fallen past them. Some of those events had occurred so long ago that no trace of the offending behemoth remained. Countless times, she guessed, redwood trunks fifteen feet through had rotted, been scattered by the elements, and been reabsorbed by trees right there. How long would such a process take? And what would be the sound of one of those beauties coming down?

Their fall made her think of hers.

She doubled her pace and within an hour returned to the campground. But she was disappointed. The trees in the named groves were not as old as in the grove she had visited with Ishi. And somehow they lacked the heart and raw power she'd felt, as if they had been scrubbed clean.

Using the map, she charted her route to Beckett's northeast quadrant, which, ominously, had no markers. For some reason tourists had not been directed to what she called the "massacre grove." At the pump she filled her canteen—so delicious the water was—and cut a line north. At some point she would work her way to the river, and the vineyard appearing on the right would tell her where she was.

Walking, she compared this place to one half a world away. Only a few weeks before, she had been showing Tsongumatta's new intern around the preserve. She was happy to finally have another woman on her team. For more than two years, she'd been the only English speaker there. True, that condition had afforded her a revered spot in the hierarchy, but she had endured long periods of loneliness. Driving the Land Rover for several hours that afternoon, she and Jamaica, the woman from Arizona, had laughed while exchanging simple truths women destined to be friends so easily share.

Jamaica was beautiful. Her long blond hair had made every African stop and turn. Their eyes filled with the glow of encountering an earthly goddess. And when Delicia went to bid her good sleep, she'd found Joseph in Jamaica's room, driving her new friend in her bed in a ritual that Delicia had shared with him many times.

Pain builds on pain. She knew that with her whole being. And the consequential price for that flagrant offense was Maya being slaughtered. A wound that might never close.

When stumbling over a root brought her to the present, the juxtaposition of this redwood world with her African one married the essence of the animal kingdom in the personage of Maya with the royalty of the plant world all around her. Both species were under threat of annihilation.

"By poachers," she said aloud. Her anger, love, guilt, and mission seamlessly moved from the elephants of Africa to the "elephants of America." On this continent, redwoods were the ivory tusks.

The river appeared on her right. Apple trees descended the hill across the water. In the distance, she heard a diesel motor, revving and idling. A few hundred yards farther on she came to the old vineyard. The engine was coming from there. She quickened her step, worried that De Boulette was already on site.

She found a crowd of people around a backhoe. They were on their hands and knees in some operation she couldn't quite imagine. Seeing Ishi among them, she remembered he'd asked for the backhoe the night before. These dark-haired workers with him must have been his people.

She would let them have their private ceremony. She assumed that was what they were engaged in. As a stranger from a different tribe and a different world, she had no place to offer or ask anything.

For a long hour she sat and watched the Pomo at their work. They were clearly celebrating little finds in the dirt, sharing them with each other. How she wished that, like them, she had cultural history, roots in the earth. How extraordinary that it had not dawned on her before that her choice of the arts of air and reaching for flight by proxy symbolized her lack of roots. She loved the earth, but she had dedicated herself to being above it. Literally. Was that the basis of her loneliness?

On occasion, the prettier of the two Native women touched Ishi in a way that had only one explanation. It didn't seem a huge revelation. There *was* something about him.

A great commotion arose around the hole. They bent as a group, paying close attention to something they had found. Time stood still. The old
man among them seemed determined to sit with the thing. When, at last,
the backhoe driver turned his machine around and drove toward the ridge
of apple trees and Ishi's people began moving toward her in the forest,
she backed deep into the trees. From there, she watched them as they ate
in a circle.

When the sun was high, she returned to her car.

Thirteen

ISHI WALKED IN to find Brodie plunking away on his keyword. When their eyes met, Ishi released a handful of the Sharps bullets onto Brodie's desktop. To Ishi's delight, their clatter created the sense of ceremony he had hoped for.

Brodie contemplated them. Eventually, he picked up a melted lump and compared it to one of the whole ones. To his credit, he understood that the melted one confirmed the burning of murdered bodies.

A seasoned journalist, Brodie resisted running his mouth off. Which left Ishi feeling as if he were standing alone in a room that was much too large.

At last, Brodie said, "Perhaps this is a first step on the road to reparations. I am happy for you, of course."

His tone had no joy.

"But?" Ishi asked.

"But . . . it never occurred to me the land sale on the hillside would become entangled with the Pomo massacre. Otherwise, I wouldn't have taken you there. Not yet. I've been holding that one so it could stand on its own, be reported in its own time. But here is the problem. I've given you a story that makes you unable to tell it."

Ishi's face must have shown his consternation.

"I don't know why I didn't see this before. But you're now a principal in this dual story of corruption, which ruins your objectivity. And which means you and I will be on opposite sides. Which, if I let you continue to report on it, would be yet another story, one that could get me dragged up before the ethics board. My strong suit is reporting on the legal side. Now I must take over what I wanted you to do, the forensic and cultural sides."

"Can't I just speak of the Pomo team in the third person?"

"Are you kidding? Other outfits are going to want to report on this. Believe me. And who's going to talk to the TV cameras? You. You are!"

"How about if I draft the articles, you tweak them, and put your by-line on them?"

Brodie seemed exhausted. "The simple solution is the most unjust. Ignore the massacre story and frame it as a vineyard takeover, essentially what history has done to the Pomo over and over. I . . . How I hate the law. But we need every inch of it. We need to focus on it and—are you willing to help with that for now? I promise we'll keep our eyes open for how to include the Pomo story."

He pointed behind Ishi to the Crime Board. Unlike the night before, it was teeming with colorful headings, with cards in bold handwriting, and with arrows making connections between cards and columns. The heading that jumped out to Ishi was *De Boulette/Murphy* with subheadings: *Political Donations* and *Quid Pro Quo/Favors*.

"How I've spent my morning," Brodie said. "The next step: We *have* to find proof of De Boulette actually doing what you overheard them say. If we move too quickly, they'll haul the *Post-Ethical Times* into court by a coach and four." When he realized Ishi didn't know what the hell he was taking about, he said, "They'll haul our ass in there, Darkhorse." He slammed his palm on his desk hard enough to make things on Ishi's desk rattle.

Ishi had arrived with a list of ideas about his massacre series. But Brodie was right; his list was dead on arrival.

ISHI WHIPPED OUT two local stories to get the paper out on time. They weren't stellar, but Brodie said they'd do and kicked him out to deal with the dark clouds hanging over both of them.

Ishi broke into an anxious sweat driving up the hill to the vineyard. As he looked at the mounds of sifted soil, they transformed into the smoldering pile Charles Gervin's men had left. He handled part of his distress by visualizing Gervin tied spread-eagle on top.

He lingered over the hole where they'd found the mortar and pestle and wondered if he should go to the Rancheria and bring the pieces back here for a proper reburial. Perhaps leaving everything the way it had been for a century and a half would be the best resolution. The familiarity of his people's pain and disillusionment might be better than dangling another promise in front of them only to have it dashed and broken.

He kicked dirt into the hole.

Wishing to expel the venom from his body, he strode to the river, jumped from rock to ledge to boulder, and pulled his body up the far bank.

Perhaps it was the color under the canopy or the protection it offered, but much of his angst stayed among the stones of the river. The trees in that grove were colossal, fourteen to sixteen feet in diameter, and standing maybe eighty feet apart. Feeling himself a dwarf forced him to consider the vastness of time. For them, the passing of a century was hardly worth mentioning.

Each tree was actually a perpetual processing factory. Year after year, each had gathered some huge volume of elements from the soil right there, had inched it along its roots, and had then hauled it hundreds of feet into the air to supply the energy and material for that year's cell division, creating a new layer of wood under the bark as well as branches reaching ever higher. The plan seemed ludicrous, the execution impossible.

And their dedication to standing was humbling. For centuries they'd stood in silence like a colossal Greek chorus, observing the dramas of life on earth—meteor strikes, fires, droughts, ice ages, species extinctions, and other forgotten events like Charles Gervin's men murdering the small group of dark people with straight glistening hair who had lived there for countless time, convinced they could build a stable and God-respecting culture on the ashes of Tribal Nations peoples.

What would trees know of drama, really? Would they know how to process it? And if they did, would they bother? Human schemes were divorced from the job of creating majesty for its own sake, from celebrating life as they knew it. Underground, the roots of these trees tangled in carnal ecstasy and competition for molecules of water and iron and phosphorous and god knew what, but Ishi didn't, because he'd never cared for chemistry, or even botany for that matter, until that moment when he stood among them.

As alike as the redwoods were in principle, each was unique, shaped by its placement, water, neighbors, light, and its history of violence—lightning, wind, and fire.

The bark was not a simple matter to be ignored. When Ishi ran his hands over its fissures, they felt both fragile and timeless. A rough tapestry of color: earth reds and browns and yellows and greens and blues and ripples of grays, laden with moss and fungi and with detritus falling from above into little cubbies where seeds had landed and taken root. Where limbs had withered and died or been sheared off, irregular scars had formed. Some hung bulbous, others were crudely stitched together. Some trees had replaced the limbs. The new ones often jutted out improbably, suggesting they would not last. Or sometimes they shot straight up alongside the trunk, not pausing to consider symmetry in any way. And yet that was the beauty of them. Sheer will and purpose in the context of time. Life force without hesitation.

How could the state ever scratch a forest like Beckett off its list of parks?

Their crowns were so dense that young sprouts were doomed to live in perpetual twilight. As Ishi wandered south along the river, he came to a colossus that had fallen perhaps a decade before. There, light reached the forest floor and a number of saplings had leapt at the chance to become the one specimen that would grow faster than the others to fill that void. In middle age—five hundred years from then—it, too, would block the sun.

Fourteen

DELICIA HADN'T BEEN aloft since leaving Zimbabwe. Seventeen days. She missed the feel of balancing on air with wire or rope under her feet. She regretted even this few number of days lost toward her goal of proving her doctors wrong.

They had given her no chance at making a true comeback. They'd said she'd actually be lucky to walk pain free. Yet here she was, fresh from Beckett's little amphitheater, ordering herself sixty feet of material to set up a slack rope. She schemed about getting some of her old circus people from the Bay Area to help her rig it, to use it for practice, and to invite small groups of people to watch her perform there. Maybe by midsummer. She had ten days to kill until the rope was delivered.

She became a regular at the café's lunch hour, hoping to reconnect with Ishi as if by happenstance. Over several days, she took the opportunity to stay current, reading the *Post-Ethical Times,* including back issues that the café saved inside. She admired Brodie's full-throated skepticism of people with money and power. Ishi wrote well, but seemed to be stuck covering run-of-the-mill subjects. He had struck her as capable of more.

The problem was, the paper had only Wednesday and Saturday editions. She feared some edition would be right on time to announce the death of Beckett. The paper's web URL linked to a page that said, "This site can't be reached."

On Tuesday, she read the Saturday edition that announced the sales of a spring on the hill and a right-of-way from it down to the border of Beckett State Forest. At that point, the purchaser—or purchasers, if they were unrelated—still had not been definitely identified.

On Wednesday, the headline on the new edition blared "Cut 'Em All." The governor had taken advantage of an obscure provision in the California Surplus Land statute that gave him the right to award the purchase of state land that had remained unproductive for two years to cash sale buyers. De Boulette was named as the buyer, with the closing date set for June 6th, 2012—less than three months away.

In the article, Efan Brodie confessed he had no proof the trees would be cut, but the events he described suggested De Boulette intended to do just that. He drove the point home by observing, "In a normal year redwoods don't produce many grapes."

Delicia looked at the patrons. By their dress, many were out-of-towners. She was pleased to see they were reading the same story. And how wonderful! Ishi was making his way toward her, holding his lunch. She stacked the papers to make room for him.

"I was hoping I'd see you somewhere," he said. "I was worried about you when I dropped you off. You seemed quite upset."

"I was. Having seen the redwoods, De Boulette wanting to put in a flagship vineyard"—she tapped the paper's headline—"is a tragedy in the making. How can they do it? How dare they!"

"Because they can. As you can see, Mr. Brodie is committed to put up a fight."

She liked that Ishi looked despondent, too.

"But money usually wins in cases like this. The only thing we can do is alert the public and hope they raise a stink, enough to rattle the governor. It's a tall order. The good news is this article will come out in the *Chronicle* tonight."

"What's the *Chronicle*?"

"The main San Francisco paper. A lot of Bay Area people come through Greenley every year, so it may touch them."

"Will the governor listen?"

Ishi's chuckle oozed cynicism. "It's an election year, and the primary is scheduled for the week after the closing date for the sale."

"So?"

"Governor Murphy has a decent Democratic challenger this time around. He might not want to concede an issue to his opponent."

"Then send this to his opponent's campaign. Invite him up here to do a photo op in the trees."

"We will. We've got a couple months. First, we have to ignite a storm at the grass roots."

Gears turned in her head. Whom did she know from her days in the limelight who could help? In the meantime, she was dying to ask him what he and his friends had been digging for in the vineyard.

"What did you find out about that rifle?"

"You haven't gotten to my article then? On page five."

She flipped the pages.

"The rifle *was* from the massacre period," he said, then took a long time chewing a bite. "I gathered a bunch of my tribe and we went back the next day with a backhoe. We found a lot of Indian artifacts." For some reason, he didn't seem ready to cheer.

"So that proves there was a village there?"

"Yes. But it was painful. We found bullets that would fit that rifle."

"Still, it's huge news, isn't it?"

He said it was, but then launched into something about reporting she couldn't grasp. The upshot was he couldn't really pursue the story beyond what was there. Something about being too close to it.

She told him it was BS. And she could see he was pissed about it. He said his boss *wanted* to cover it, but not in a way that would take away from the cutting the redwoods story, which he he was sure could become national. And the boss, Brodie, was too busy with everything else to cover the massacre story.

"But there's no law I can't make the story big from the inside," Ishi said. "Dump my reporter position and get others to report on it. I'm going to see if that apple grower Minkle will let the Pomo bands hold a traditional dance on the site. Big event. We'll try to get TV coverage and let other media spread the word. My girlfriend and my father are seeding the idea to the other bands in the tribe. It's rare to get us all together."

"That'll be a good start. But then what?"

"I don't know. At the least, it'd be important to get the state to acknowledge what happened there and to make a memorial. The Pomo need a win. All the tribes do."

"But the site is not on the road," she said. "Who would ever see it?"

Fifteen

BRODIE GREETED ISHI on Monday. "There you are. Good morning. This gentleman here is Stephen R. Baskin. He is . . ." Brodie made a show of looking at the card in his hand, because he knew perfectly well who Baskin was. "General Deputy Counsel for External Affairs and International Acquisitions, De Boulette International, LLC, which stands in this case for Lugubrious Long Crapola. He has done us the kindness of paying us a visit, though the argument he carries seems intent on making others pay for his corporation's rapacious charter."

"We've met," Ishi said. He pretended to be too burdened with his papers and coffee cup to extend a handshake.

Unlike when Ishi had met him in Minkle's vineyard, Baskin was in full Sacramento regalia: impeccable navy blue suit, California flag lapel pin, three-pronged flattened breast pocket handkerchief, pants creased to a knife edge, and deep mahogany tassel loafers.

"Perhaps you can tell Mr. Darkhorse what it is you told me," Brodie said, "because I will have trouble sorting my way through the nonsense to make it intelligible."

Baskin received Brodie's derogation as if being lauded for years of fine service. His smile was slight—hinting toward the humble spectrum—and genteel. He had the kind of Caucasian markings Ishi saw often in higher-ranking Corps officers: refined features, smooth skin, delicate crow's feet by grey eyes that looked carefully without revealing one fraction of judgment or opinion, or even hiding any. In short, a snake.

He proved this by waiting for Ishi to set down his load—at which point, he closed the distance between them with his warm hand extended. "Yes, we did meet. That was a beautiful day."

Ishi shook his hand, expecting the rock grip of their meeting in the vineyard, and yet Baskin's hand was smooth, welcoming.

"Mr. Brodie and I know of each other by reputation, but this is the first time I have had an opportunity to come by and see your operation." Baskin turned his head as if taking in architectural splendor.

"It's a pleasure, of course, to have you, Mr. Baskin," Brodie said imitating Groucho Marx. "But you've come to the wrong place. Our *operation* is out *there*." He made an arc with his upturned palm. "Out there where corruption runs thick. We use this little hole in the wall to package our insights." He pointed to the haphazard stacks of the *Post-Ethical Times* issues he called his external hard drive.

"I am happy then, to be *inside*," Baskin said, with a chortle. "I don't get to read your paper as much as I would like." He cast a generous look in Ishi's direction. "But I did happen upon yesterday's headline while in the Greenley Market."

"Cut 'Em All," Brodie said, perhaps to ward off the wave of inordinate decency flooding the room. "You like it? Take a bow, Ishi. That was his. He's getting good at them."

"It *is* catchy, of course. But it strikes me as introducing a horse to a buyer with a recording of his flatulence. Really off the mark. And I've come to the—what—this castle of vision here in Greenley to rebuild, or perhaps to establish properly for the first time, good relations between your paper and De Boulette International."

"*LLC*," Brodie said, followed by a Bronx cheer. "We know all about you. In fact, I am willing to bet I am one of three people in the world who knows the full shadow side of DeeBeeInt."

"We do our best to—"

"Baskin, cut it right there. I have no intention of rolling over to allow your legally sanctioned desecration of this town any oxygen. And I think you'll find you're not just dealing with a cranky editor on his way out to pasture. There is a tenacity in the folks who live on this land that you would do well to observe and, in my opinion, to personally absorb.

"Here's what I know about you and the people you speak for with such regard. Your generosity is the kind that will strip the land and water out from under those of us who live here, in the process of creating profits for investors who never take the time to examine what extraction even entails."

"Now, Mr. Brodie," Baskin said, as if soothing an irritable aunt in a nursing home. "And I hope I may call you Efan—"

Brodie barreled on. "Yesterday, I gave Ishi a list of towns where DeeBeeInt has succeeded in devouring the way of life. Check me if I am correct, Ishi. In France—Petit Sommes, ring a bell, Mr. Baskin? And L'Eglise Mouchant. And Sverovbonda on the Dalmatian Coast. And the three villages in Algeria that when your parent company had finished serving itself to the local gold and pulled out, triggered a run on the banks that put the whole country into a decade of pain. And—"

"Mr. Brodie, please. The problem with news is that it focuses on the bad. Because it sells papers, like pictures of car wrecks. I get it. In some ways, we are both in the marketing business. And when news runs out of that, it *redraws* the normal to look positively awful. You people are prone to forgetting that there are two sides to every story because you dwell on only one side.

"De Boulette has brought uncounted benefit and wealth to communities around the world. And we haven't even mentioned the products themselves, which bring delight. I prefer that you not attack the goodwill I bring and will continue to bring. If all you are capable of is resistance, mark my words, you will eat yours."

"If we are going to talk about eating," Brodie said, "pull up a chair." He walked to his crime board and tapped a column heading all the way on the left that needed more attention. Ishi wondered why he'd chosen that one.

"De Boulette is the dark shark that's going to attack, dismember, and do away with the last apple orchard in this valley," Brodie said. "Minkle is entirely expendable to you. He is the first real casualty. You are going to destroy him personally and take his land. He is beloved in this town."

"Stop, Efan. This is exactly what I mean. I'll admit, De Boulette has tried over the years to negotiate a way to acquire Josh Minkle's property as our headquarters in California. It's no secret. You reported on it accurately at the time. It was before I came to the corporation, but I have read your campaign to protect him. And I agree even, that, in hindsight, De Boulette should have made more ethical choices. We have learned from those early days. I assure you we have no plans of any kind to disrupt Mr. Minkle's business."

At certain times in the service, due to issues of rank and engagement, Ishi had been obliged to stand in offices, in hotel conference rooms in Kabul, and in the shade of stone outcroppings in the fields near battle while his superiors spun out linear yards of linguistic hostilities. He took pleasure, now, in being free to take a seat on the corner of his desk. As he did, to his surprise, he found both men looking at him. The dynamic in the room flopped open for him to speak.

"To capture *market share*," Ishi said, "De Boulette will take down one of the last great stands of old-growth redwood and plant grapes the world doesn't need. As if that weren't enough, it will suck dry the last of the functioning headwater springs in the Greenley River watershed. And what Efan and I have learned in the last few days is that your corporation and the governor's office have been in long-term collusion to make this go smoothly *under* the radar until it's all too late for the people you market to, and say you care for, to have a chance to pull in your bridles.

"If you must know, I have personal reasons to have my dander up about this sale, beyond what will come out in the *Post-Ethical Times*."

Baskin was nodding sympathetically. "I understand, Mr. Darkhorse. We do our research too. I have learned that you are Pomo, a noble tribe that has been treated badly."

In Ishi's lifetime, no one had ever given Pomo this much deference. While wanting Baskin's line to be authentic, he prepared for what would come out of Baskin's mouth next.

"*And y*ou have served your country well. I gather you dodged horrors in doing so. *And* successfully sidestepped culpability, at the company level, in Bamiyan Province night raids that went badly. And for that I am grateful. I served too. So I know.

"But please grasp this. We are not pushovers, and we'll not be fall guys for what you see as wrong with the earth or more particularly with humanity. We have a generous reinvestment policy for all our activities.

And if it matters to you, the mission statement to leave the earth a better place than we found it hangs over my desk in Dallas.

"And you, Mr. Brodie—we know what you're *not* telling Mr. Darkhorse. No one is clean here. That, too, is a private matter and we will respect that, particularly if you extend to us some intention of getting along."

He had brought no hat or folder, but seemed to be gathering himself to leave. "I will check in with you in a few days and test the waters of what I hope will be a new set for the changes that will be coming for the Greenley community.

"Don't get up. I'll let myself out."

WHEN BASKIN'S FOOTFALL on the stairs had disappeared behind the low hum of traffic on Main Street, Brodie collapsed into the stuffed chair beyond the crime board and exhaled. "*That* is why life is so damned difficult."

Ishi rose from his desk to examine additions to the crime board.

Brodie's phone buzzed with a text. "Would you mind logging my computer into KWDZ?" he asked. "The governor is holding a press conference. My snitch tells me it has to do with a little town in Ackerman County."

A minute later, the gentrified face of California democracy stood in front of a bristle of microphones. Having just had a demonstration of corporate power, Ishi could easily draw a line through the personages of Baskin, Stephen R. and Murphy, Thaddeus J.

Ishi and Brodie jotted notes as Murphy explained the intersection between the little-known Surplus Land statute, a governor's duty to lead, the long-view planning required, the huge deficit his predecessor had left him to remedy, the unemployment situation and how that impacted wine, and several other pro forma staples that often find their way into press releases when a politician needs to obfuscate graft.

When Murphy was done, Brodie said the governor had helped him see where he needed to drill down further into the only part of his defense that made sense, the Surplus Land statute.

Ishi left a message on Minkle's voicemail asking for permission to hold a ceremonial dance on the massacre site as part of creating some memorial to the victims. He didn't mention Baskin.

Sixteen

MID-MORNING ON THE day set for the Pomo dance, Delicia's aunt Stephanie dropped her off at the foot of the road leading up to the old vineyard. Delicia had been doing way too much sitting since leaving Zimbabwe, and insisted on walking up the hill.

A number of vehicles lumbered up the road, passing Delicia because it was too steep to stop. Each showered her in a cloud of a fine red dust. The pickup truck beds were loaded with humans with coal black hair, checking her out, hanging on as the drivers careened over the bumps. Some acknowledged her with a raised hand.

When she reached the top, an impromptu parking lot had appeared along the northern edge of the vineyard. People of all ages and ambulatory capability were walking with armloads toward the spot where she had seen Ishi's group digging. But today, it was transformed by a ring of pop-up canopy tents set up among the old vines, some with tables, others with beach chairs and blankets on the ground. There were tents for water and food. Pomo of all sizes were getting dressed in feathered and beaded regalia, though most of the older people were going to be spectators. Comfort with this ritual permeated the gathering.

She spied a small stage—really a plank laid over two wooden crates—and behind it, yellow police crime tape strung on stakes driven in a circle around the piles of sifted soil and the holes the backhoe had dug. That excavation into what Ishi had said was the funeral pyre had no look of being sacred, but knowing what it was gave it weight.

Delicia volunteered to carry loads from newly arrived vehicles and found herself invited to settle down with two separate groups.

An old Pomo woman wearing several layers of skirts was seated in a chair. "Where're you from?"

That was a hard question. "Oklahoma originally," Delicia said.

"You got Cherokee in you?" The woman was missing teeth.

"Not that I know of."

"Have you seen us dance before?"

"First time."

"How'd you hear?"

Delicia looked around. There were only about twenty whites. "I met a guy named Ishi Darkhorse a few weeks back."

"Yeah, he's over there." Ishi was engaged near the stage with a woman and several men.

"Looks like it's going to be hot today. How are the dancers going to do it?"

The woman waved her hand as if she was patting the head of a boy only she could see. "Heat's part of the offering."

"Wouldn't it be cooler to dance under the trees?"

The old woman took a moment to grasp this notion, then she laughed with a big shake of her head. "Ground's too soft. Everybody would fall down."

A Pomo shaman-type started singing over the site of the pyre, which stared at the sky like an open wound. His voice drew people's attention. Delicia couldn't tell if it was a meant to be a celebration, a lesson, or a dirge. Next, a high pitched electronic feedback squeal came from a speaker on a metal stand near the stage. A thin Pomo man jumped to adjust the PA volume.

The older man who had been at the dig took his place in front of the stage. He waved the microphone away, but just the same, a woman held it near him to pick up what he was saying. He introduced himself as Eli, the elder of the Dead Creek Rancheria, and told the story of the last fifty years of his band shifting "from outhouse to piss pot," he said. Everyone chuckled. He acknowledged that his Pomo sisters and brothers had traveled on short notice from as far away as Clear Lake, Middletown, Point Arena, and Geyserville. He welcomed them and introduced his son Ishi.

Ishi took the stage wearing a beaded throw over his shirt. Delicia didn't see a strong resemblance between him and Eli, except that he, too, was uncomfortable with the microphone.

Fortunately, he spoke well. He said everybody knew why they were there and that he preferred not to dwell on what had happened. He told the story of Brodie bringing him to the site, and of the Dead Creek Pomo sifting through the soil. He named the Pomo who'd helped that day. And he thanked Josh Minkle for letting them dig and allowing the gathering. He thanked the man who had driven the backhoe.

He said they should treat the site as a cemetery and holy ground. He hoped the dancers would know what kind of rituals were appropriate, because he didn't.

A young Pomo woman approached him with a piece of paper and whispered in his ear. The beautiful hair cascading down her back identified her as the woman Delicia had taken to be Ishi's girlfriend when she'd spied on them from the grove. Ishi seemed reluctant to receive what she was handing him.

A middle-aged Pomo man with a sun-weathered face cried out, "Go on. Read it. It's all of our history."

Ishi looked the paper over. "What we don't know," he said, "is if any of the people who lived in this village survived that day. I'd like to think so. That somehow a few escaped. Maybe some of their descendants are with us right now and don't know it. That would show the resilience of our tribe."

And he began by setting the scene of the village that had thrived where they were standing. Of families going about their daily lives, moving in their late summer harvest rituals between their fire hearths and the drying racks for salmon and steelhead that they hauled from the river, making baskets and arrowheads, grinding acorns into meal, gathering wood for fires, and repairing their dwellings, all in the shadow of the great trees.

On their drive to the woods that first day, Ishi had told her he didn't know anything about his tribe's actual history. He said no one did. The stories had been lost in the years of running landless, homeless, without respite or shelter. Which meant he had clearly been doing a lot of thinking and research in the past days.

Without transition, he lifted the page the woman had handed to him and began to read. It was perfect timing, symbolically beheading the idyllic scene that had gone on for centuries to describe the arrival of the militia. He read of the author seeing signs of the village from the ridge, sneaking down the slopes in the evening, and then under cover of darkness, surrounding it.

Ishi waved his hand in a circle to indicate the vineyard. His voice became charged with emotion, and it seemed he was speaking a greater truth. All eyes were on him.

As he read, Delicia felt the distance between her and the Pomo dissolve. She imagined herself as a wife in one of the wikiups that night with her husband and children, experiences she had never had and rarely craved. When Ishi got to the part about the lead flying from the Sharps rifles so thickly that the wikiups were collapsing, the paper started to shake in his hands. He seemed to have trouble seeing the print. His voice wavered.

Delicia started trembling as well. Before she knew it, she was dragging her children, through her home's south-facing opening and running toward the river. She heard shrieks all around and felt herself out of breath and out of hope. And there for an instant she thought of Maya's herd scattering when the big guns brought the matriarch down. How she wished she could have taken Maya's place.

With a child under each arm, she jumped over a white man who was reloading, sprinted through the river, and somehow without air made her way into the gloom that the early morning lent the redwood grove.

Back in the present, Ishi tried to hold steady, and when he couldn't, he rebuked the document, slamming the fist that held it against his thigh.

Voices around Delicia encouraged him, told him to keep going. Kind voices. Plaintive voices. Pomo of both genders were wiping their eyes.

An elderly woman in a shawl and what looked like traditional dress made her way forward. She stopped in front of Ishi, looked up to him standing on the plank, hands resting on her skirt. When he focused on her, she nodded her head, flicked her finger at the paper he was holding and kept nodding until he raised the sheet and read it to the end where the author seemed to express his humanity by regretting the death of one of his men.

There was a long period of silence, Pomo standing there as if watching their own funeral pyre burn behind where Ishi stood.

Finally Ishi turned to join them in their tribute and looked at the piles of soil.

She couldn't gauge how long they stood like that, but became aware that the Pomo children had also stopped. Perhaps they had never seen their parents be this dedicated to stillness. Or perhaps this was part of their culture. She longed to know which it was.

A resonant stroke on a skin drum broke the spell. And another, and another. The patient spacing between the strokes brought the Pomo back. Women and girls in dresses, holding fabric scarves, and bare-chested men in headdresses of feathers and bead spires attached to bands of fabric and leather wrapped around their heads, and other ornamentation on their waists made their way to a central point, among the tents, waiting for something. They were not smiling. Their minds seemed far away or deep inside.

The drum cadence gradually sped up and a voice began singing in that lilting style unique to Native Americans. The women began moving forward, stutter-stepping, swinging their arms and animating the scarves. They were gentle. They spun slowly around and danced off in another direction. Their steps were relaxed, every aspect of their movements the opposite of high European ballroom dancing.

The men moved more in a block, lines of them, taking a skipping step on occasion, and moving backward as often as forward. Rituals depicting sexual courtship and tension so many cultures throw into such things seemed secondary, unnecessary. The display was soft and lovely, like watching fish negotiate the changing currents in a stream's circling backwaters. The woman Delicia linked to Ishi moved like a leader among her Pomo sisters, aware of them without looking. Her body was happy.

Now and then, the dances stopped until the drummer banged out a new rhythm. Occasionally, a dancer joined or withdrew. But the large body of the dancers showed no signs of tiring. They saw each new rhythm and chant as unique theater and were eager to explore it. What struck Delicia as remarkable was that she saw no jostling for hierarchy.

All the while, Ishi was moving from tent to tent, stopping and talking. There was no boisterous conviviality. No backslapping. Their interactions had a degree of gravity. Gentle nodding of heads as they spoke to each other. In the people around her, the phrase *an important day for the tribe* passed from mouth to mouth. Contrary to its meaning, it sounded flat, the way people at funerals said, "I'm sorry for your loss." She wondered if the Pomo lacked a legacy of important days.

Twice, she caught Ishi looking at her from a distance. The second time, she realized she was swaying with the rhythm and absorbing the moves the women were making. The men started flipping the featherladen fabric that was tied around their waists. Delicia thought of the tail feathers of big birds in Zimbabwe doing their courtship rituals. Yes, and the women responded with subtle, coy turns.

Ishi kept progressing around the circle. Was it her wish that made it seem he was moving faster? It was a bad instinct to think that way. All wrong. She saw him stop to talk with a large white man, older, with a substantial camera around his neck. She hadn't seen him earlier. He posed Ishi for a picture, an opportunity Ishi did not seem to enjoy.

Ishi finally made it to the tent where she was standing and held out his hand. It seemed awkward to shake it. He thanked her for coming.

"I love the headgear and the feathers," she said. "Do you dance?"

He blew out a breath. "I've been away too long."

She imagined he was referring to his time in the service.

Then like an owl diving for prey, that pretty Pomo dancer with the long black hair streamed right up to Ishi and Delicia. She grabbed his arm with only a slightly concealed proprietary energy. The music hadn't stopped since Delicia last saw her dancing, so she must have simply pulled out.

"I'm Amber," she said. "Who are you?"

"Delicia Fortunado."

"This is the woman I told you about," Ishi said. "The circus lady."

"Oh yes. You fell. You seem to be moving all right now."

Delicia gave her a puzzled look.

"The truck I was in passed you on the way up," Amber said.

"You dance beautifully."

Ishi said, "I've got to keep moving." And he was gone.

Amber smiled. A complex smile that she tempered by raising her index finger and shaking it to say *Don't even think about it*. Then she too departed.

A moment later, Amber led her sister Pomo out of the dance ground over to the hole where the pyre had been. Dancing, they made a tour around the crime tape. The rest of the community stood up and pressed close. Delicia imagined generations of Pomo, back and back, dancing on this site just as they appeared that day.

Ishi's father, Eli, found Ishi's arm. He spoke into Ishi's ear and then pointed up. It made her think they were looking at the souls of dead Pomo lifting out of that ground, finally heading to freedom in the sky.

Seventeen

FOR ALL THAT the people and the media in northern California noticed, Brodie's article about the Pomo dance at the massacre site might as well have been minutes from a Cub Scout leaders' meeting. The only other paper he got to publish it was the *Indian Country News*. But a picture of a tribal dance at the site of a long-ago massacre couldn't compete with the top twenty concerns of injustice to the many Tribal Nations that week.

Judging from De Boulette's increased presence in the town, the powers that be had apparently decided to present their upcoming foothold in the valley as a *fait accompli*. Corporate officers of different standing began preparing Greenley's inhabitants for the felling of Beckett's redwoods. In the one De Boulette op-ed Brodie printed, the corporation proposed to leave a group of fifteen large redwoods surrounding the Park Service Campgrounds. This "grove" would enclose a "recreation unit"— whatever that was—with audio and visual kiosks sharing media for visitors to reminisce about times gone by.

A particularly irksome ploy involved De Boulette's promise to create a label called Redwood Cabernet. Brodie's letter from the editor that week stated that the wine would have "a robust body of shamelessness and finish with hints of sawdust and drought."

Members of Team De Boulette appeared in the café and restaurant, on the street, cruising in their darkened window SUVs, in the pews of the Catholic Church, and at any community meeting they could find reason to attend. They had an impressive array of polished speakers to represent the "good fortune that was coming to Greenley Valley," in language to meet the agenda of any valley gathering, be it senior lunches, League of Voters, sports meetings for parents at the high school, and even sewer negotiations in the planning commission.

But "quitter" was not in Brodie's resumé. He and Ishi were driving the point of their spear into proving that the deal between De Boulette and Governor Murphy was a quid pro quo.

One angle continued to research major donors to the governor's re-election campaign. Noting that De Boulette had dropped off the radar in Greenley in 2009, after Minkle definitively rebuffed their efforts to purchase his holding, Brodie and Ishi cast their net further back. Over the course of the next week, in addition to their other work, they got access to a list of hidden and secondary tier donors, including mandatory contributions from De Boulette's vast administrative staff to a slush fund account. De Boulette's donations to Murphy dwarfed those from all other entities in the fall of the year that Minkle refused their offers.

Quietly that next June, Governor Murphy entered the already-closed Beckett State Forest into provisions of the State Surplus Land Act. Two months later without fanfare, De Boulette and the state signed the promissory contract to close on the sale when the two-year fallow period ended in June 2012. Circumstantial happenstance that was very cozy.

A week after the Pomo dance, Minkle showed up at the *Post-Ethical Times* office.

"I have more crappy news, Efan." He picked a callus on his palm.

Brodie switched off the office's music program. "Speak, Josh. Is it okay if Ishi records this?"

Minkle nodded. "Looks like I'm going to have to sell my land or just lose it all."

"This *is* bad. Why?"

"Wells Fargo Bank called my accountant. They're demanding full payment plus penalty fees on my loan within ninety days. My recent late payment on it is my thirteenth, which exceeds the terms of the note. The bank says"—he inspected a scrap of paper with handwriting on it—"it's, 'simply exercising its right to recall the loan' and to place the property for sale. I can challenge the ruling, but they know I don't have the money to go to court."

"The vineyard parcel is a separate deed, right?" Brodie asked. "Can you let it go and save the orchard? Does the success of your business depend on it becoming productive?"

Minkle coughed theatrically. "My wife left me over the *success* of my business. Against her advice, I used our equity in the orchard as collateral for the vineyard loan. This can't be coincidental. I suspect De Boulette is licking its chops to buy everything for pennies on the dollar the day the bank forecloses on me."

Brodie let out a sympathetic sigh. "Josh, I guess you don't know. De Boulette is a major shareholder in Wells Fargo, and I learned the other day that Stephen R. Baskin is now a member of the bank's board."

The injustice hit Ishi in the gut just as it had when he was reading the massacre document to the dancers. Whites were going to take that land again.

"All bankers have their price," Brodie said. "That's the blurb on the back of their business cards."

"I know you guys are working hard to save the trees," Minkle said. "But if you can fold my land into this, I'll do anything to help."

He asked if they could think of any local vineyard that might want to buy his orchard. Brodie said that seemed a long shot on such short notice.

He was uncharacteristically kind to Minkle, but after the farmer left, Brodie said, "I don't see how he can help us on this end." Then he threw his pen at the crime scene board. "Since the shit's in the fan, Ishi, I need to come clean with you."

Ishi thought he'd seen all of Brodie's emotional palette. But the old man's eyes grew red, somewhere between grief and fury. His head bobbed hard and fast. "It's been eating me up, and Dori has been telling me I have to do this *now*."

"And *I'm* the person you need to tell?"

"Hold still, Darkhorse. I'm gonna need your best day."

Ishi took his seat and turned off his phone.

Brodie had no gift for hemming and hawing. "The massacre document. I told you it came to me a couple years ago."

Ishi's pulse ramped up.

"You never asked how it came. So I let it slide. Longer that I ever thought I would. I told you it was in a trove of papers. What I didn't say is it came from my great uncle after he died. The author of that piece— I'm sorry, Ishi. Charles Gervin was my great-great-grandfather."

Ishi took in the sheer balls of Brodie's machinations in waves, each one grinding him into smaller pieces until he lost contact with the room.

The only other time he'd felt that dissociated from his surroundings was in the first seconds after his squad took a mortar round that had killed two of his buddies outright and made a mess of Fitzpatrick's face and shoulder. The Taliban unit across the valley had gotten a bead on them.

Brodie's confession settled it. Everything that could have gone wrong in the last 156 years had done so. The worst of it was being lied to by the hand that had fed him for the last however many months. The only option to survive the attack in Afghanistan had been to pour over the edge of their trench and risk taking direct fire. As on that day, Ishi knew every second was precious and that he had to move.

He stood, scooped up his electronics—everything else belonged to Brodie—and left without a word. Brodie's calls to him from the top of the stairs to reconsider clattered around him like pencils hitting the treads.

AT THE TRAILER, while packing his gear into his truck, it occurred to him that he had a near-perfect resumé to do what most decent people would want done—even though the chances of succeeding were one in a thousand. Not only was he a Marine, he was a Pomo Marine. Maybe he would be the new incarnation of a Pomo warrior returning to finish the fight.

Minkle had asked for help. Ishi was ready to put his body on the line. The redwood groves and the massacre ground were linked historically and deserved to be dealt with as one thing. The imbalance of power between the parties meant the story—if he found a way to tell it—would have to inspire many people.

De Boulette had picked up Charles Gervin's baton to finish the slaughter. Gervin's militia had had rifles. De Boulette would bring chain-saws and the power to contort the law.

No matter. The descendants of the Pomo were regrouping to counter-attack. Justice for his tribe would require an uphill climb and luck, lots of it. Ishi's weapons were his body and his ability to tell the story of his people—over Brodie's dead body if he had to. He would take it to the *Chronicle* direct and to any other paper he could find.

As he pulled out to travel north, Ishi realized he'd left the Sharps rifle and Pomo artifacts in the office. His bulldozer mode climbing the office stairs announced him.

Brodie met him at the door. Ishi held up his hand—*I'm not talking*—and marched to the closet.

"I understand, Ishi. And if you're quitting, I'll let you go—with two weeks' notice. And I want your best work in those two weeks."

Ishi's face contorted into a *you've got to be kidding me* expression. "Mr. Brodie, I don't care if you accept it or not. I'm walking. I have to put my body in a more important place."

"Hold on, Darkhorse." Brodie waved his index finger vigorously. "I actually agree with you. The good thing about being old is I've seen it all. *And* I've played by the rules for"—he turned his right hand palm up to count and added the thumb of his left—"in two years it will be six decades.

"In all that time, in spite of my best efforts, this cockamamie world has barreled on mistaking the building of sandcastles in the tidal flow as progress. Which is to say damn near diddly. There is still war and graft and power plays and desecration of beings and the environment beyond our imagination, let alone our ability to do much about."

He took a couple breaths to get his next line right. "But one thing I'll *not* be party to is letting you, sir, go to waste."

Ishi was dropping the arrowheads and bullets into manila envelopes. "That's not your call anymore, *sir*. It's one thing reporting on a crime that has already happened. Nothing we can do about that. People need to know. But knowing a crime is *going* to happen and reporting on it as if it is a baseball game, counting balls and strikes? That's a waste of my life."

Brodie's softening look caught Ishi off guard. "Here's what Dori said about you last night. You've made me the best she's seen me since I was in my thirties. She attributes it to you wearing down the calcium deposits in my cranky old heart. Don't look at me like that! What I love about that woman is she can be eloquent when her dander is up.

"Had the Pomo massacre story played out the way I originally thought months ago when I hired you, I would have told you about my ancestor right off, and our Plan A would have been right: get the governor's attention to drive him to grant your branch of the Pomo recognition. I don't know. This being an election year, the occasionally honorable Governor Murphy might just jump at a chance to create a touchy-feely stroke of policy to lift him in the polls.

"As for your resignation, it makes sense. But hear me out. The dissolution of our society may mean it's time to throw out the rules. So here's my proposal: However you want to do it, America's Last Real Newspaper will take that stand with you. Let's take it to the limit and accomplish all we can. And then after all the cards are played, your job will still be here—that is, if you want it, and if I'm not in jail."

Ishi fingered the back of his chair, staring at the floor and taking time to assess the change in the wind.

In the next minutes, Brodie apologized three different ways for the gross omission about his lineage. This put Ishi in a position new to him., above his commanding officer. At last, he sat in the chair to signal accepting Brodie's apology and listened to him praise his wife and Ishi.

When Brodie was spent, Ishi told him the particulars of the plan he was cooking up. Brodie's complicity would help immeasurably.

"I like it a lot," Brodie said. "Go work it out. But know you're probably kissing your career at a major paper goodbye. For now, if anybody in the business calls us out on it, I'll say it's the ultimate in embedded journalism."

"For an old guy, you're not stuck in your ways."

Brodie bowed ever so slightly. "All I ask is a piece from you every day. A thousand words. Can you do that?"

"I can," Ishi said. He left having no idea if he could. Instead of heading north to the Rancheria, Ishi passed the entrance to Beckett State Forest and took the windy mountain road over the coastal range to the big town on the coast. There, he picked up camping equipment to complete his kit, including two small solar chargers for his electronic devices, a tarp, a hammock, and a special weighted arrow to go with the bow he had bought. He threw in a large box of ammo for his Sig Sauer.

From there, he took the road he knew well from riding the school bus in the years before his family fell apart and came to the Rancheria from the west. He arrived just as Eli's physical therapist was leaving.

Eli responded to his idea by saying it was about time Pomo had their own Sitting Bull.

Amber, home after working at the drug treatment facility in Leggett, was giddy to see Ishi. But her mood collapsed when he told her his plan, particularly the part about not knowing how long they would be apart. She liked his idea of having Marco bring him supplies. It would give him responsibility and bind her brother to him. She said she'd come, too, when she could.

Marco said he was ready to join Ishi up there, but she shut him down.

"No way. It's too dangerous for you."

Amber and Ishi retired to her room early to do what they would not be able to do for a while.

Eighteen

I SHI ARRIVED AT the massacre site as the sun was breaking into the valley. He unloaded his gear on the bank of the Greenley River not far from the digging site where they had found the Pomo relics. Then he parked his truck on the far side of the vineyard near the road leading to the highway. He placed the key on the console in case he left in the custody of law enforcement or in a body bag.

Every time he had been in the grove, a particular tree had captured his awe. It was sixteen feet wide at the base and its trunk was arrow-straight. That morning he had awakened from a dream in which it had been holding up the sky. And his first thought was the name he would give it: Atlas.

In successive trips, he carried his equipment across the water and laid it at Atlas's base. Then he filled his water bags in the river, and leaning back against the trunk, he reviewed his plan. He had brought four large packs, 250 feet of half-inch six-braid rope, a similar length of light nylon cord, and the canvas tube that held the weighted arrow and his bow. Unlike any other trees nearby, Atlas's first limb extended level. It ran roughly forty-five degrees to the riverbed, a giant spar ten stories overhead. It would make a good platform to stand on as he hauled up his supplies.

He just had to get up there.

Atlas was one of seven giants that formed a rough circle. Pacing among them to gather his will, Ishi wondered if he really *could* change the fate of the forest . . . and with it, of the massacre land. Would his climb get noticed? What kind of reception would he get when he finally came back to earth?

To calm his nerves, he went through his equipment, a habit he'd developed before going out on a mission. He checked the zippers and velcro fasteners on each compartment of the four large packs. He ran the 250 feet of the half-inch six-braid climbing rope through his hands, looking for defects. He hefted the similar length of light nylon cord. Lastly, he unzipped the canvas tube that held the bow and the weighted arrow.

He tied his packs in ten-foot increments along the part of the rope he would haul up last. Next, he secured one end of the nylon cord to the tail of the arrow and uncoiled and arranged the spool of it onto the forest floor so it would lift off without snarling. He tied the other end of that cord to the lead of his climbing rope. He visualized the arc of the arrow several times, then nocked it in his bowstring. At last, with his right hand, he drew the string behind his ear, aimed the arrow's tip to fly over that lowest branch, and let it go.

It flew well, but passed under the branch. He changed his location, laid out the cord again, and pulled the bowstring back farther. That shot flew haywire and thudded into the trunk, still short of the branch. As he pulled back on his third try, he thought of the Pomo men running from their wikiups, knowing they only had one shot. This one flew true, cleared the branch about five feet from the trunk—perfect—tipped back toward earth, and landed fifty feet from him with barely a sound.

He freed the cord from the arrow and pulled on it until it lifted the lead end of his climbing rope. With deliberate drawdowns on the cord, the rope rose up and over the branch and back to earth.

He repacked the arrow and the bow in its tube and added that to the luggage train. Lastly, he hooked a six-inch pulley to his belt for use later, made a loop for his foot in the free end of the rope, and set a hitch under his left thigh and around his waist to secure himself as he ascended.

Pulling down on the baggage side of the rope caused the loop with his foot in it to rise a good step. He held his weight one-handed and reset the securing hitch. Repeating these steps, he climbed. At times, the rope passing over the branch got caught on the bark, forcing him to jump and shake it free. The friction of his weight on the rope was doubling his labor. In sweaty increments, he rose along Atlas's trunk.

Eighty feet from the ground, he rested for a long spell. Then he climbed furiously until he was able to throw an arm over the branch.

Scrambling aboard a rough, round object was typical for Marine training, but he'd lost a few steps since boot camp.

After he caught his breath, he stood and walked to the trunk. He secured his pulley to a branch overhead, clipped the climbing rope into it, and hauled up his train of gear, belaying each piece as it arrived. A little after 10 a.m., he had rested enough to explore the tree.

BY MID-AFTERNOON, HE had set himself up where three large branches joined the trunk about 220 feet off the ground. He had strung his hammock between two branches overhead, and hung the tarp to cover it in the unlikely event California decided to break its drought. He fastened his little gas stove into an irregularity in the bark that seemed made to hold it. His water bladders, with three days' supply, hung like kielbasa at a butcher shop. He texted Amber to let her know he was safe and Marco to make sure he was on board to bring supplies.

The third branch was the most level of the three. It allowed him to walk out and peer through the cloud of needles to catch a view of the valley. As he looked east, the massacre ground was directly below him, Minkle's orchard was in the near view to his right, and in three directions countless tracts of vineyards filled the vast flat land and ran up the hillsides in creative plots—vines staked and trellised with an engineer's precision.

Higher still, the steep, untended open land that should have been green with the new season's grass was still golden brown from last summer. The helter-skelter of third- and fourth-growth forests rose out of the gulches and gullies, and capped the hills in dark green.

He hung his solar collector in a sunny nook to charge the extra batteries for his phone and iPad.

Brodie had texted him.

sorry about yesterday and all of it

where are you

Ishi replied:

in my new home will connect soon

He climbed another hundred feet to where the top got bushy and found a cluster of branches angling up toward the sky. They were strong, but thin enough to respond to his weight. From there he could see long sections of the two-lane highway bordering Minkle's land. It was a third of a mile away.

Descending was dicey, like backing a truck down a mountain ridge with a foggy rearview mirror. He saw the value of primate tails and prehensile toes.

To fuel writing an opening piece worthy of West Coast papers, Ishi gobbled an MRE. The stakes were high. How to reach readers who might never have seen a redwood—or for that matter, who'd never met a real Indian?

His first humiliation was that his hammock failed as a writing station. A half hour later he found a wide limb tipped up at a slight angle from level. With the trunk at his back, he could sit cross-legged or straddle it and work with his iPad on his lap. His first order for Marco would be to bring a cushion.

He began with what he thought was a good idea, but his mind couldn't focus. At last, he tipped his head back into the trunk, looked at the needles overhead, and slept.

The grove he awoke in was altogether different. The late-day onshore wind had blown a great bank of fog over the hills, which blocked the sun and swallowed the trees. Ishi sat still as a rock, but the world was moving. Constantly moving. He tried to join with the solidity of the tree. And failed.

Once, from deep inside the trunk he heard—no, maybe he felt—a muffled thud, some resonance as if the tree was an enormous wooden drum being struck. It was then he realized the tree was moving. Though it was six feet through where he was sitting, the trunk was swaying, slowly swaying. Like the arm of a metronome passing through thick water. Or was it carving a circle? Or an ellipse? In any case, its motion wasn't regular, as if it were on benzos. Occasionally, it froze briefly in its course, then jumped free.

As the breeze and traffic noise diminished, a subtle range of clicks and creaking came from every quarter. Some from the branches themselves. At other times, from inside the trunk. It was a slow-motion symphony with no time signature. After rehearsing for millennia, driven by the sheer love of making sound, it was playing for an audience of one. Atlas was not a static resource but an artist, lacking only the ability to walk away.

Brodie wouldn't print a piece describing all this, but Ishi descended to his nest knowing some paper would. He prepared his first meal on his stove. Then, exhausted from all his climbing and listening, he crawled into his hammock.

There was no mistake. The tree was rocking him. When the coming of night hushed man-made sounds, the clicking grew louder. All the trees in the grove were clicking and groaning. A great redwood chorus.

For the first time in years, he smiled as he fell asleep.

BEFORE DAWN, THE grove offered another kind of music. Tiny timpani, with no resonance, provoked Ishi to irritation. Unwilling to be roused, he covered his ears. But when it continued after the sun rose, he rolled to make sense of it.

All around him the tree glistened as if covered in ice. Beads of condensation hung silvery on the end of each redwood needle. As the drops swelled, they fell. Some were plunking onto the tarp he'd hung overhead. Water pooling in two places—a piece of magic he hadn't seen coming—meant he wouldn't have to rely on Marco for this main resource.

Nineteen

As was to be expected, the emperor's announcement of the Temple of Listening project was beautifully timed. It came with the first signs of spring, a mere thirteen months after the Tohōku earthquake and tsunami. With great fanfare, he presented the project as one of renewal for the dispirited people of Japan. The public response had been overwhelmingly positive.

By the end of March, Tadao had made good progress on the designs. He had lived and breathed the project for many weeks in order to overcome the glorious and yet static nature of Japanese tradition. Without question he had shared the stages of his contemplation as well as his sketches with his master, Sensei Watanabe. As it turned out, much of his hard work had involved dragging Sensei from his entrenched rules of art and form into a new way of seeing. Gradually, Tadao felt the older man's conservative habit breaking free as if links of chain were snapping under tension.

At last, he and Sensei felt the temple's innovative design had succeeded in maintaining the vaunted *feel* of Japan's historical architecture while laying the groundwork for a new paradigm that would better call in the ocean *kami*. The creativity and the care were to show the *kami* that the Japanese people meant to be better stewards of the earth in the future, and in that way to gather the considerable power that *kami* wielded as a force for good to protect the land and its people.

From the designs, he prepared a list of the timbers needed to build the frame that countless pilgrims would see for 1,000 years. From that, he worked backward to create a tally of specific logs that would guide the sawyers in locating the trees they needed to fell.

For the last five centuries, four family firms had been entrusted with the responsibility of maintaining and harvesting trees from Japan's imperial forests, which were the sole source of wood for the nation's traditional buildings. The devotion and technical skills of planting, pruning, guarding, harvesting the trees, protecting the soil, and sawing the timbers had been passed down father to son, which is to say, master to disciple, in unbroken lineages. These firms employed thousands of workers, and in modern times, whole departments dedicated themselves to take every advantage of the latest scientific developments for care and assessment of the trees.

After extraordinary preparation, Tadao sent his timber lists to each of these firms, along with extensive notes. It was his first time using the Watanabe and Son wax seal on a missive. Of particular note, Tadao discussed the characteristics for three of the tie beams in the main roof. Their size would be as large as the revered Hinoki Cedar could ever yield. Of all the woods available in Japan, this species of cedar was prized for good reason. Trees of this age would be the very best available to resist damage from the elements, particularly heavy fog and occasional ocean storms. They were Japan's best hope that the buildings would remain erect to fulfill the emperor's vision.

Since the timber drying process and the construction will take many years, Tadao wrote, *it is my hope you will be able to quickly locate excellent trees. It is our goal to complete this project in time for our beloved Emperor to visit it and bless it in his lifetime.*

As usual for beams of this nature, we consider it wise to have you harvest at least two trees for each beam we seek so that we can be certain to have one free of defects.

It was normal to expect it would take a considerable number of weeks for the sawyers to locate and reserve these trees. Tadao spent that time working with masons, gardeners, sculptors, statuary craftsmen, electricians, painters, landscapers, and the like, both to get their input and to reserve their services so the project would go smoothly and the result would be pleasing from every angle and modality.

Barring unforeseen consequences, he was confident he would be ready to present the plans to the emperor for his approval on the date Sensei had reserved to meet him.

Twenty

ADJUSTING TO LIFE off the ground was full-time work.

First was the sheer physicality of it. Every action required movement across and around uncertain surfaces. Ishi realized how most mammals took for granted the simplicity and predictability of walking on the earth. In the tree, feet, knees, hips, hands, and a cavalier confidence all played important roles in getting from here to there. Any tension in a body part while moving made missteps more likely. For pointers, he watched videos of monkeys.

Next was the logistics conundrum: he had to strategize a place to store each item where it couldn't come loose and would be safe to handle. Everything he dropped vanished with a simple *whoosh* and soft thud, or seemed to hit every branch on the way down. On his three visits there, Marco had already retrieved a number of items: Ishi's hatchet, his toothbrush, a cup, the cutting board, a small pillow, a sock, and most important, the packet of nails he used to secure the string and tape that held many items.

Checking the ground under Atlas with an eagle eye became Marco's first task when he showed up, which in that first week had been after school. Amber's rule was that to help Ishi, he had to have perfect attendance. She would visit on weekends as she could.

Marco didn't own a car, but Eli and Amber agreed to let him use their vehicles. He would park across the river, whistle to announce his presence (as if Ishi couldn't hear him climbing the grade to the vineyard) and ask what he should be looking for. Ishi would lower a nylon bag for the items. On that first visit, he warned Marco to step carefully in the area Ishi had dedicated for his toilet.

Ishi had managed to hold onto his phone, the solar chargers, his iPad —his lifeline to the world of journalism—and his laptop. This last was quickly becoming an albatross because of its weight, size, and slick cover. It wanted to slide away no matter where he put it. He was making do with the iPad. That high up, the signal made his articles easy to send.

Each time Marco came, he had a new ploy to get Ishi to let him into the tree. It quickly moved from a running joke to an annoyance. Marco brought food and treats to salve Ishi cravings, which seemed to grow as the days went by. The fact that he was collecting his own water meant there was less for the boy to do. So for an hour, they conversed—about girls in school, Amber's moods and her messages for Ishi, Marco's plans to join the military, and as much as Marco could stand of Ishi's need to talk about his tree sit, Pomo history, and De Boulette's evil.

BY ITSELF, THE story of a Pomo's residency in a massive redwood at the site of a newly discovered massacre would have been well-received. The news that Ishi was writing articles while two hundred feet in the air proved seductive to many readers who normally might have had little interest in environmental issues or that part of history. He wrote every day, and Brodie's close relationship with the *Chronicle* provided a venue for those pieces. Ishi's byline was getting known.

Brodie had guaranteed that Ishi's series dedicated to Pomo history and culture would be placed on the front page of the two weekly editions of the *Post-Ethical Times*. Ishi interviewed anthropologists at Sac State and Cal Poly Humboldt, and Pomo elders of various bands. He pored over histories of early California settlement, including the periods of Spanish missionaries and Russian traders. What Brodie liked was how Ishi always brought these pieces back to the land and the trees.

Ishi's other articles were about the present. Some described the acrobatics and humorous considerations of living in a tree. Others addressed the discovery of the massacre in the Greenley Valley and the current state of the Pomo. These latter ones cross-pollinated with Brodie's articles on De Boulette and state government collusion. After a few days, the *San Francisco Chronicle* seemed to know they had a captivating angle, and dedicated half a page to Ishi's and Brodie's work every day.

ON ISHI'S SIXTH day aloft, Brodie sent him a text about his first piece in the massacre series.

I'm getting lots of emails about it. It's heartening to think there is a thread of justice that still runs through this American culture. It is battered, bruised, and emaciated, but it endures because truth and justice are intrinsic to part of every human culture. Without having to be coached, first-graders protest all acts that, on their face, aren't fair. (Unfortunately, as the little ones develop, they learn to sublimate their pique in order to partake of the goodies that power and favoritism bestow.)

Classic Brodie-speak.

To my sensibility, the image and majesty of the California coastal redwoods embody that thread of justice. Your ancestors were drawn to them because of their intrinsic power. My ancestor and his ilk were drawn to them through the Doctrine of Discovery, with its overt racism and domination over indigenous cultures, and its love of profit.

With each passing day, Brodie was warming to the notion of Ishi *being* the story *and* reporting on it. He said there'd been surprisingly few raised hackles in the West Coast media. He attributed this to the spell redwoods cast on the culture, combined with the guilt people who ended up in journalism felt about the genocide their ancestors had perpetrated on the indigenous population.

And now the *Los Angeles Times* wanted to pick up his series.

ISHI WAS WORKING on a piece exposing the underbelly of De Boulette's American CEO, Archibald Crockett, when he heard a sound new to him: an irregular scuffing and scraping somewhere below. When the white noise of car tires in the distance covered it, he turned back to his writing.

Several minutes later, he heard the sound again. Louder.

He saved his work, secured his iPad, and climbed down to his main quarters to hear better. It was not a threatening sound. He stood by the trunk a moment. The sound seemed to be directly below him. He pulled his pistol from the bag hanging on a nail, slid it into his waistband, and headed down.

Because the noise he made obscured what he'd been hearing, he halted several times. Breathing. Yes, some large animal below him on the tree. A few branches above his landing limb, he got a broken view to the floor of the grove but saw nothing. He was about to move again when forty feet down he caught a glimpse of black hair parted in the middle smack against the trunk. Was it a Pomo? Climbing freehand? For a second he wondered if it might be Amber, who was the only one with motive to try. She had teased him about it. But she hated heights.

Had Marco just given up waiting? He was tempted to call down, but realized that could cause a fall. A death on the site would end his project.

The bright color of a backpack strap on a shoulder caught his eye. A woman's shoulder. Fit, climbing straight up the bark on the trunk, using the huge crevices in the bark for hand- and footholds. She was fifteen feet below his landing limb.

He worried. Transitioning from climbing the bark to mounting the branch was a complicated move. But she moved laterally with grace, so she could ascend past the landing limb. When she glanced up again, he recognized Delicia.

At the prospect of her company, of any company, his heart beat hard. She climbed higher than she needed to, made a smooth lateral move, and stepped down onto the wide limb with the surety of someone getting out of a taxi.

She exhaled a hard breath, like a blue whale surfacing. Then she slipped off her backpack, leaned against the trunk, and folded her arms. She wagged her head back and forth slowly.

"Delicia," she said to herself, "you got some ovaries on you."

No great first line came to Ishi, but with each passing second, it seemed his silence honored her more. She would see him soon enough, standing two limbs above her. She would know he had watched her.

Now he could honestly say she was lovely from every angle. Her sheer top had three-quarter length sleeves and no collar. The day was not warm, but her sweat had stained it front and back.

Seeing him when she turned to climb, she didn't flinch. "Thought I'd pay you a visit. May I come up?"

"Too late to be asking that." He withheld his smile, maybe because it was the only way he could appear as unruffled as she seemed to be. "How'd you know which tree I was in? It would have been a pain to climb the wrong one."

She reached overhead and tapped the pulley.

He was embarrassed to have been outsmarted. "I'm all out of fresh salmon, but I can give you some tea if you are not all climbed out."

"Deal," she said.

It was stupid to check on her progress, but he did, as if to confirm he wasn't dreaming. And he learned from her when, in places, she took her own route.

She slipped up into his nest and scanned it. "I love it."

"You can sit there." He pointed to the hammock and bent to free his gas stove from its strap.

"So this is the tarp that's solving your water problem. Very clever."

She'd been reading his articles.

"Luck," he said.

"There's much less luck in life than we think," she said. "Both good and bad."

"Was there luck in your fall?"

She saw the branch that led to the view of the valley and walked on it as if it were a sidewalk. She spent a minute looking, then returned. "Can't answer that. You know, I thought you had disappeared. I was hoping to see you after the Pomo dance."

She sat on the hammock.

"What did you think?"

"Of the dance? It was great, but even Brodie couldn't give it much juice, you know, to save the trees. What *you're* doing is better. More dramatic."

"Is that what you came to tell me?"

"Nuh-huh. You've got to get people *here*. Or at least bring them in remotely. I can help with that." She pointed to her backpack.

"You have a clown costume for me?"

She chuckled. "Maybe on my next trip. You need visuals and, no, the selfie you sent to your boss is not what I mean. He's a media animal. If the world had a hundred like him, crime would probably become a quaint relic."

"He'd be happy to hear that. What *are* you doing here?"

"I know some things about media."

The tea water boiled. Ishi filled his only cup.

"You paint well with words, Ishi."

He was about to thank her.

"But what you need, if I may say so, is another approach. To save these trees, you need to get people to pour in here."

He handed her the cup. "I don't disagree. But there's only one of me. The real work has to happen in Sacramento. Ultimately the governor is in control. If he lets the sale go through, the sawyers will come and drop these trees. That's Game Over."

She blew across the surface of the tea. "You're more depressed than your articles let on."

"Touché. It's hard to stay positive with all the forces arrayed against us, against the Pomo and the trees. This is a last-ditch effort."

"You ask me," she said, "De Boulette needs its head smacked. And the governor, too."

"Why do you care so much?"

"Because the *taking* has to stop. That's all humans do. Take, take, take. We even kill the things we love . . . *for* the things we love."

Images came to him to affirm her point: the massacre, the logging, the lack of salmon in the river. He thought of the elephants she loved in Zimbabwe and—

She interrupted his thinking. "I think this world is in a war few are willing to acknowledge."

She seemed so sure. But he didn't like how close it sounded to religious fervor. "You said you brought something."

"Yes, a visual. Maybe it will shift things. As soon as your article came out and I saw where you were, I started making you a banner."

She saw his skeptical look. "The world I come from is based on getting attention. Listen, this valley has only one road through it, right? Well, the other day I checked it out. There are a couple places where the tops of these trees are visible. Every driver who looks over will see it. All the locals and a lot of rich people come through from the coast."

"I don't get what good a flag will do."

"It's not a flag. It's a protest banner. Don't worry, I made the letters three feet high."

Twenty-One

A LITTLE AFTER THREE o'clock, Ishi and Delicia stretched her banner taut from limb to limb across the top of Atlas. He wondered how long it would take the news to get to Brodie, and how many drivers would get the reference.

With a promise to bring the other half of the banner soon, Delicia headed back to her aunt Stephanie's sewing room. She was grateful to ride down on Ishi's rope. She put her foot in the loop, grabbed hold of the haul line that Ishi had secured into the pulley, and virtually jumped off the limb. She dropped with the ease of a fireman on a pole.

After she left, he sifted through their interaction. She didn't treat her beauty as a tool. He was disarmed by her intelligence and passion about a task that he was still feeling his way through. In publicity, he was way out of his depth. He'd done a lot of listening.

An hour and eleven minutes after the banner went up, Brodie called him.

"You're stunning me, Darkhorse. Did you get your girlfriend to make that?"

He answered truthfully. "No."

"You have a secret admirer, then. One of my oldest subscribers sent me a picture. I damn near split a gut."

"So they can see it from the road all right? How's it look?"

"Reads loud and clear. Let me put it this way. I expect *Charlotte's Web* will soon see a bump in internet searches. And if we play this right, in sales too. I should call the local bookstores to see if we can get a five percent kickback. *Some Pig.* Really! How on earth did you come up with that?"

"I had help."

"Well, keep it up. What are you going to do next? I assume you have it all worked out."

"Yes, we have another one coming to finish the thought. I was hoping you would like it. If we can get the TV stations in Santa Rosa to do a piece on it, we'll time the punchline for a couple days later."

"Listen to you! You aren't going to tell me what's coming, are you?"

Ishi was listening intently for irritation in Brodie's voice, but heard none. "Not yet."

"Great. I now have a reporter going rogue. You're going to be the death of me . . . right after you bankrupt America's Last Real Newspaper."

"Nonsense . . . with all due *respect*. I've just taken on a PR person. I predict your subscriptions are going to jump." Ishi shook his head. He'd never guessed he would be so cavalier with Greenley's intellectual heavyweight.

"At some point, I'll want to know who this fellow is. Write me a piece on him, willya, that we can print on a slow news day. There are bound to be a few of those, 'cause I think we're gumming up De Boulette's plans nicely. If we can slow them down a little and extend this —how shall we say—*pas de deux* until the primary election, we might be able to force the governor out of his Camelot castle to have to address it."

"I will write that. But my expert is a woman. And if she has her way, there won't be too many slow news days."

AS PLANNED, MARCO came that afternoon with a bag of supplies. Ishi descended to his landing to wait for him. When Amber stood glaring up at him with her hands on her hips, he was glad to be a hundred feet above her.

"I know you can't thread a needle," she called up first thing. "So who made the banner?"

"Do you like it?"

"I don't know. Depends on how you answer."

Marco was smart. He knew to stay back in the trees. But Ishi couldn't retreat. "I was writing day before yesterday, and damn if that circus lady didn't climb up here freehand. Unannounced."

"That circus lady? The one who came to the dance?" She stamped her foot. "I warned her. And I'm pissed at you. I gave you *my* blessing to sacrifice *our* time together so you could make whatever statement might call attention to the tragedy that happened here. And the goddam prettiest white woman in northern California pays you a visit?"

He'd seen glimmers of this energy from Amber before, when other Pomo women felt emboldened to flirt with him. She would rear up in a hissing display but thirty seconds later would practically sashay off with her sister Pomo, laughing, their arms around each other. She'd never felt threatened because she was the only Pomo who had ever caught his eye.

"Tell me. Is she stupid? I gave a warning as big as a thunderhead."

"Before we go any farther, don't forget I'm here to prevent the *next* tragedy." He gestured toward the grove, throwing up whatever obstacles he could to keep things civil. Amber probably was too smart to not see that, but he needed time.

He also needed Marco, and Amber had complete sway over the boy coming. In the beginning, she'd thought—and he too had thought—that Marco coming would help maintain Ishi's bond with Amber. Now Marco was a mere appendage.

"Look, I didn't call her. She showed up on her own *with* the banner."

"But you hung it." She folded her arms. "So you encouraged her. What's that bitch's name?"

"Delicia. Fortunado."

"This whole time I've been worried about you falling out of this tree. If you do another kind of falling, I swear I'll get all our ancestors to lay out jagged rocks underneath wherever you go."

"Come on, Amber. You gotta realize, I can't be here without the help of lots of other people."

"You *got* people. Marco's coming. I'll keep coming. Lots of Pomo will help . . . when they get it together."

"Look, she's gone. Come and gone. Brodie says her banner's going to help a lot. So can we stop this? It's not easy being up here . . . and away from you."

Gradually, Amber saw she'd cast herself into her own pond, and to get to land, she'd have to swim.

"It's not bad, the banner," she said. "Kind of funny, actually. Sorry to be so pissed off. I know you understand. Marco didn't get the reference of *Some Pig!* I had to explain it to him."

Charlotte's Web had made the rounds in some of the tribes, because the spider was a totem creature. It was one of the few books Ishi had grown up with. The story didn't treat Indians badly. It didn't treat them at all. A white narrative, not offensive, because it relied on the animal world. There had been hardly any books by Indian authors before the new millennium. That was changing.

"No way I'm coming up there, but can you come down to let me apologize?"

She tapped quickly on her phone. Ishi's pinged.

I'll tell Marco 2 take a walk

Can U come down 4 a quick one?

She added a smiley face and a heart.

This good day was seriously at risk of choking. He smiled broadly so she could see. "I wish I could," he said. His shine drooped. "My commitment to stay up here is what gives it power. If people find out I come down for this or that, they won't take me seriously."

She hammered another text.

Sex isn't 'this or that'

I am not this or that

Marco became the hero then, way ahead of his years. He marched over and put his arm around Amber. "How about Amber hugs me, and I come up and give you the groceries and her hug?"

"You are not going up there, got it? You're all the family I have."

Marco looked to Ishi for a counter-edict.

"Sorry. She's right. After you do your Parris Island tour and you can get yourself up here, then we'll talk."

Even from a hundred feet up, Ishi saw Marco's hand curl into a fist.

Ishi had his best idea in their whole relationship. "Would it make things better if you make me another banner?"

Amber swelled to be asked. "Yes, it would. What should it say?"

"The strongest thing I think you can do is make one that says, *Ghost of the Pomo.*"

Amber left almost dancing.

Twenty-Two

ALOFT WITH ISHI, Delicia had felt both the ease of moving in the limbs and the importance of the stand Ishi was making. It led her to an obvious conclusion. She finished the addendum to the *SOME PIG* banner and took off for two days to gather supplies.

When she returned, contrary to her expectations, her Aunt Stephanie got on board with her plan. Stephanie cackled and said she wished she was young again and hadn't trashed her body when she was too naive to know any better.

Delicia read Brodie's jubilant editorial about the press conference a spokeswoman for the governor had finally given to address the goings-on in Greenley. According to Brodie's analysis, she was trying to thread several needles at once: showing awareness of the subject that was garnering print media, hoping that "the tree sitter" didn't fall, and on top of that, acknowledging that the trespass on state lands was both illegal and foolhardy—"the 1990s proved such protests were feckless *and* dangerous," she said—and expressing concern for the state of the redwoods now that Beckett had come back into the public eye. The meeting's oddest moment was when she commented that there were no portable toilets for the tree sitter to use. But overall, her expert tone of lightheartedness and clout was part of the message.

Brodie pointed out the glaring hypocrisy of "the state being complicit in arranging the clearcutting of the redwoods that it supposedly treasured." And the spokeswoman overlooked the fact that Ishi was not some "eco-terrorist tree-sitter, but a published journalist of the Pomo nation calling attention to land where his ancestors had been slaughtered and roasted."

Brodie's related article outlined the incredibly coincidental tragedy of Wells Fargo's action to put Minkle out of business in time for De

Boulette to add his property to their land grab. To add insult to injury, Brodie found a logger who was irate enough about the sale to estimate, free of charge, the timber value of the Beckett redwoods. When all the wood made it to mill, it would bring in four times the price De Boulette was paying. Which amounted to it being a giveaway of state resources.

In all this, Delicia knew she was making the right decision.

She had Stephanie drive her up to the vineyard and across the dusty road to the riverbank. She portaged her bags into the grove, waved to Ishi, who had dropped to his landing limb, and returned to help Stephanie make her way through the river boulders. Stephanie had insisted on seeing her niece's talent in action for herself, and she'd brought a sandwich to make her morning's entertainment complete.

Delicia shrugged off feeling watched and laid out her gear at the base of the tree to the left of Ishi's, also a beautiful specimen though its lower branches provided a more difficult landing. She had taken good mental notes on what Ishi had brought, though her gear included one thing he had not—the sixty-foot section of rope she had ordered for her slack rope routine.

It was auspicious that Marco appeared while she was clipping her bags to her climbing rope using carabiners. After he sent Ishi's supplies up to him, he hovered a little close for her liking. "I was hoping you'd come," she said. "Any chance I can piggy-back on Ishi's orders?"

"Sure," Marco said, acting cool. But his eyes got huge when she handed him two one-hundred dollar bills. She added his cell phone number to her phone.

She made a loose coil of the top section of her climbing rope and fastened the end of it to the belt at her back.

Stephanie hugged her and promised to collect her when she came down. "Call me anytime, dear."

Delicia scanned a possible route up the trunk and glanced up at Ishi. "Lieutenant Fortunado reporting for duty . . . sir."

Ishi's salute was half-hearted, but she was confident that he'd realize her value when the second banner went up, and her name became attached to the project.

She climbed around a burn scar at the base of her tree and she was off. Her hands kept finding solid holds in the bark's fissures. Below her, the rope lifted smoothly from its coil. And her foot behaved well. A few stabs of pain.

About ten feet from the low limb, she heard Stephanie call up. "Dee, I think you mis-measured. Did you mean to drag the first bag up before you get there? That's going to be heavy."

Delicia looked down. "Dammit."

But Marco leapt forward and unhooked it. "All clear," he called up.

Getting herself into the crotch of the first branch was harder than she'd thought it would be. But at last she was aboard.

Ishi clapped with more enthusiasm. Stephanie and Marco hooted below.

Like Ishi, she had brought a pulley and used it to haul her bags up.

"D'you mind if I tie a loop in the end and haul myself up to join you?" Marco asked.

"You're cute," she said. Her voice had a slight fetch in it. "Maybe some other day."

"Don't encourage him," Ishi said.

ISHI SEEMED DISTANT while Delicia made her tour of the tree. Some thirty feet below his nest, she found a serviceable group of limbs to set up her own. It placed her on the far side of her trunk, which saved them the awkwardness of living like suburban neighbors.

Her next priority was a pair of limbs to which she could fasten her slack rope. She found them twenty-five feet below her nest. And to her delight, a good way above Ishi's nest she found something else she needed: a beautifully level branch on which to stretch and train. That it extended toward a similar branch coming from Ishi's tree made it possible to consider talking with him at close quarters. If she only had a ten-foot bridge, she could walk to Atlas.

IN MID-AFTERNOON SHE sent him her first text.

hope UR not mad this'll B good wait n C

The minutes crawling by without a response hurtled her back to junior high school. At last, her phone vibrated.

why didn't you tell me UR plans?

this needs to be a Pomo statement

this is R land

She was mortified.

Later, she heard him climbing down, then saw him. He was mastering the art of moving limb to limb. She took a seat where he could see her. He came level and squatted on a branch. They were fifty feet apart, a distance that allowed both candor and hiding.

"This is your fight," she said. "I'm here to support you. But if for any reason you want me gone, say the word."

He stared somewhere below her. Finally he said. "If you mean it, fine. We can try it. At this point, no one knows you're here. Maybe we should keep it that way. You say you have a banner?"

"Yes. Let's hang it. If people don't respond, then I'm mistaken." Her skin prickled. It had been years since she'd had to audition for anything.

"I've put in my article for the day. So now is good."

She rose and pointed. "See you up there."

"I thought you were going to toss it over."

"No, this one's longer. It'll go from tree to tree."

He went still a moment. This seemed hard for him. At last he said, "Let's try it."

She'd been so excited these last few days, Ishi being resistant hadn't occurred to her. Brodie had already touted the first banner. Northern California papers had printed pictures of *SOME PIG*. "Guerrilla marketing," they called it. Several TV stations had run it, too. Even in the few hours since she'd climbed, she'd heard a number of drivers on the highway honk. It was almost as good as applause. According to Brodie, people in the valley were nearly of one mind in wanting De Boulette to stay in France.

She pulled the throwing weight she'd made and the banner from the case that also carried fabric she had precut and hemmed for future banners . . . if Ishi didn't kick her out.

That he was climbing quickly and already a good ways above her gave her a competitive jolt. She snickered and let it go. Wasn't she past that?

At the top, she found him looking across the space.

"So what's your plan?" he asked.

She replied by tying the weight to a long length of cord. She swung it back and forth, getting it ready to throw. Timing and force were everything. Seeing the parallel with swinging on the trapeze, she let it go at the far end of its arc. It landed near Ishi's feet. First try!

His look of doubt softened.

She tied her end of the cord to the grommet next to the word "Wants," and he hauled his end of the banner to him. He read it upside down and laughed. They spent twenty minutes stringing it between the trees and getting it level. Horns on the highway started before they even finished. Those few words were going to kick Ishi's protest to the next level.

Well, Ishi's and *Brodie's* protest. Those two made a good pair, though from what Ishi had said about his boss, they were opposites in some ways. What couldn't be denied was how the number of comments from readers ballooned after the new *SOME PIG* picture was printed. Opinions covered the usual gamut between enthusiasm and hate, but the publicity was the important thing. Papers from British Columbia to Tucson had run some of the *Post-Ethical Times*'s best articles.

AS DELICIA HAD hoped, the banner addendum—*WANTS TO CUT US DOWN*—roared out from Atlas like a tidal wave. Those seven words in that location caused media to call them "a cudgel wrapped in laughter." In passing, some wondered about the logistics of one man tying a banner to two trees, but rather than assuming the obvious, most people simply added this to the list of Ishi's superpowers. She hadn't anticipated how this detail made it easier for Ishi to accept her presence.

They had several conversations over the next few days, across the distance, a method they named 'the jungle phone.'

She said she'd decided her tree needed a name, too. "We've got to keep equality in mind." She beamed and patted her tree's trunk. "I'd like to introduce you to Her Majesty."

He liked it and sarcastically admitted she knew a bit about publicity. Her Majesty, it was.

Ishi admitted having a sense of triumph that readers were doing what Brodie had been sure they wouldn't: merging sympathy for the Pomo cause on one piece of land with wanting to defeat a multinational corporation that had designs on a neighboring piece. Brodie had thought this kind of nuance would go over the head of most Americans. But as Ishi's sit ripened into its third week, several pundits in the Northwest noted that this scenario of a single man against a corporation was stirring Americans' best instinct: cheering for the little guy. Ishi was quick to point out that for four centuries, Tribal Nations people had never *risen* to the level of the little guy.

Commentators conjectured that the power of the trees and the tragedy awaiting them allowed readers to overlook Ishi's tactics and his bloodline. Of course, some thought he was only fighting for the trees. That led to one jungle phone talk where she found herself trying to calm him down.

Some readers were charmed to learn that a tribe named Pomo even existed. The Pomo lifestyle of fishing and basket weaving in the California garden of Eden that Ishi presented in his articles dented the white stereotype of Indians as diabolical. In comparison to the Plains Indians, who'd fought back against ethnic cleansing, the Pomo seemed almost cuddly.

She and Ishi kept Brodie in the dark about her being up there. The campaign to save a small chunk of land in a remote California valley was gathering momentum. Brodie's main objective was to get under the governor's skin and have him, by political necessity, help them with publicity that would cut his own legs out from under him. One of Brodie's maxims was *Silence is our most insidious opponent.*

Some days later, Delicia had still not risen from her hammock when several car doors slammed across the river.

Ishi texted her. *Company. De Boulette. Crap, it's Baskin.*

She'd seen Baskin the day Ishi had first brought her to the redwoods. Ishi had characterized him as "a hit man in a suit."

Baskin was the guy responsible for Wells Fargo pulling the rug out from under Minkle's mortgage. This off-stage detail had struck her as the most vicious of the whole affair. Minkle was just a stubborn farmer, minding his own business. Had he collapsed under De Boulette's pressure to sell five years earlier, the dirty dealing with Murphy that led to their taking Beckett State Forest might never have been necessary. The trees might never have been under threat. Evil made insidious turns.

Even from a distance on Delicia's first sighting, Baskin's upright arrogance reached across the river and lent a whiff of sulfur to the air. During her time in the spotlight, she'd encountered a lot of men like him. She had learned how to decline their many creative offers to get her into bed. True, Tsongumatta's Dr. Joseph Massama had evaded her radar by catching her as she was rising from four months in a hospital bed.

She jumped into her jeans and slithered down the branches to see what would happen. Something told her to slow down as she got near her lowest limbs. Might Baskin and his partner be armed? She pulled out her phone to record the event.

"Mr. Darkhorse, this is Stephen Baskin from De Boulette. We met in your office on the twenty-first. I want to talk with you. Off the record."

"I'm here. But I'm *on* the record." Ishi's voice was below her.

"Well, can we have a civil conversation? And by that, I mean practical?"

"All right. This will be practical. Do you know a fellow named Charles Gervin?"

Baskin looked at the ground a moment. "Sounds familiar. Why?"

"A hundred and fifty-six years ago, Charles Gervin stood out on that vineyard with a ragtag group of armed men and, like you, he would probably have said he was being practical. Though he lacked your manners to knock on doors first. Your corporation has different weapons, but your aim is the same—"

"This early in the morning," Baskin said, "I'm not good on romantic narratives."

"Then let me give you some pointers. If you spend some time in these woods without the agenda of counting board feet and dollars per vine, it might give you a new way of appreciating the world."

"Look, Darkhorse . . . of course you have a point. We all love these trees. But they have outlived their usefulness. There's only a few left, and with climate change they're in the process of dying. De Boulette will carefully cut them down and sell the wood to the most respectful buyers. There's just no sensible reason to let this resource die on the stump."

"And you'll make a ton more selling them than the 1,457 acres are going to cost you. That's a pretty sweet deal. But you're ignoring half the argument and most of the reason I'm up here."

Delicia hadn't seen this side of Ishi before.

"I've read your stuff. Your argument about history is weaker than the one about saving the trees. You can't bring back dead people."

"Oh, I must have misheard. I thought you wouldn't waste your time reading romantic narratives."

"I prepare for all my meetings. So I acknowledge your points. But face it. In time, people will get tired of your argument and you'll come down. It would be best if it happens in the near term and without a lot of fanfare. If you don't, consider that we're prepared to publicize your unit's—shall we say—tragic activity in Bamiyan." He shook his head in mock concern. "No telling how that could beat up a young man's plans for his future. Let alone revealing him as a hypocrite of the highest order."

Ishi let barely two seconds pass. "How do you like our banner?"

"You're a piece of work, Darkhorse . . . for a piece of shit. And to answer your question, not much. Though it's impressive to consider the trouble you went to, stretching it from tree to tree. Wish I'd seen *that*."

Delicia had been barely able to hold her phone steady for all the venom rising from the SOB. The words just poured out of her. "Then for the next one, we'll be sure to send you an invitation."

Baskin and his vassal wheeled at the sound of her voice and looked up, straight into her camera.

"Turn that thing off, damn you. You had no permission to film this conversation. You got a girlfriend up there with you. I should have known."

"I doubt you asked Josh Minkle," Ishi said, "if you could drive over his land this morning. Probably because you're the guy driving him into bankruptcy."

Baskin had no reply.

"And you are obviously a little deaf when you're talking to tribal nations people. Cause I can hear him coming across the vineyard clear as day. I couldn't help myself. I texted him as soon as you arrived."

Baskin slapping his pant leg showed his hearing had quickly improved. His vassal dashed along the riverbank, trying to see what was coming.

"Steve," the vassal called back, "the guy's got a backhoe . . . and at least four men with him."

Baskin turned and trotted toward the place where he had crossed water.

"Thanks for stopping in, Steve," Ishi called down.

Baskin raised his middle finger behind his head and kept moving.

"Nice contribution," Ishi said to Delicia. "I'm going up to my 'window' to see what happens. Do you think you can get to the top to film the event? It might be good to have a bird's eye view on it."

Delicia didn't waste a second. She dashed up her tree, hearing an engine roaring and some loud human voices. When she got to the place below the banner where she could see almost directly below her, she watched through her phone's camera.

Minkle had stuck the bucket of his backhoe under the tailgate of Baskin's SUV and lifted its rear wheels two feet off the ground. Minkle's men had surrounded Baskin and his vassal, who both looked poised for the impossible: to enter the driver's cab and escape. Was Baskin armed? He didn't seem to be the killer type.

She held the phone away from her mouth and yelled down, "You're on film."

Twenty-Three

IN CONTRAST TO Ishi, who was haunted by Baskin's threat, Brodie loved every part of what he called "the Baskin episode." He decided to hold it for the time being.

"It'll be valuable as leverage," Brodie said on the phone after viewing Delicia's footage. "We can exploit missteps De Boulette and the governor are sure to make.

"And, I must say, your teaming up with the Delicia woman is providential. Her sex brings a one-two punch to the protest, and her backstory, such as I have had time to peruse it, will prove endlessly helpful in calling attention to our cause. The governor's going to have to reckon with us. If *I* were his advisor, I'd say *sooner* than later. So though I don't really need her permission to name her, I'd like to get it to start us off on the right foot. Can you give me her contact?"

Ishi worried that things might get out of control. "She *is* compelling and, of course, very beautiful—"

"I've looked at her pictures."

"—but she's a bit of a loose cannon."

"That could be good. Loose cannons keep everyone looking for the next move. And in the case of Murphy and the state, the power of her social media following should keep *them* worried. I mean it is hard to stay one step ahead of an unpredictable force."

Ishi gave Brodie Delicia's phone number. Shortly after, she used the jungle phone—to say Brodie had reached out. She'd consented to being part of the articles.

"I am impressed that he said he'd consult with you," she said, "on how and when to use my presence. But he *is* going to announce that you have company. Are you all right with this? I'm going to wait until he does before contacting my network of people. I think it's been a good day. And it's still early."

DELICIA DOVE INTO doing her own thing. He saw her moving around, climbing way above him as he worked. At an early hour, she texted him that she was heading to sleep.

It was such a weird dynamic to text a neighbor he could talk to at any moment. He brooded in the dark on various scenarios with Marco and Amber until he caught himself nodding off where he was sitting. A fall from up there was another way he could make the news.

Nights in his hammock were becoming more and more delightful. Wrapped like a papoose, or maybe like a fetus in the womb. Held close, almost floating in the dark. He looked forward to the music of the dew dripping from the branches, and the day's first croak of ravens. Even the sound of tires on the road as carpenters headed off seemed part of the fabric of nature.

THE NEXT DAY, his handful of oats was coming to a boil when he heard several voices. Delicia's was one. The other was male.

Ishi sprang to his window to see if he recognized the vehicle that might have arrived. At the far end of the vineyard, Amber's burnt red sedan was parked next to his truck. Why had Marco come so early and parked so far away? Hoping everything was all right, he dressed and headed down.

Delicia was sprawled on her landing branch, and someone was hauling himself up using her line. Marco! The boy's strength made it look easy. But his inexperience was causing the rope to gyrate. That he wore only a small pack caused Ishi to look again. Below, he had attached a large duffle to haul up after he arrived.

Delicia was stabilizing the rope.

"Marco, you're being a complete ass."

"Delicia doesn't think so," he called out. He didn't even sound winded. "She invited me when I told her I wanted to help."

Delicia didn't change her focus.

"Send him down," Ishi bellowed. "He's going to get himself killed." And he knew Amber was going to kill him no matter how this turned out.

"I want to give him a chance," she said, still facing Marco. "He's giving us good service. It's just for an overnight. Look at him. He's fearless. That's great," she called down. "Just a little more. You're a natural."

Marco let go one hand and gave a Tarzan scream. "Hear that? She says, I'm a natural."

"At your age, idiocy is natural."

"Now is not the time, Ishi. He's got to focus. I know what I'm doing."

She was right. Military field protocols said, 'If interfering will make moves dangerous, zip it.'

Ishi leaned against the trunk and watched Marco clamber aboard Delicia's landing limb. He couldn't hear what Delicia was saying. Her body language was showing Marco how to move. She took his backpack herself, and Marco began hauling up his duffel.

Ishi realized his meal would be boiling over and he climbed at a good clip to save the pot, if not the meal.

The oats were crisp. He ate them, chewing on the fact that his mission had become more complicated. He had liked the balance of politics being "out there" and the grove being a refuge. But now, it seemed, politics were coming to the trees. His interactions with Delicia were already complicated enough. Having a third body up there would send a more complex signal to the governor and to everybody paying attention.

For a second he saw the whole Pomo Nation in the grove's trees. They would be the first aerial tribe in the nation! He mulled that over. The idea pleased him. If 187 Pomo climbed, they could manifest as ghosts of the villagers murdered down below. Would the press be interested in that?

He put the idea away and began that day's piece for America's Last Real Newspaper, though he was aware he was polishing his voice in anticipation of being read in bigger papers.

Movement in Delicia's tree distracted him. She was leading Marco up her route to the top.

Marco looked over. "She's going to set me up in quarters up here."

Ishi said simply, "Be safe. No clowning around, okay?"

"Ho!" Marco called back.

"And do what she tells you. She can save your life."

Marco's sloppy salute made Ishi's skin prickle.

"Don't worry, I'll watch over him," Delicia said.

Ishi texted her some parameters to get things straight without Marco hearing.

Later, he was buried in his work when he heard several muffled sounds that he couldn't identify. Then came the sharp zinging of rope being pulled over a branch, a sound his own preparations to climb had made. Something was completely off. He stashed his iPad in a shot and began dropping through Atlas's limbs.

Somewhere lower, Delicia called out, "State foresters! It's a raid."

As Ishi neared his platform limb, two men were scampering up lines to limbs above the one he was on. A third was coming to his landing limb. All seasoned climbers in state camo uniforms. Ishi's knife flashed in his hand, and without hesitation he cut the rope of the man who was closest to the ground.

The fellow fell back with a cry. A fall of less than 20 feet into the needle duff. He jumped up. "You're gonna pay for that, you bastard. We're from the state and we're here to take you down."

Ishi heard Delicia cussing. For some reason she was higher than before.

Ishi crossed to the line of Atlas's second highest climber. The forester was thirty feet up when Ishi reached out and shook the man's rope. From the training these men had had, Ishi presumed they both knew a thirty-foot fall could easily kill a man. "You're next."

The man dared him with a look to commit murder and kept climbing.

Ishi hesitated only long enough to think, *the sooner the better.* One stroke, and down the climber went.

The climber proved his skill by landing in expert control, with a roll, but he swore, freeing himself from his line as it toppled on top of him.

Ishi dropped to his landing limb. The man climbing the line looped over it stopped and looked up. Bravado would not improve a fifty foot fall, and Ishi had shown his ruthlessness.

"He's crazy," the first forester called up.

The second forester was standing, looking up, rubbing his shoulder. "You are resisting arrest, you know!"

Ishi stared the remaining climber in the eye. The word "manslaughter" flashed in his head. "I'll cut you down. I promise I will." His bark masked his decision that he wouldn't. A bluff in the game of aerial poker. For a long minute he and the climber froze, eye-to-eye.

"I mean it," Ishi said.

"Okay. Don't. Don't cut it. I'm going down." The climber released his his tension hold and zipped to the ground.

For good measure, Ishi cut his rope. At least those three were done for the day.

But two other foresters were ascending Her Majesty. They were already too high to cut down, even if Delicia had a knife and could reach their ropes. It looked like Ishi was going to lose his teammate.

There. He'd said it. Teammate. Amber was going to have to deal with reality.

The only weapon he had was his phone. As he filmed them chugging up their lines, his mind flew through the arguments. He had put himself and his mission in great peril. He was on state land. Trespassing. And by cutting those men down, he'd endangered the lives of two state officials. What was that? Reckless endangerment. Even if they were unharmed, statutes could make everything a crime. Ishi was cooked. No savior anywhere nearby. He saw himself in the marble hallway of a generic state court.

His whole response had taken less than two minutes. His defense that it was in his training to repel an attack would probably be laughed out of court. But a new element was coursing through him these days. Any prosecutor worth her salt could use the fury lightly buried in his massacre articles to turn a jury against him.

Ishi had changed since returning to the Rancheria. And in the last month, his commitment to not capitulate to authority that was married to corruption had come to a boil.

He looked down. The climbers of his tree were assembling their gear, coiling their cut ropes, watching their colleagues climb to Her Majesty's lowest limbs. They had sent three into his tree and two into Delicia's. They'd planned how to prioritize their power, which probably meant they had been spying on the grove. And they had come in through Beckett to hide their arrival. Baskin must have informed them about the situation. And for what? To facilitate the state's intention—actually the governor's—to drop these trees to benefit a corporation. To level a resource that belonged to the public.

Ishi erased that thought. More and more, he subscribed to the point of view that resources didn't belong to any public but to the Earth directly.

The state climbers in Her Majesty moved up their lines like Navy SEALs. Their skills made Ishi's merely commendable. They were at about the same height off the ground and they were goading each other, bantering, competing, as if this were a fun jaunt with the boys. A state-sponsored antic to brag about for years to come.

"Remember when we ripped that circus broad out of her tree?"

"Are you kidding? One of the best days of my life. De Boulette still sends me a case at Christmas as a thank you."

Ishi looked for Delicia. She was not in view, must have climbed. But to what avail? Once they were in her the tree, she was stuck. They were going to haul her down. He'd have to watch helplessly.

And Marco. Was he up there still? He hoped Marco had left Her Majesty for some reason while Ishi had been in his writing tunnel. Otherwise, Marco would have been hollering, wouldn't he? Probably defying them. Too bad he would miss his big opportunity to come face-to-face with the kind of people he wanted to be. Would he try to take their side? The foresters probably didn't even know he'd climbed that day.

He texted Marco.

if UR in Delicia's tree hide in the top

stay put

the foresters don't know UR here

If they haul her down maybe U can take over her job

Next, he texted Delicia.

if Marco is still aboard tell him to hide in the top

they don't know he's here

She texted back.

check

i hope UR filming this

He hated being relegated to voyeur. They only other tool he had that could help or obstruct was his rope. Could he pull off some kind of rescue? And not die?

He filmed the climbers reaching their limbs, then shut his phone down to take off up the tree, thinking as he went about getting a rope between the trees. Marco and Delicia could walk hand over hand and then he could cut it. But the climbers would do the same thing. Ultimately, there was no escape.

Video, then, would be their best weapon. He set his phone to upload live to the internet and began again. He made a short introduction, telling viewers what they were watching.

Soon the climbers came into view below him in Her Majesty. Still no sign of Delicia. He climbed higher himself. She probably grasped that the higher their confrontation with her was, the more troubles they would have removing her. And the more danger to all of them.

Ishi reached the level of her nest. And Jesus, she was standing there naked. Unfathomably strange, but he looked a second time.

She appeared a minute later in a red spandex swimsuit, with a slim, yellow fanny pack around her waist. She bent and seemed to be tying on some footwear. She was moving smoothly and fast, and with no tension. In the end, maybe she saw this all as a publicity stunt for herself. She was hoping to play them and get captured in her circus attire. That could actually be smart. Or was she just a narcissist?

She caught sight of him, flashed the OK symbol, pointed up, and began climbing. Still no sign of Marco. The only good news.

Ishi climbed too. Forty feet higher, Delicia crouched on a limb that pointed straight into the grove.

The two climbers were making good time, considering it was their first climb in Her Majesty. They called strategy back and forth. Not looking overhead often enough, in Ishi's opinion. They were that confident they were going to catch a woman. If they fell, Ishi thought, the helmets they wore would prevent absolutely no injuries.

They were talking into hands-free radios. They had coils of rope on their hips. One also had a clutch of zip ties hooked to a waist pocket. It looked bad, as if Delicia had given Ishi instructions to film a car wreck in which she was a driver. He hoped she intended to make a spectacle of being captured, to keep them from realizing Marco was aloft. The opposite of narcissism.

"Where is that little cunt?" one said.

Delicia stood. "The little cunt's up here." Her red was glorious against the green. "You should respect women more. I'll make a note to contact your supervisor." She waited for them to turn away from the trunk, so they could see her. She was quite a ways out on that limb. "Now, let's see if you *boys* can catch me."

Just like that, she laced play into the machismo seriousness of the event. The tension between the two forces kept Ishi's eyes glued to his screen. He whispered into his phone for the benefit of future viewers: *"She has just dared these two muscle boys to catch her."*

In the time it took the men to turn back around, communicate the most rudimentary tactics for fulfilling her command, and reset themselves to climb, Delicia scooted to the trunk, disappeared behind it, and appeared on a higher branch, this time on the vineyard side of Her Majesty. An old branch at that spot had snapped off ages ago. Now, a vertical spar grew out of it, reaching for the sky. Delicia knew this tree like a playground hero, and had a plan. Too bad the endgame was clear.

The men couldn't decide whether they should stay close together or separate. Over the next few minutes, they tried both options. It looked like an animated game of three-dimensional chess. When they were close, she circled around them. When they tried to come at her from two directions, she slipped between them. As good as they were at the vertical climb, they were clearly outmatched in the lateral scrambling department.

Mocking and laughing, Delicia missed no opportunity to point out their inadequacies. She even gave them directions. When they followed them, she changed course. When they ignored her, she appeared where she'd told them she would and chastised them. But not in wholly demeaning terms, as she explained to them. "It wouldn't be ladylike."

The men's talk became a constant stream of profanity. Both ripped off their helmets and mopped their heads with their sleeves.

"Real men like the chase," Delicia said. "Aren't you real men?"

"Listen, bitch! You can't do this all day. We've got more men below. Play all you want, but you're not getting free."

His fellow climber was coughing, gasping for air.

The viewer count feature on Ishi's video app started exploding.

"I'm worried about your friend," she said. "Maybe you need to go take recess. Call your mother. Shall I take a picture of you for her?" She produced her phone from her fanny pack.

But the men were right; another climber appeared in Her Majesty's lower limbs.

Ishi called to her. When she turned, she followed his gesture to see the threat.

"Ahh," she said. "Big Billy Goat Gruff has come to help his little brothers. Tell me your mother's email." She put her phone away and climbed.

Something about her movement showed the stakes in the game had shifted. She vanished above and Ishi climbed, letting his phone run and narrating the scene. As he passed through his own living quarters, thinking options were narrowing, he stuffed his pistol into his belt.

Delicia appeared on the limb he'd seen her use as a balance beam. She did a few stretches, as if to make herself ready for more feats. Or was she just teasing them?

With three climbers, the foresters were better able to climb without leaving much room for Delicia to escape between them. She tried to outsmart them once, but turned and scampered up again. They were moving more deliberately, confidently, sensing their humiliation was almost over. As if setting the jaws of a trap.

Delicia seemed to know she was out of options. She returned to that balance beam branch, eight feet above where Ishi was filming. Maybe she wanted a safe place to surrender, so as not to risk anyone falling.

Ishi reconfirmed his choice to capture whatever was going to happen. It looked like they would have her in less than a minute when Marco appeared just above her.

"You guys leave her alone." He was brandishing a pistol, moving cautiously because he had only one hand to use.

The foresters stopped cold. One held out his hands in surrender.

"Get out of this tree. This is ours!"

"Marco," Delicia said. "Don't shoot them."

"Tell them to get down," Marco said. His voice wavered.

The late-arriving climber produced a weapon of his own and took a practiced crouch. "Don't make me shoot you, you little Indian fuck."

Marco moved to put the trunk between him and the threat. Ishi slid his pistol from his waistband. For the moment he concealed it behind his leg.

"No one should die here," Delicia said. "He's just a boy. And we're filming this." She pointed at Ishi.

That seemed the first time the climbers noticed how exposed they were. Still, the forester with the gun fired off a round. Not at Marco, but at Delicia, though if he had meant to hit her, he would have. She made a bright target.

"Surrender now, lady."

Ishi raised his gun and readied his soul for a shootout.

"Okay," she said, putting up her hands, turning, and walking toward the trunk. "Okay," she said more submissively.

At the trunk she turned and faced the length of her branch. Then in a graceful and powerful stride, she trotted along it until it bent under her weight. She took one more long stride, leapt into the air, and landed farther out. The branch bent like a diving board and launched her into the space between the trees. She curled into a tight tuck, traveled the distance to the branch on Ishi's tree that reached toward Her Majesty and landed on it in a beautiful pike position. It bent under her, raised her back up, and she bent her knees to stop its momentum. She turned and curtsied. "Try that," she said. Not submissive anymore.

Ishi managed to catch the expression of awe on one of the first two climbers' faces.

"No bother," the forester with the gun said. He motioned toward Marco. "We'll catch this little prick and run the law up his butthole. That'll be a good start. Then we'll break for lunch, call for reinforcements, and come up and get your asses."

Marco emerged from behind the trunk where Ishi could see him.

"Don't, Marco," Ishi said. "Put the gun down. You want to join the Marines? This isn't the way."

Marco seemed to hear. He held the gun out as if it were nitroglycerin. "I'll come down. Back off a little."

The foresters conferred and agreed to a tacit sign of retreat if he would drop his gun. Marco said he would. He descended to Delicia's balance beam. He laid the gun where the branch met the trunk, turned, and followed in Delicia's footsteps . . . more or less. Amazingly, he made it to the end of the branch and jumped to make it sag. But it seemed he couldn't decide between going into a tuck and making a regular long jump. Halfway across, he knew his mistake and scratched at the air. To his credit, he reached the branch Delicia had landed on, but he hadn't gained her height and it caught him high in the chest. His head snapped back. He barked something between a warrior cry and a wail. His right arm stopped working. He was holding on with his left, trying to throw a leg around the branch from underneath. He turned his head to see Ishi. His look was pathetic, desperate.

Ishi headed up and handed his camera and his gun to Delicia as he squeezed by her. He went out as far on the limb as made sense and went down on his belly. He reached for Marco's hand, or his hair. Anything. Blood was oozing from Marco's mouth. Several teeth were shattered.

"Hang on tight, buddy." Ishi snaked forward another foot. The branch sagged under the weight of the two of them. For a second, Ishi thought it might break.

Honoring his commitment to Amber, he worked himself forward a few more inches. The bark tore at his chest, and he got his hand on Marco's good arm. But it was clinging to the branch with such effort, it offered Ishi nothing to haul in. He slid his hand down Marco's flank and hooked his belt. Got a good hold on it. He was opening his mouth to give instructions on what body part to move, when Marco let go his good arm. His body dropped. Ishi yanked hard on the belt, but Marco's momentum swung him head down. One of Marco's boots belted Ishi in the face. And in the instant of taking the blow, his fingers released just enough for the belt to pull through them.

With a cry, Marco's arms swam helplessly. He passed through several branches, merely grazing the needles. Then one caught him right below his chin, which fired him into a backward spin that continued until his torso drove his head into the ground.

Twenty-Four

Maybe a raven croaked in the canopy. Maybe a truck ground its gears on the highway. Maybe Delicia screamed. Maybe the state foresters cussed or yelled condemnations. Maybe they were decent enough to turn silent. But Ishi remembered the moments that followed Marco's fall as devoid of sound, as if he had been transported to the dark side of the moon.

Gone was the air of deep bluster that had permeated the grove on all sides until the moment Marco's feet left Her Majesty. Gone, too, for a few clicks of time was the tension that had both raised the testosterone and emerged from it. The foresters' hatefulness gave way as they adjusted to a wholly different reality. Ishi would have liked to think they were tasting humility.

But it didn't matter. Everywhere his mind traveled, he saw consequences.

The state's lawful act in a redwood grove—however unnecessary— would fuel reactions to his Pomo band's status . . . in the government's storyline, in the courts, in his project, in his career, and perhaps even in De Boulette's course of taking the trees and rearranging that land along the Greenley river.

And it would vomit consequences into his relationship with Amber.

With the return of sound came the slow, deliberate movements of the foresters. Forty feet away, they were adjusting their equipment and communicating as much with body language as with simple words, most of which Ishi couldn't hear. One was coiling rope. One was looking-some two hundred feet below, perhaps wishing Marco's body would move, so they could all reassume their previous roles. The two foresters whose ropes Ishi had cut were kneeling by his body. That thing that was no longer Marco, boy of boisterous pomposity.

"No pulse," one called up.

This prompted the last forester to climb into Her Majesty, a man who fit the definition of commando to a T, to lift his radio from its pocket on his left breast and dial a knob, searching for a channel. As he spoke into it, he looked at Ishi for the first time.

"Dispatch, California State Forester Siemens. We got a coroner call in Beckett State Forest. Ping my phone for co-ords."

"Copy, Siemens. Cause of death?"

"Catastrophic collision. Fall from a tree. No pulse. Male, late teens. No other injuries on scene requiring ambulance."

Ishi pried himself up to sitting on the branch and turned, expecting to see Delicia. For an instant, he wondered if she too had fallen. But he saw her elbow sticking out from behind Atlas's trunk. He took some deep breaths, got his feet under him and went to her.

"Are they coming for us?" Her face was white, waxy.

"I don't know."

"He fell for me." She shook her head at how that came out. "He took the fall *I* should have taken."

"Stop."

"I'm a complete fuckup, Ishi. I've ruined everything. I killed that boy."

"The *fall* killed Marco. *He* put himself here. The state—"

"I let him up. Don't you see? If I hadn't—"

"Stop!" He pointed to the foresters, then mimicked the hopelessness in her body language. "If the *state* hadn't. If *I* hadn't. If De Boulette hadn't. If Charles *Ger*vin hadn't." He grunted disgust. "We're *all* in on this."

Delicia shook her head, clamped her jaw, and put her arms around him. He held her while she hyperventilated into his chest. At times, her whole body flexed as if she was screaming in silence.

Finally, she released her hold on him. "I'll go," she said, "if they agree to let you stay."

"They're moving slowly. Let's wait to see what they do."

WHAT THE FORESTERS did was descend. Siemens, the radio commando, headed down last. Before he did, he called over to Ishi.

"We're in a major clusterfuck now, pal. Command has ordered us to stand down. But make no mistake, we'll be back for you and your little hottie. This is state land, and you're interfering with state business."

Ishi mulled words to meet the moment. "I hear you. Killing Indians is an old tradition."

"Don't blame us. Your protest set this in motion. The rest is above my pay grade."

"Must be nice," Ishi said, "to be so dissociated."

Siemens shook his chin one time to purge what he'd heard and followed his men.

Ishi's head swam. The story was already out. He couldn't stop it. If he and Brodie could, they'd want to get ahead of it.

He whispered to Delicia. "It's going to be rough for a while. To keep them from destroying your gear, I suggest you go climb down Atlas and let them see you filming them."

As she dug for her phone in her fanny pack, she found his too.

"How much did you film?" he asked, knowing there would be no good answer. When he powered it up, the YouTube view counter was over at fifteen hundred and rising fast. The raid on the redwoods was rocketing around the internet.

He watched her go. Even carrying a load of grief and guilt, she was a miracle of grace. She had almost too much beauty for one body. But was it good fortune or bad?

He was about to call Brodie when Brodie called him. "I've just seen it, Ishi. The Santa Rosa TV station folks saw it almost live and called me for an update. Dammit. I thought all we were doing was investigating the sale of a spring. We have major work to do. And fast."

Ishi regretted the road ahead. "Here's my list. I have to call the boy's sister. She's my girlfriend."

Brodie groaned.

"When I do, she might succeed at doing what the foresters failed to do."

"You mean get you down?"

"Yeah, by killing me."

"Let's avoid that."

"Then if my Pomo sisters and brothers will let me, I've got to start coordinating a Pomo funeral. . . . But, Efan, I may be heading to jail."

"That would be a stunning political mistake for the governor to make. Then again, never underestimate the cruelty of people in power who have a lot to lose." Brodie thought a moment. "The silver lining is, your video just might accomplish everything we've been trying to do."

"It's not about me any more," Ishi said. "As cold as it sounds, I refuse to let this interrupt my series."

"*Yes*, Darkhorse! *Now* you're a journalist. If it's any consolation, Martin Luther King did some of his finest writing in jail. And I'd say you are *embedded* up to your eyeballs."

He went on. "My list is to be all over the governor. If his administration even thinks of doing something immoral or predatory on your stand up there, or anywhere, I'm going to get all the West Coast editors to join forces to make him wish he was running for dog catcher in Paradise.

"And De Boulette? Their Redwood Cabernet gambit is going to render them a dead company. That's the goal, anyway.

"Lastly, I want you and Ms. Fortunado down safe. By the way, since she is flying around the internet—literally—I'm going to name her immediately. It would be the worst turn to have other outfits beat us to that. She's going to carry a lot of this story."

AFTER THE FORESTERS dropped from Her Majesty, Delicia reported that Ishi had been right. "Being filmed, they left my stuff alone. Their radio traffic says the coroner is on his way. Do you think you should go down when they come? Will your girlfriend forgive you if you don't?"

Ishi heard Amber screaming in his mind. "Both options suck. Staying up here, she'll want to kill me. If I go down, they'll arrest me. I got to call her now."

"I'll give you privacy," she said. "By the way, in the last ten minutes, your video has earned 9,300 more views."

"Keep your video, too," he said. "We may be able to use it. How are you going to get home?"

She shrugged. "The same way I got here."

AMBER'S CELL PHONE was out of range. He told her to call him. He reached his father.

"Got bad news, Pops. Marco climbed the tree with the circus lady in it, 'cause I told him he couldn't come up here with me."

Eli said nothing.

"And he fell."

"He dead?" His father's voice jumped with regret.

"Yuh."

They both let it lie a minute.

"But it's more complicated. The state sent foresters to bring us down. I cut the ropes of two of them. But others went after Delicia. She managed to jump to my tree. Marco tried to copy her."

"He's just that way."

"It was a bad fall, Pops. But he didn't suffer."

"Does Amber know?"

"I left her a message to call. If you see her first, try to explain it."

"He's all the family she has. This is going to be . . ." He used a Pomo word Ishi didn't know, but even the sound of it carried horror.

"I always liked him," Ishi said. "I always wanted a little brother. He probably didn't know it for how I squashed his enthusiasm. I think he wanted to do good." He thought a moment. "Maybe he has."

"Are you going to write a piece about him?"

"I hadn't thought of that. Good idea. Just so you know, you might get a crowd of news people there. For now, I'm going to stay up here. But I might wind up in jail."

A chuckle covered Eli's resignation about the endless pain of being a Pomo. "Runs in the family."

Twenty-Five

THE COUNTY AMBULANCE kicked up dust as it left Minkle's vineyard.

Watching Marco take his last joyride, Delicia wanted to die. She had no doubt she deserved to. There was so much she couldn't bring herself to tell Ishi—or to tell anyone, particularly not Aunt Stephanie when she called. Nor could she hide from the fact that her attraction to Marco—which had fallen somewhere between mothering and desiring the container of his boyish power—had played into her defying Ishi about bringing him up.

History was proving this field and the river edge land to be a death zone for Indians. And now the mounting body count in her own wake was crossing tracks with its tragedy. In equal amounts, she lamented her fate and worried about Ishi being the next to die.

Minkle had been a player in this drama not by choice but by proximity, through ownership of the vineyard. Land that had never yielded him anything. If she understood Ishi correctly, Minkle's owning it was the cause of his loan for the whole property being called in. He was going to lose a glorious apple orchard for trying to bring back a field of dead grapevines.

It seemed nothing good could happen on this perfect spot for a village.

SHE HAD OTHER things on her mind when she talked to Ishi the next day on the jungle phone. She thanked him for forwarding Brodie's article about the raid and Marco's fall before it came out in the next morning's edition of the *LA Times*. They agreed the man had a talent for shaking a bushel basket of shame at the governor as the "public servant" who pulled the trigger that had resulted in another Indian death.

What she really wanted to know was how his conversation with Amber had gone.

"She's a wild mess," Ishi said. "She told me she'd come over here and cut all the trees down herself if she could, and she'd make sure to put me in the top of each before it came down."

The dual loss in that image distressed Delicia. "She thinks she's lost her family and her boyfriend all at once."

Whatever Delicia's conjecture, Amber's arrival an hour later put it to rest. Delicia vowed to stay out of sight while Ishi faced a woman in her cyclone who was a hundred feet below him. But she couldn't resist finding a place close enough to hear and to peek.

Amber had dressed inappropriately to commit murder—a skirt and an embroidered top. And she had brought a fancy enough bouquet of flowers to ruin anybody's budget. The first question she asked was where Marco had landed, though if her eyes had been drier, she would have seen the depression in the ground and the wrecked needle duff. It was under Ishi's tree.

She knelt and laid the flowers in the hollow. Keening some modal melody, she ran her hands over the duff as if it were Marco himself and the sides of his coffin. The authenticity of her grief triggered Delicia's powerlessness at not getting to wail next to Maya's body, at having no way to make amends to the herd. She wished she could be as free as Amber and saw Amber's outpouring as the best method to put her brother to rest, as the best route to free herself from the teeth of injustice. She hoped Amber would exhaust herself, saving Ishi the worst of her anger.

But Delicia had misgauged Amber's stamina. She stood and in a fury of footwork, kicked enough duff into the void Marco had made to fill it. All the while she hollered judgments and accusations at Marco, and at men who were not there, and at the stubbornness of the past because it refused to rewind and let Marco live.

She saved her last verses for Ishi. Tipping her head to see him seemed to open the lid to her rage. "You promised me you wouldn't let him up there. You fucking promised. You *know* how he is—dammit—*was*. He was a lost boy. A damn idiot. With a father as worthless as used shit paper. He worshipped you. And if you have any integrity, you'll come out of that fucking tree and stand here beside me so I don't have to do this alone. I have no one left and my dreams have melted into sky."

"I ordered him not to come up," Ishi said. "I thought he'd obey my command. We both told him not to try. And I couldn't be watching for him every minute."

"Well, you should have. You're sitting right there."

"I would give anything to have this morning back," he said.

It pained Delicia to listen to Ishi squirm.

"You said you were going to be up there two weeks, maybe three, until you made your point. And you put me over a barrel asking Marco to help you. So, of course, I had to allow it, which I see now was the worst mistake I could have ever made. Like telling a child not to touch a bowl of ice cream you've left on the floor. With a *spoon* in it, *goddammit!* How could you? How am I going to live with this, Ishi? I've lost him. I've lost you—"

"You haven't."

"I have too. You invited that high-end piece of candy to protest with you—"

"Come on Amber. You know she came on her own."

"Don't think I don't know what you're up to. Do you think I'm blind? She puts on that little 'fuck me' suit and—"

"She just showed up—"

"Don't defend her, dammit. I saw the video. The one *you* took. She was flirting with the state guys, and where did she go when she needed help? She jumped into your tree like she'd been doing it every night since she got here. With a flip! That would turn any man on! Say you weren't ready to fuck her."

Ishi's struggle to find words made it sound as if he was slow to deny it, which was all the proof Amber needed.

Delicia empathized with Amber's despair and with her ruthless tactics to deal with it. She had torn into Joseph Massama in the same way after finding Maya slaughtered. But that morning she finally grasped how hard it was for a good man to be on that end of the spear. Unable to let it slide, she hustled down through Her Majesty's limbs.

When she got to her landing, she saw Ishi had lowered himself down on his rope and was hanging a foot off the ground trying to hug Amber, when he let out a yowl and fell out of his hitch. His hand cupped his face.

Whatever grace he'd brought down, he was over it. He fought Amber off while getting himself back into the tether and began to haul himself up.

Amber switched from recrimination to begging him to come back down. When he kept climbing, Amber dug into her purse and fiddled with something. She found what turned out to be a knife.

Ishi wasn't looking at her getting set to cut his rope.

Delicia called, "Amber, I'm the one you want to blame."

Ishi halted in mid-stride. Amber froze, too.

"Direct your anger at me. Then both you and I can hate me. 'Cause I have thought of throwing myself out of this tree several times today. The only reason I haven't is 'cause I knew *that* would immediately take the honor away from Marco. The world is watching. Say what you will about him, but he has turned a huge number of people onto the Pomo fight here. There have been 200,000 views since yesterday. Which makes him the most important member of this team."

Amber's body posture went from wounded warrior to conqueror. "Shut up, Diddle Dee. If it weren't coming out of your faithless little mouth, maybe I'd give a fuck about what you're saying, but as far as I'm concerned you have too much to pay for to ever make it up."

The upward blast of Amber's heat stung.

"I'm prepared to dedicate my time up here to making Marco's sacrifice worth it. For the trees and for him. Then when I come down, I'll let you use that knife on me if that's what you need."

She took a deep breath. "It's none of my business, but I think you should arrange a funeral for Marco right where his ancestors died. Right out there. Maybe you can cremate him there and you Pomo can finally have a chance to grieve for all you have lost. And Ishi could attend the funeral too *and* stay on his protest, which is heroic. You should be glad to have him love you. Marco told me how much he liked Ishi, and looked up to him, and was afraid of him."

She trembled as the image of Maya's desecrated body once again overwhelmed her. Elephants knew how to grieve. She saw the rest of the herd's bellowing and their raised trunks as lamentations and honor that Delicia, in her anger and guilt, hadn't recognized.

"That way, whoever comes here in the future will praise your brother. Don't waste his death on getting even."

That would have been a good moment for a second crew of foresters to capture her and Ishi with barely a struggle. Ishi had reached his landing limb and seemed disoriented. Delicia was spent. Amber was not the running type. They could zip-tie her and charge her for aiding and abetting redwood terrorists.

THE FIGHT BETWEEN the women was not done, but Amber left that day with an apology for her tone, if not her words. Ishi got Minkle's permission for an interment— but with the land ripe for a wild spark, cremation was out of the question.

Four days later, after the state said it wouldn't object to the burial— an executive decision driven by, in Brodie's estimation, a rattled Governor Murphy—Delicia concealed herself behind the WANTS TO CUT US DOWN banner and watched Pomo from many bands circling the spot where their ancestors had been burned. They sang and they danced for hours. And though Delicia couldn't hear her words, Amber spoke, waving her arms in grief, and read a tribute to Marco that Ishi had sent to Delicia earlier for her feedback. Ishi's father, the chief, spoke too. The wind scattered flower petals and herbs that he threw into the air.

Watching Pomo toss dirt onto the coffin, Delicia flashed on Maya's bones blanching in the sun after every carnivore Zimbabwe had to offer had picked them clean. At last, when the dust of the Pomo vehicle caravan settled, Minkle's backhoe driver finished the burial and smoothed the scar.

Amber pitched a tent across the river from where Marco had landed. This time when she crossed the river and stood under Atlas, Delicia climbed up to give her and Ishi privacy.

While she was perched on high, the casting chief for the scintillatingly hot daily show, *Takes On America*, called her cell. Someone had sent him the video of her jump. He and his staff were excited beyond all reason, he said, to do a show with her. He already understood it would require a crane to reach her nest. And he had found a willing construction company in San Raphael. He had no doubt his viewers would love to hear how the moonwalking aerialist had gone from a career-ending fall in Moscow to saving elephants in Zimbabwe and now to leaping from one redwood to another like Butch Cassidy and the Sundance Queen. For calling attention to America's greatest symbol of natural beauty, he said, she deserved to be supported in every possible way.

Delicia told him she would inquire about permission from the landowner.

Twenty-Six

"I SHI, MY MAN."

Brodie was the second person to interrupt Ishi's morning ritual of staring overhead at the gift of water puddles sagging in his blue tarp, listening to the ticking of the drops. Earlier, a text from Delicia about the call from *Takes On America* had poisoned that ritual.

"This piece about Marco's funeral is hypnotic. You put readers into the bird's-eye point of view, literally, and impart the clarity and breadth that comes from that height. Its thread of sadness is palpable. Well done.

"On a side note, I found myself wondering if that's how being up there is affecting all of your experience.

"In any case, your development in these past few weeks has me clicking my heels." He laughed uproariously. "Can you imagine *me* clicking my heels? Think of a hippo on roller skates. *Don't* mind me. Dori told me not to call you this early, but truth is, the office is lonely. I want you to stay up there as long as you have to, to cut De Boulette's power lines, but at the same time, I want you down ASAP.

"The drive in your serial massacre narrative would make Dickens proud. I *can* say without speculation you're breathing new life into America's Last Real Newspaper. Standing on the sidelines—well, in the coach's corner, I guess—it feels as if I'm watching the blood of history joining the tragedy of the present."

"Efan, how many cups have you had already?"

"My usual. Two." He sounded honest . . . until he hemmed. "Actually, I *am* on the second pot. But I'm feeling good, mighty good. Probably because I have incredible news, courtesy of burning midnight oil. I finally had a moment to dig deep into the Surplus Land Statute legalese. And"—he slipped into a bad Deep Southern accent—"well, shuh mah maooth. Down at the bottom, in print that ants need glasses for, it says,

'Properties owned by the State subject to the force of this Statute must be declared in well-publicized markets and be open to unbiased bidding. To avoid all appearance of'—they drop in a long unmanageable sentence that essentially means, *corruption*, and the paragraph ends with, 'the State must choose the highest bid.'

"I don't have to tell you there was *no* open bidding on Beckett. They would have published a notice in *our* paper. So I *have* written to Murphy's chief of staff that if the Gov doesn't abrogate the quid pro quo with De Boulette by noon today, I am running this puppy in the *Chronicle* as soon as they'll have it. More on this later.

"The sad thing is, nothing can be done about De Boulette owning the spring and the right-of-way, and they can satisfy their vengeance in several ways. Wouldn't put it past them. Water *is* this valley's gold, and they've got it. To make matters less sure, whoever becomes the top bidder and buys Beckett can also cut the trees.

"But I'm an optimist. I keep hoping some cranial-rectal-inverted soul from Silicon Valley will forego parting with a few hundred million to purchase a senate seat in Oklahoma and will instead buy Beckett to simply leave the trees standing."

Brodie exhaled in self-deprecation. "I'm sorry. I know I'm rambling. What's up for you today . . . other than *you*, and that leaping phenom neighbor of yours?"

"I was going to call you shortly." Ishi swung his legs out and onto the limb. "Delicia messaged me last night while I was writing Marco's funeral piece. Just saw it twenty minutes ago. That weekly show *Takes On America* wants to do a segment on her . . . *in her tree*. And they want to have her reenact her jump. She asked if I can get Minkle's permission for them to use his land."

"This is *all* great!"

"It is and it isn't. I know that you try, Efan. But do you see what you blew right over? They want to exploit a white girl's jump without putting it in context of a brown-skinned boy pile driving himself into the ground." His jaw was tight. "It will help her relaunch her career, I s'pose. Good for her. But I've been lying here thinking that a crane that size might have to set up right on the site of the Pomo pyre. Symbols, Efan. Most of life comes down to symbols."

Brodie fell quiet. A raven's wings scraped the air as it flew by Ishi's tree.

"You're right." Brodie's voice was humble. "I try, but I fail. Listen, I have a lot of purchase with Josh Minkle. Would you be offended if I call him to ask permission? Between you and me, I'll see if he's willing to grant it only if *Takes On America* also interviews you, so you can tell what happened there."

AND THAT WAS how it came about that the Honorable Governor Thaddeus J. Murphy abrogated the contract that had ensured De Boulette would make an ungodly profit buying Beckett Sate Forest and selling the redwoods; that the State of California promptly placed a notice in the *Post-Ethical Times* and in papers up and down the state that announced it was taking bids on the land; that the governor agreed for the time being to look the other way while two mismatched humans occupied trees in an old-growth redwood grove; and that *Takes On America* agreed to foster, in some small way, a band of Native Americans, one among many, who had been left holding crumbs since white people arrived. The show's top brass wanted Delicia that much.

THREE DAYS LATER, half a dozen self-proclaimed eco-warriors—young, white, and long-haired—came in through Minkle's orchard gate and set up tents along the riverbank. Ishi's protest had just been getting back to normal, and this was another invasion.

Hot under the collar, Ishi called Josh Minkle.

"Chill, man," Josh said, "I've decided I've got to enter the fray, because since losing the inside track at Beckett, De Boulette is redoubling its efforts to strangle my business. Listen up! I'm not going down without throwing everything at them. So I've invited anybody who wants to camp on my land to come."

He confessed that opening the vineyard piece to the Pomo archeological dig, the dance, and then the funeral had overtaken his shame about never planting it in apples.

"You and Delicia protesting there are making the timing perfect for me to join forces with you. The last thing this valley needs is another vineyard. And I don't own the woods, but I don't want to live here without them. I think if we get enough of these young people, their presence will shove a wrecking bar into the state's gears when they come to take you down again . . . and they will. So those eco-hippies will be your scouts. They're young, they're angry, they see corporations as the devil incarnate, and they have cell phones."

"Are any of them carrying weapons? A shootout down below will end everything."

"They said they weren't," Minkle said, "but we never know anymore, do we? Maybe that uncertainty will be in our favor."

He'd saved the point he most wanted to make for last. "It'll be a pain in the ass to have *Takes On America* come through here. But all I need in return is for them to drop a sentence or two during the show about De Boulette's driving a simple apple orchard into ruin. Maybe a compassionate hedge-fund type will see the broadcast and step up to pay off my mortgage."

In the end, Minkle was no different from everyone else.

AFRAID THE PROSPECT of the massacre land ever becoming a sacred Pomo site would slip away under a wave of white protesters, Ishi inspired Eli to get more Dead Creek Pomo to set up tents.

"I've been thinking," Ishi added, "that maybe getting rid of the race element will make for a more far-reaching story. Who knows? It could be a good closure for the massacre."

Whenever new arrivals came, Ishi gathered them under his tree and asked only that the Pomo be allowed to set up in the best spots along the river.

Two weeks after Marco's fall, lights in the vineyard lit up the early evening. For a short time, anyway, the past and its village were joining the present.

Twenty-Seven

I N MID-APRIL, Tadao traveled with Sensei to Tokyo's Chiyoda Ward for an audience with *Tennō Heika,* His Imperial Majesty, Emperor Akihito. Spring was well underway, and the weather was pleasant.

As their taxi approached the gate of the Imperial Palace, Sensei wore a strange look. Tadao feared his illness may have taken a sudden turn for the worse. Sensei withdrew his handkerchief from his sleeve, spit up a small ball of green goo, and wiped his face.

"It has been a long time since I've been nervous."

Tadao took this as a sign that was almost as bad.

For his part, Tadao had increasingly been on tenterhooks about the state of his order of Hinoki timbers. It was highly unusual that he hadn't heard back from any of the imperial forestry firms.

Once inside the palace, the unbending quality of the guards, the personal remove of the attendants that greeted them, and being made to wait in rooms where nothing else ever occurred seemed designed to rattle the confidence even of samurai warriors. When they were summoned into the audience chamber, Tadao noted that Sensei relied on his cane more than usual.

Sensei wore a black robe with simple white lining at the cuffs and the hem. Tadao was dressed in loose-legged pants and a large-sleeved gi, distantly related to his working uniform. He had never before worn one made of silk brocade. The top's panels crossed over his breast and were held in place with concealed buttons made of ivory. The diaphanous quality of the silk gave him the sense that he was mostly naked. And the gold designs on the deep blue field surely called attention to how nervous he was.

Seeing *Tennō* sitting at a large lacquer table, however, impeccably dressed in a pinstripe suit and backlit by floor to ceiling windows, Tadao was overcome by a feeling of poverty.

They had been instructed to make formal bows to *Tennō*, to not sit in his presence, and to wait for him to ask something of them before speaking. As they crossed a vast woven rug, Tadao prayed they wouldn't have to stand too long in silence.

An assistant spoke into the emperor's ear. *Tennō* turned. All Tadao could focus on was the mirror-shine on the emperor's shoes.

Tennō rose and, abandoning all remove, reached for Sensei's hand before any bows took place. Tadao let go of his master's arm and risked a glance at Japan's most powerful descendant.

He was older than Tadao expected, older than Sensei, though grace made him seem ageless. The emperor lifted Sensei's arm that held the cane and guided him into the chair next to his, which happened so fast Sensei was sitting before he could protest. He grinned in the new way of his that had come with carrying less responsibility. He patted the seat for *Tennō* to sit next to him as if they were old family friends.

Tennō sat, poorly disguising a charmed smile of his own. They looked like compatriots from another time waiting for a train.

"Is this your craftsman who will build the Temple of Listening?"

At first, Sensei seemed not to hear. Finally, he bade Tadao answer.

Tadao had trouble making his throat work. "Yes, Your Excellency. But in truth I am one of sixty-three craftsmen who will construct it."

"Sensei Watanabe has informed me he has chosen you as his heir and that you have a created a design."

Tadao suddenly remembered the long roll of drawings in his other hand, and at the same time became aware he hadn't yet bowed. He agonized for too long about which order of next steps would be proper. Finally, to end his torment, he bowed clumsily. "The design is informed by many hands, Your Excellency. And these are rough sketches. All can be changed." Armpit sweat raced down his flanks.

"As I wrote in my request to see Your Excellency," Sensei said, "the temple we think will invite *kami* in this modern age has a few innovations to Japan's traditional designs."

Tennō signaled for Tadao to unroll the sheaf of drawings on the table and rose to examine them. He studied the photographs of the site, and he pored over the plan view of the temple and its three elevations. His eyes lingered on the perspective rendering of the interior courtyard, taking in the huge natural obelisk of almost pure black onyx that was its centerpiece. This was not a surprise.

This preexisting feature of the site, looking as if it were erupting from the earth, had spoiled Tadao's sleep for many nights. Twice he had returned there, hoping to find another orientation for the temple. Attempts at hiding the obelisk behind the temple broke the building's intimacy with the forest. Leaving the stone as an entrance monument looked as if the design was mocking *kami*.

The drawing showed what Tadao and Sensei and Sensei's son, Satoru, had settled on—the obelisk was to remain prominent and off-center in the courtyard, with the rooflines of the buildings taking their slopes from it. Spanning the courtyard was the trunk of one of the site's great twisted conifer trees as if it had blown down, its globe of bare roots looking like a medallion on the clavicle of space.

"It has been a long time since I've been there," *Tennō* said at last.

Tadao was surprised at how the emperor conveyed conflicting emotions while barely moving his face. Since he hadn't asked a question or made a request, his words floated in the room.

"My uncle took me when I was a boy of fifteen. It is the prow of Japan into the Pacific." The emperor said nothing about the black stone, but used his hands to mirror the rooflines around it. He nodded to himself.

Next, he pointed to the arrangement of eight raw logs near the cliff face to the right of the temple. They were roped, one beneath the next, like the slats of a giant's Venetian blind. "And what is this?" His tone said he didn't like them.

Tadao's arm felt heavy as he moved his hand to show the path of the onshore breeze. "Giant flutes, Your Excellency. When the wind blows over the hollowed ends, it will generate tones so low that only *kami* can hear them."

Tennō's eyes widened. "How clever. Rugged and handsome at the same time." His eyes darted, picking upon more abnormalities. He tapped the huge iron wheel that would stand upright on the far end of the courtyard. It held four urns, positioned as if marking the main directions of a compass. "And this?"

"It is a water wheel, Your Excellency. Its movement initiates the striking of a gong. This urn in the top position is slightly off-plumb. When rain fills it, its weight releases a catch holding it upright. Gravity causes the wheel to suddenly rotate ninety degrees counterclockwise. Like a grandfather clock, the torque trips this huge wooden hammer here to strike that hollow log. Its resonant sound will again call *kami*. The urn, of course, empties out, and the next one sits in position to catch more rain. We estimate it will ring irregularly, about six times a year, but only those in attendance at that moment will hear it." Tadao waited until he wanted to jump out of his shoes.

Tennō walked to the windows overlooking the imperial gardens. For those minutes Tadao and Sensei remained standing, awaiting direction. When His Excellency turned to face them, he drew himself into a most dignified posture.

"I am affected by your design. It combines our Buddhist tradition's wonderful sense of masculine skill with Shinto's feminine mutability. I believe it will gather *kami* from the sea, from the sky, and from the land."

He walked toward them with simple ceremony and when he arrived, he pressed his right index finger onto the mirror-like surface of the table. "We have a problem that we have been investigating for many months. I received confirmation last week that after much testing, it appears our beloved Hinoki cypress is adversely suffering from the effects of climate change."

When he looked Tadao in the eye, Tadao dropped his gaze to the emperor's finger.

"To build this temple, Sensei, I am afraid we must find another kind of wood."

Twenty-Eight

THE GROWING COMMUNITY in Minkle's vineyard brought Delicia back to the years when being in a crowd—and, more importantly, being *above* a crowd—gave meaning to her life. It was a delightful turn, because the days of voluntary confinement in Her Majesty were often too long. The noise of others and the new faces who brought deliveries of food and supplies to her and Ishi quickened her pulse. The nighttime lights in tents below spoke of a sweet city. The squeals of children playing in the river drifted up and made the hair on her skin stand on end. She was cheered by two magazine stories that had come out featuring her career and the political turn it had taken. For the first time since the tragedy in Africa, her life force was not struggling for air.

Someone without her background might have been offended by Mr. Brodie's characterization of the Beckett protest against De Boulette as "fast turning into a circus." The man never missed an opportunity to entertain while presenting the issues. Why was it, though, that the name of the art form that dazzled virtually everyone could also be a slur? Delicia chose to take it as a man of words tipping his hat to her. But she wondered for the first time if Ishi felt slighted by her presence and whether, unable to be honest about it, he had pushed Brodie to write that.

Almost as if tempting fate might serve up just punishment for her part in Marco's death, the day after he fell, she'd hung her slack rope between two of Her Majesty's limbs. The rope the men had set up for her in Zimbabwe was at the traditional height—six feet off the ground. Falls were part of mastering every act, but at six feet they rarely yielded more than bruises. The stakes of a misstep in Her Majesty were clear.

Her first session showed that in the seven weeks since Maya's slaughter, she had lost her peak strength, though only her old circus pals would have been able to see how she overcompensated for her muscles going a little soft. But each day as she got stronger, the unique setting and the slight flex of the branches that held the rope inspired her to create new ways to move her body along the rope.

A week after *Takes On America* set their date to film the protest, Ishi came to watch her. His presence improved her focus. Most slack rope performers mounted their rope in the middle of its sag, reaching up from the stage and mounting with a simple pull-up. Delicia's only option in Her Majesty was to hook a leg around the rope where one end was fastened to a branch and slide down to the center. When she got her feet under her, she bent, grabbed it, and pushed straight up into a handstand, using the flex and sway of the line for balance.

Ishi disappeared. Her Majesty disappeared. The possibility of falling disappeared. Existence became rope and gravity and muscle and freedom. She walked forward and backward. She went from standing poses to a split and to the Serpent, where she corkscrewed her body around the line without stopping. She hung, swung, kicked her thighs and feet to the sky, let go as in her gymnast days on the uneven bars and tucked into a ball. She opened to catch the rope as she flew by.

Her foot wasn't bothering her at all. She got the rope swinging side to side and balanced on one foot, then on one hand. Two moves from her distant past just appeared—a cartwheel into a bridge and a shoulder stand. As a finale, with a jiggle, like an upside-down jitterbug dancer, her shoulders came free from the line and she dropped headfirst, catching the rope behind her bent knees.

Ishi was a good audience. His first response was awe. Then he clapped slowly, making almost no sound. "You're crazy good," he called over. "And just plain crazy."

"It's an older art form than the tightrope. I used to warm up on it to get in shape for the wire."

That afternoon they hung the new banner Delicia had been making during those long days. *SOME PIG* had come and gone. THE GHOST OF THE POMO banner that Amber and her Pomo sisters made had also done its job. This new one would generate more publicity and make a broader statement for the filming. A forward-looking one. Ishi seemed all right with it. And as the people gathering on Minkle's vineyard now included a contingent of Pomo, she felt a balance between honoring his people and saving the groves.

WE BREATHE FOR THE PLANET

SIX DAYS LATER an enormous crane made its way, not up the road from the highway—the turns were too tight—but directly from Minkle's orchard, lumbering across the vineyard from the south. The operator happened to be a Paiute tribal member. He understood Ishi's concern about defiling the site of the Pomo pyre. He managed to place his outriggers in a configuration that did not intrude on the spot.

Vans emblazoned with *Takes On America* unloaded crates of gear. Riggers and grips fashioned the basics of a film studio onto the large yellow steel platform that the crane would lift and dangle in front of and, if all went well, in amongst the limbs of Atlas and Her Majesty.

Delicia had risen early and done a full course of stretches and strengthening. She was strong enough to repeat her viral jump, but to make the jump on demand? Though she had welcomed the idea when *TOA* proposed it, she awoke with a dream like those she'd had in the early months after her fall. It was reassuring that the producers could do little to her if she backed out.

It wasn't *Takes On America*'s policy to give questions to their interviewees in advance. But along with being able to speak about the redwoods' place on this earth, she hoped they would give her a question that would allow her to segue to her experience at the Tsongumatta Wild Animal Preserve. She had rehearsed a paragraph on the beauty of elephants and the precarious position of the remaining pachyderms on earth. She would politely sidestep follow-up questions that called for her to address allegations of abuse on the preserve, some of which she had made herself in the two days before she got a ride to the airport to escape to California. She didn't want things to get out of control.

Part of her research delved into Alton Profft, who would be conducting the interview. By reputation, he was wired to twist the flow of conversation into salacious territory. For that, she practiced replies to misdirect him. He was a large, affable man, still popular but on the downhill side of his career.

Before the roar of the crane engine and the *TOA* generators made it impossible, she had a jungle phone session with Ishi about the day. He was obviously uncomfortable with being on film. To buck him up, she reminded him about the success of his massacre series. Although the *New York Times* wasn't running it, they *had* done an article on him: "Warrior Out On A Limb."

He countered her points, saying he didn't deserve to speak for the tribe, because he'd been adopted out. The Studebaakers *had* been well-meaning. They'd given him the education that had set him on this course. They had given him a foothold in the white world. But they hadn't been helpful on questions of how to handle his identity.

"Of all Pomo, I know the least about the pain they live with. And when you look like me, you're only in the white world by permission of those in power."

She gave up trying to solve his problem.

To make a schematic of the "scenes" they would shoot, the crane lifted the platform with only the producer and cameraman aboard. She and Ishi took their three-way call to guide them to places in the trees. After a month of living rarely seen, having the platform dangling twenty feet away felt surreal, as if she had become a doll in a child's fantasy.

The producers found a place from which to film her on her slack rope and discussed how they could capture her making the escape jump. They overrode her concern about it triggering the Pomo community because they lost one of their own in the event: "Our demographics show they don't watch *Takes On America*."

They found Ishi's nest perfect for filming, but he seemed disgusted that they wanted him to reenact his cutting the climbers' ropes to repel boarders.

As the production staff prepped the platform for the full load of gear and its crew, Delicia hung the small mirror she had ordered and readied her face with makeup—not in the garish strokes of paint that worked for circus divas sweating under bright lights, but by copying the fine shades TV make-up crews had used for her the world over.

At 12:30 p.m., the producer used a bullhorn to demand quiet on the set and the crane operator sent the platform aloft. The trouble the electricians and cameramen had gone to in the setup confirmed this shoot was a big deal. To make the audio pristine, all the equipment was powered by batteries in the biggest of the vans. A hefty bundle of cables swooped off the back of the platform to the ground. One sudden jerk of the crane's controls would disconnect the whole affair, not to mention dumping a two million-dollar crew into the Greenley River.

The platform was made safe with a three foot-high pipe railing, also bright yellow. Inside it were two mounted cameras, a handheld one, a cameraman, an assistant to touch up Delicia's makeup, a ruggedly built grip, a techie seated in a warren of equipment, and the producer. In the middle of them, the handsome, white-bearded Alton Profft sat belted into a long-legged director's chair. He gripped its arms and was staring straight ahead. His skin color spanned the spectrum between ice blue and dead white.

The platform parked between Atlas and Her Majesty, where the producer ran through the order of the scenes. But it was clear the cameraman was running the show. The techie transmitted his desires to the crane operator 150 feet below. When all was perfect, the operator shut down the diesel motor.

During the sound check, Profft showed he was not just a dancing ornament behind the mic. "Ms. Fortunado, there will be a thirty-five second intro to the piece that captures your backstory—a short clip of you on the wire from Reno 2008, and a pan shot of the land in Zimbabwe with a voiceover about the tragedy that occurred there. We'll then have a statement about the fusion of war, poverty, and resource extraction, and how Maya's death led you here to care for America's elephants, as you call them. We're looking for six minutes of footage with you, which we'll intersperse with interviews with Messieurs Brodie, Darkhorse, and Spencer, the governor's chief of staff." He tipped his nonexistent hat. "So when you're set. . . ."

First, they filmed her slack rope routine—to loosen her up, they said. And they were right. It opened her emotionally. It disheveled her just enough to appear authentic—she noticed when the show ran—as she took them on a tour of Her Majesty. Her old confidence rising allowed her to make short shrift of Profft's premeditated questions, such as if her choice of name for her tree showed her love of monarchy.

With the speed of a gunslinger drawing her pistol, she said, "The strutting of kings and queens doesn't compare to the dignity of this tree."

The lights on her made it hard to see Profft perfectly, but his smile showed his seasoning. The color was returning to his face.

His preparation, his skill with language, his ability to adjust his follow-up questions to answers Delicia gave, and the quality of his voice all showed why he was in that position. In the interview section, taken of her sitting in her nest with Her Majesty's trunk as backdrop, he got her to weave her life choices, her lessons learned, and her hopes with the determination and sacrifice her activism required.

He prefaced his series of questions regarding the raid with a paragraph that informed viewers who had not heard about the tragedy that it led to.

"We understand," Profft said as a wrap-up, "how difficult this may be to talk about. But how has this event changed your intentions and your daily life?"

Delicia weighed her words. "The fall of that young Pomo man has galvanized my commitment to stay in Her Majesty until humanity decides to protect this forest forever. At that point I'll have made my payment for his loss, and I'll be willing to come down to face any consequences of trespassing on state land." How she loved speaking in front of cameras!

Profft made no effort to hide being impressed. He threw her, though, by next giving her a chance to "bury forever the narrative of your choices in life being guided by a death wish."

"I thought I'd cleared that up *long* ago." She blinked for a number of seconds, which she hoped the editor would cut out. "We circus performers don't generally speak of it directly, but here's what I think. No one can really live in a meaningful way unless dying is included in the equation. We simply won't rise up—maybe 'wake up' is a better way to say it. We can't be our best if we don't reflect on how *our* death enhances our experience of living, of how it gives meaning to the present.

"Politics and greed promise payoffs of happiness that never really come. Compare that to these trees existing here and now, without any voice or corruption. This is where I come in. Their existence is like a performance. They blaze in the present. When they are gone, no amount of memory or film footage of them will yield the power they have now. Cutting them down will diminish us forever.

"So I've danced on the wire to remind us all of our special blessing to live. Danger is beside us in all we do—if you will—on the left and right of our wire, but death isn't the point. Joy is. Reverence is. Love is." She dipped her eyes to cover the feeling that blew through her—that she was a charlatan because she knew so little about love.

How she wanted to check in with Ishi at that moment, wanted confirmation that it sounded credible. But he was too far away to hear. She glanced in his direction. He was watching.

"Our society has the Death Wish talk backward. It was the white men who came to California who had the death wish. They *slaughtered* Native Americans. For *gold*, they brought death to every corner of this state, including this one. And that has *never* stopped. Now it wants to kill this forest." As she looked for Ishi again, a tear formed in the corner of her eye. The close-up on that tear made the final cut.

Knowing the climax they were building toward, she decided it would it appear more spontaneous if it came from her. "May I demonstrate the Perfect Present? Would you like to film me making the jump again?"

They had other ideas in mind for that shot. So next, they filmed Ishi at the stations in Atlas, the last being in his nest where he gave his plaintive explanation about humans who had been disregarded. His footage, too, became iconic.

As the late afternoon light was bringing out the forest's richest green, yet again they swung the platform to Her Majesty. Delicia had warmed up again. She had dressed in that same red spandex outfit she'd worn the day of the raid.

The problem was, this jump sequence suffered from being deliberate. It could never measure up to the powerful moment Ishi had caught on his phone. This was performance, pure and simple. It was ironic: she had longed for such a moment since her fall in Moscow, and now she was finding fault with it being at hand.

She'd been away from an audience for a long time, but she knew that to make it work she would have to draw on something deeper. Although only a few eyes were on her as she stood on the limb that extended toward Atlas, she thought about the millions who would see it later.

When that alone proved inadequate, she dug deeper. She found Maya, faceless and robbed. She found the vibrant Pomo boy whose hormonal response to her was evident even as she stood a hundred feet above him when he delivered supplies. And she lifted the lid of her guilt's sarcophagus for having let him climb up.

This jump was a purification. Her body glowed as she took her swan pose on the branch. From there, she let go into a simple walk that became a dash. She hit the end of the branch better than the day she escaped the climbers and launched herself into a double flip. She added a half rotation so that she landed facing where she had started. And she stuck the landing.

"That," she said to the camera. "Just that."

As he had been on that previous jump, Ishi was standing there. She turned and went to him. When she watched the program, she was devastated that the editor in New York cut out the most important part—the audio of her asking his forgiveness. It simply showed the hug they shared.

Twenty-Nine

IN THE DEAD dark of night, awake in his hammock, Ishi heard pick-up trucks. They entered the vineyard from the grade road to the highway. Having lived in Atlas for seven weeks, Ishi was well attuned to the sounds of vehicles on that access road. But these had made no sound. They must have crawled up. He heard them only when they accelerated across the vineyard.

Seeing the sky *not* light up with headlights, he was up like a shot.

He knew the branch to his "porch" well enough to walk it in the dark. The moonlight revealed large trucks—three of them, accelerating across the level ground.

He cried out to the people camped in tents below. Their night lights had gone out long ago. He guessed it to be at least 2:00 a.m. when the dark forms of men with baseball bats poured out of the truck beds and went after those sleeping in tents. Some had been awakened by the trucks and Ishi's cries. He saw a few of them struck down. Worse was the scene of men beating lumps caught inside the fabric.

He called Minkle. "Josh, we have another raid. Men in trucks."

"Christ. Have you called the sheriff?"

"No reason to. They'll be long gone before sheriffs can make it over the mountain. Here's what I think you should do."

Just before they hung up, Ishi said, "If you have a rifle, bring it with you."

NATIONAL MEDIA HAD a field day with how the lone California orchard owner had sacrificed his main field truck to capture thirteen men. Minkle had floored it up the highway—Ishi heard his engine in high whine—and he'd parked his truck across the access road in a place where no traffic could drive around it. Then he'd hunkered down nearby in the woods with his rifle.

Because the grade behind them was a steep single lane, the invaders who raucously drove down found themselves with few options when they came upon the stopped vehicle. The last truck of the three tried to get away by backing up the hill, but in the dark, in the fury—or was it humiliation?—and with the gravel slipping under his spinning rear tires, the driver backed right off the road and rolled his vehicle. Two of his passengers were injured. One broke a clavicle and punctured a lung. The other broke a femur.

Because EMTs are unbiased about whom they treat, the injured attackers were taken to hospital and when patched up, to jail. The small light of justice, though, was that they were last of the injured that night to be transported. The county's ambulances flocked to the massacre site by way of Minkle's property to take all the tent people to the emergency room.

The idiots had burned Minkle's truck, thinking somehow that burning it would make it disappear. Sheriff's deputies arrested those the ambulances didn't take.

The injury toll among the tent community was astounding—broken bones and concussions, but remarkably no fatalities. Only three had managed to escape unharmed. In the darkness, they had bailed over the bank into the river and escaped into the trees.

To get ahead of the story, spokespeople for De Boulette blamed the encounter on racial tension between the Pomo and eco-warriors at the site, whom they characterized as wired for violence and having wildly competing agendas. Eco-warriors wanted to the save the trees, while the Pomo wanted God-knew-what that had something to do with old grievances settled long ago that they couldn't accept. In short, these groups tried to beat each other to death.

With Brodie's help those stories went down in flames. Confessions from the attackers revealed them to be vineyard workers from Santa Rosa, recruited for an extracurricular night's work. They weren't sure of the identities of the men who paid them each $300 in cash and who had supplied the baseball bats. But within three days, the local athletic supply store came forward with the receipt. The credit card belonged to the assistant of a man named Stephen R. Baskin.

When the *Takes On America* piece aired, it included a short synopsis of the De Boulette raid as text on the screen before the credits rolled. According to the show's headquarters in New York, their phones lit up, with 85% of calls in support of the protesters.

Brodie's editorial on the incident suggested that De Boulette's staff overseeing terrorist activities was underfunded and that, for the time being, "they should stick to advertising Champagne and wine."

But the legal arm of the corporation pressed forward to wrest Minkle's land from him. The higher-ups were confident their reputation and clout could weather a local disturbance that was "unfortunate for the victims and the perpetrators alike." Minkle had only six weeks left before he had to pay up to keep his land away from the bank. In corporate time, six weeks was the blink of an eye.

But Brodie's damning exposé of De Boulette's abuses in other countries, coupled with what he termed 'the Minkle raid,' was the first that Americans heard about this part of the company's business model. Almost overnight, De Boulette's bid to take Beckett and its trees became a long shot. More stories of their wrongdoing surfaced in the national press, and the corporation lost numerous lucrative advertising contracts. To control the damage to his reelection chances, Murphy fired an underling for vague causes that made it sound as if favoring De Boulette had all been that person's scheme.

The tent community was left in literal and psychological ruins. Only a few of the people who had been camping there made their way back. The rest didn't have funds to replace their equipment, or the blows they took had broken their protesting hearts. There was talk of a human rights violations charge. But that would take years, and the lawyers experienced in that kind of case knew that most of the would-be plaintiffs would have moved on by the time a trial date was announced.

Of those who carried on, members of Pomo bands around Santa Rosa were first to set up again, and they outnumbered members of the

Dead Creek Rancheria. Ishi was happy to have them all. Over the next five days, new eco-warriors from the white world came in clusters, some tastelessly adorned in war paint. To keep county sanitation inspectors happy, an anonymous donor paid for portable toilets.

AS ISHI FIRED off what he thought might be the last of his massacre series, a caravan of four large vans and three overloaded cars broke into the vineyard. They did not park on the far side where the other campers had. They came forward slowly, as if making sense of the scene. They halted between the new tents and the river. Ishi heard Delicia whoop and then ululate. People stepping out of the vans echoed her, transporting him to a wedding celebration his unit had come upon in Afghanistan.

"Why didn't you tell me you were coming?" Delicia called down. "I would have brewed a vat of redwood needle tea."

The caravan significantly increased the population of the temporary town of Minkleville. These new arrivals were older than most of the eco-warriors and even from 220 feet up, Ishi saw their authentic outrageousness. Their uniforms were taut musculature, and they had the swagger of rock musicians.

"Ishi," Delicia called, "we have the best of reinforcements. Now Murphy is going to have to bow down."

Ishi couldn't see Delicia, but he heard her near-hollered conversation with a pair of the women.

"I thought you were in Lisbon? Our gain, their loss. And you, Becca. You said you were done, done, done with everything circus!"

A woman with dazzling red hair called back, "I *am* done with circuses, but *this* is *life*. And I wouldn't miss this for anything."

Pomo protestors gathered to assess the new tribe. They displayed no tension; it was more curiosity. Some of the new men went straight to them and slapped high fives, as if they were celebrating old friendships.

The Pomo pointed almost as a group to Ishi, who was out on his front porch limb.

The men from the circus saluted. "Ishi Darkhorse," cried out one with a booming voice, "we of the Provisional Beckett Circus pronounce you ringmaster on high."

Ishi attempted an Elizabethan bow and produced cheers.

"We're here to make sure this stand of yours has a surplus of joy." Fists were raised.

One sinewy new arrival with a bandana rag holding his long hair in check draped his arms over a Pomo man and woman, one of the few couples in Minkleville.

The woman of that pair, Silver Weaver, had been shuttling back and forth as mediator between Ishi and Amber, who was making herself scarce after seeing Delicia embrace her man "on national TV! The only thing I want to know," Amber barked via her messenger, "is how many times that slut with the fake Spanish name has leapt into your tree."

Ishi had answered honestly. "Twice. Both filmed."

OVER THE COURSE of the afternoon, the Provisional Beckett Circus members unloaded an extraordinary conglomeration of supplies. One van carried a full tent that housed a propane-operated kitchen, which members set up between the Pomo and Eco encampments. It came with solar collectors to run a music system that played dance music from all over the world. And they made no bones about ignoring Murphy's stipulation that there would be no camping in Beckett's groves. Tents for various interminglings of performers sprang up in sweet locations out of the easy view of sheriff's deputies who came to check on living conditions within walking distance of Minkleville.

Before dusk, from across the way Ishi watched the whole crew haul themselves into Her Majesty. Their boisterous gathering highlighted his loneliness to the point that he considered dropping down his own line and crossing over to join them.

Delicia explained to him later that she had worked with most of these women and men on the world circuit. A number of them had been laid off as circuses shrank in size and personnel due to relentless pressure from animal rights organizations and the rise of digital entertainment. Some were newly retired and were suffering from quitter's remorse. For them, life without applause had little meaning.

Hours later, after discussing all manner of stories and ideas, they slid down Delicia's line and wandered, laughing, into the forest.

A text from Brodie lit up Ishi's nest.

Remember how I killed your story idea of Fukushima radiation poisoning California?

Turns out you were right on the $

Sharpen your pen. Gird your loins. The big fight comes.

Thirty

WEARING IMPECCABLE EARTH-TONE robes trimmed in black that Sensei had had made for him, Tadao turned at the ramp to the airplane and waved farewell to the three most important people to him: Sensei; Sensei's son, Satoru; and Kumezo, the head of construction.

"Stepping out of the pages of history will improve your impact," Sensei had said when the robes arrived. "If we could, we'd send a samurai on horseback with you. Wear these robes like armor to protect yourself from all the strange things you will see."

Throughout the flight to San Francisco, Sensei's words spawned images of American crowds dogging his mission. Tadao countered them by thinking of the victims of the tsunami and nuclear meltdown. Close to his heart were the pregnant women around Fukushima who would give birth to children whose lives, like his, were destined to be shortened by the effects of radiation.

During the week of preparing to travel after making the offer for the redwoods, *Tennō Heika*'s Office of Public Affairs had counseled Tadao that they were not bargaining for Beckett State Forest. The honorable State of California had placed the land for sale, and the sum the Japanese government offered was more than four times the appraised value. In addition to the huge deposit, the offer came with a kilogram bar of gold and a two-fold contingency: because of the extraordinary funds pledged, California would entertain no other offers until Tadao had inspected the wood. If he found it suitable, Japan had thirty days to close the sale.

Tadao had other worries. His fever-pitched study with a tutor in advance of the trip had not revived all of the English he had forgotten since leaving the orphanage. He also fretted about what would upset him more: whether Americans would feel guilty when he arrived carrying poison from the atomic bombs they had dropped on his country, or if they wouldn't even remember that they had. Certainly, he would not broach that subject, but it raised other questions. Were the Hinoki forests victims of the bombs America had dropped that had killed his grandparents and his parents? Had the trees weakened and finally become sterile?

Rocketing through the dark, Tadao saw the situation with America the way some Japanese media had expressed it: Japan's generous purchase was an apology for its aggression against America, and in return, America allowing Japan to take old-growth redwood trees was a gesture that asked Japan's forgiveness for unleashing the nuclear age on its cities. If nothing else, perhaps this purchase and building the Temple of Listening would bring the two countries closer. That rapprochement would certainly please *kami*.

He fell asleep with moonlight reflecting off the plane's wings and the roar of engines in his ears.

IT WAS AFTERNOON in San Francisco when his airplane touched down. Tadao found the rush of human energy in the airport's long halls unsettling.

While the Japanese press had barely covered his departure, a gaggle of journalists confronted Tadao and two Japanese embassy officials while they waited in the baggage claim area. He didn't know what to make of reporters wearing shorts, or of them yelling over each other to be heard. Feeling insecure, he abandoned his prepared statement in favor of letting an embassy official answer questions. And for the first time, he listened to Americans speaking their version of English.

One question was about how he planned to handle Americans being upset with Japan purchasing their wood. A reporter in dark glasses and baseball cap asked if they realized this purchase would rekindle passions left over from the war.

A contingent of white men in grey suits—governor's aides, Tadao learned later— rescued them from the need to answer and drove them to the Miracle Hotel in Sacramento.

The trappings of his hotel room caught him by surprise. He worked the gold faucets in the bathroom. He opened the little refrigerator. On the counter were an elegant teapot and a selection of teas, though they smelled different than teas he knew.

The bed was too large, too soft. For company, he let the TV news run. But when he saw video of himself arriving at the airport, he sat upright. The screen displayed trunks of monstrous trees, followed by a map he recognized as Northern California. A red circle pulsed far north of San Francisco, in the area where the redwoods grew. Next, a beautiful woman stood on a branch, gesturing to the tree behind her as if imploring people to buy it. A banner tied to the top limbs said: WE BREATHE FOR THE PLANET.

Tadao had never heard of anyone protesting in the imperial forests. People honored the trees' place in society. If a woman ever had a concern regarding some trees, Sensei would write her a letter explaining history, religion, and *Tennō*'s wishes. He would invite her and her family to the opening ceremonies of the temple. Tadao looked forward to meeting this woman.

But he was thoroughly confused when in the closing shot, she raised one foot like a dancer and held it above her head. This seemed disrespectful. In fact, if people in America honored *kami*, he had seen no signs of it in the two hours he traveled from the airport. And the hierarchy of the physical elements in his hotel's lobby seemed designed by a child.

What, he wondered, kept Americans aware of their place on the land and their duty to it?

AS HE AWAITED the designated hour in a high-ceilinged alcove across the hall from Governor Murphy's office the next morning, the air in the building seemed to vibrate with schemes. Men in dark suits and women in skirts and heels strode by with urgency. In a glossy, soft-cover folio bearing the California state flag, Tadao found a picture of the governor and his note welcoming people to witness government in action. Even dressed in a suit, the governor seemed like a cowboy.

The large double doors across the hall swept open. Aides ushered Tadao and the Japanese deputy ambassador past three secretaries standing at attention and into a conference room. Some twenty men hovered near a long table made from one piece of cedar. Its grain was straight and its growth rings were gloriously tight. Tadao was comforted that Americans knew the value of wood.

Heads turned as the governor swooped in late. Wearing a blue suit and a garish tie, he approached Tadao with an outstretched hand.

"So nice of you to come to America. How do you like it so far?" His smile was overpowering.

Though Tadao had understood the question, he waited for the deputy ambassador's translation and thanked the governor in Japanese for seeing them. He presented the governor with a carefully wrapped box.

The deputy ambassador explained, "This is a gift for the people of California from *Tennō Heika*. And this second one is for your wife from Mr. Kitamura's sensei."

The gifts caught the governor off guard, but with reasonable grace he handed them to his aide. He bade everyone to sit. Tadao was seated across the table from him, with the deputy ambassador on his left.

Not wanting to leave the governor's question unanswered, Tadao said, "It is my first trip out of Japan, so everything is new." But the charade of translation felt heavy. He blurted out in English, "You have many Japan cars."

The governor erupted in laughter. "Yes, California is Japan's greatest customer. Now we're happy to offer you something in return. You'll love the part of our state where the redwoods grow. It is very beautiful, the heart of wine country." The governor kissed the fingertips of his right hand and opened them like a flower blooming.

Referring to a sheet his aide handed him, the governor said he was happy Japan had expressed an interest in this extraordinary forest. "The emperor's offer seems a fair price for a stand of the best timber in the world." He gestured to the man on his left. "My economic minister, Mr. Bellows, has been communicating with your emperor's office and he'll be taking over the meeting. I assure you we want this to work for everyone and for it to be handled fairly, because there are other parties interested."

The deputy ambassador shifted uneasily in his chair.

Rising, Mr. Bellows attempted a formal Japanese bow. "Mr. Deputy Ambassador, Mr. Kitamura, as I have discussed with the emperor's representative, in your country it is common that when you buy timber you also purchase the land. But in this case that is not necessary, which would make your purchase cheaper. Several American parties would be happy to own the land after the trees are cut." He looked down the table to a man wearing a pink dress shirt and a brown tie.

Tadao used the time of translation to consider what Mr. Bellows could possibly be driving at.

"What makes sense, of course," Bellows went on, "is for you to inspect the trees to see they meet your standards." He laughed. "We are certain they will. This forest has been growing undisturbed since before Buddhism came to your country."

"That is good," Tadao said. "*Tennō Heika* ask Watanabe and Son to build a temple living one thousand years."

At this, people tilted their heads. Apparently, they didn't know what wood could do.

"You may have heard there *is* a little protest going on with the trees," Bellows said. "But it is temporary." He pointed to a man in a drab green jacket with an insignia on the breast pocket. "Mr. LeCale, chief of California's Department of Forestry and Fire Protection, is working to resolve it. Here in America, we have the right to free speech."

"We don't see what harm one woman can do," the deputy ambassador said.

Mr. LeCale stood to speak. "We are encouraging her to come down. Of course, her safety is our highest priority." The man seemed quite confident.

"No need," Tadao said. "I talk her. I talk *on* her. I talk on her about *Tennō Heika*'s temple, and she come down."

Judging by the silence in the room, Tadao's words had allayed everyone's concerns.

It did seem, though, that the governor and Mr. Bellows had not completely understood *Tennō*'s proposal to buy the land. Japan intended to harvest the wood for centuries. He trusted the deputy ambassador would clarify this in private.

After the meeting ended, the man with the pink shirt dragged over a fellow with a belly like a pufferfish. His hair needed cutting and the suit he wore did not fit well.

"Excuse me, Mr. Kitamura. My name is Gunther Flaggenbauch. And I would like to introduce Mr. Grayson."

Tadao bowed to both men.

"Mr. Grayson is a logger of excellent reputation, and if Japan's bid is accepted, he will give you wonderful service." Mr. Grayson's hand engulfed Tadao's. It was rough and had grease in the creases.

The deputy ambassador asked Mr. Flaggenbauch if he worked for the governor.

Flaggenbauch stuttered a reply that Tadao didn't catch. The deputy ambassador translated, "He says he is acting as a go-between."

Tadao turned to Grayson. "In Japan, trees for temples one meter." He held his hands apart that distance. "You come north with us tomorrow?"

Mr. Grayson's speech was hard to understand. He spoke, as Sensei would say, like a dog chewing a rock. "Yes, I live in the valley."

"You cut big many trees?"

Flaggenbauch jumped in. "There aren't many trees this size left in California."

"Really?" asked Tadao. "California has many trees, no? You cut big tree, Mr. Grayson?"

"When I was young," Grayson said. His eyes shifted in a strange way.

Tadao guessed he was paying deference to the magic of a man wearing robes.

THE NEXT MORNING'S drive to northern California took Tadao through land where vineyards dominated every view. Eventually, that broad inland valley died at the mountains. The winding of the road made him feel at home. Their driver was a state forester, happy to answer questions. He confirmed Flaggenbauch's statement about big redwoods being rare. In fact, for the first part of their climb, they saw no redwoods at all.

"In the old days," the forester said, "trees containing 40,000 board feet were common. They had annual rings almost too fine to count. The wood was almost impervious to rot."

When Tadao converted the math, he remembered Sensei warning him that Americans were famous for overstating size of things

"Making a fortune in California's gold rush," the forester said, "was unpredictable. But our *forests* were gold standing in the open. Frustrated miners and poor immigrants poured into the woods by the thousands to take them down.

"The first cut of the coastal forests took about sixty years. For the next forty, fellers cut trees that had been too small to take on the first pass through or that had sprouted out of the old stumps. Without competition, those trees grew between three to six feet in diameter in a hundred years. Remarkable, but the quality was not nearly as good as old growth."

The forester explained how early loggers had floated logs down rivers to mills on the Pacific coast. Clear-cutting encouraged weaker species to compete in their place, and when left open, the land tended to burn more often. Winter rains eroded the hillsides. Since the war, all former forest land that was tillable had been bulldozed for livestock and apples. Now the transition to vineyards was almost complete.

They came, at last, to a beautiful valley of vineyards. The hills had stands of small and medium-sized conifer trees.

"An acre of grapes yields up to 2,400 bottles of wine a year," the forester said. "There's more money per acre in wine than forests can produce."

They drove over an arching, one-lane bridge from another time and climbed a short way until they came to an overgrown entrance to what must once have been some official place. Two vehicles with state insignia on their doors led the way. Beyond an unmanned guard post, the forester slowed and pointed out the first redwoods. Because they seemed little bigger than Hinoki, Tadao nodded. Sensei had been right about Americans' need to exaggerate. The undergrowth was chaotic, thick with shrubs.

He was relieved when they passed bigger trees. Two meters wide. Another kilometer further, they came to a parking lot.

The size of the trees in the campground area thrilled Tadao. Two and half meters through, at least. If the wood was truly impervious to rot, it was going to save Japan's temples far into the future. The woods had a spontaneous yet settled quality that challenged a basic tenet Tadao had absorbed in Japan's imperial forest—that regimented planting and nobility were linked. He felt thrilled and uneasy, the way he might when a new craftsman arrived armed with better techniques.

The forester pointed to a large map. "The green area," he said, "has been carefully surveyed. The surrounding blue is wild forest."

"And," Tadao asked, "*Tennō Heika* buying all, correct?"

A second forester answered, "Yes, if the deal goes through."

"There are 549 acres of mapped groves," continued the first. "Altogether, it is 1,457 acres and it is all in redwoods."

For their hike, Tadao was happy to be wearing his workman's black, loose-legged trousers and a linen gi top. The forester produced high boots for him to wear.

"Where is the woman?" Tadao asked.

"She's a ways from here, in a grove along the river. We can walk the other groves first."

"She and I talk today?"

The forester nodded. "If she wants." Did he seem amused?

A woman with a camera joined them and they headed down well-marked paths that had begun returning to nature. Tadao picked up a handful of duff, smelled it, crumbled it, and rubbed it against his cheek. He grabbed a fresh sprig of needles that had fallen. They were soft and inconceivably short for such huge trees.

He stopped in a grove of trees that each measured more than three meters in diameter. The forester walked on until he became quite small. Still, he hadn't reached the neighboring tree. Tadao marveled at the color and lines in the bark and at how it was thick and flaky. He knew at once that the design of the Temple of Listening must pay homage to this paradoxical union of size and vulnerability. He made a rough calculation of the beams in the tree behind the forester and realized it held enough wood for perhaps the whole temple. His respiration quickened.

High above, some of the lower branches were thicker than mature Hinoki. The canopy was vibrant green, shading out any undergrowth. Tiny cones lay thick on the ground. The redwoods in America were still healthy. So this was what forests looked like when no bombs had fallen nearby!

Tadao rotated several times, feeling like a minnow in a rice paddy. The setting was too large to comprehend.

There were no paths in the woods when they set off for the grove where the woman was. It seemed they were walking back in time. The trees got bigger still. The forester estimated they were 1,500 years old, older than The Temple of Listening would be built to stand. Their trunks looked as if imperial foresters had been caring for them since they sprouted. And if young trees kept coming, there would be wood to rebuild the temple in the fourth millennium.

As they approached the groves by the river, the forester explained that the woman protestor was not alone. "She has other people helping her, but they are across the river on the neighbor's land. And her boyfriend is in the neighboring tree."

Struck still more by the size of the trees in the next set of groves, Tadao halted in dramatic fashion. Working on impulse, he washed his hands in water from his bottle, rinsed his mouth, and spat it out as when entering a Shinto shrine. He bowed at the waist and clapped twice firmly to alert *kami* he was entering. When this seemed not enough, he remembered Sensei on occasion bowing to the ground. Now he understood why. He placed his palms together at his chin, knelt, and brought his head and hands to the ground. When the forester squatted to ensure he had not taken ill, Tadao waved him away.

From then on, each time the placement of trees and light touched him, Tadao stopped and bowed to the ground that nurtured them. At last, they came to the grove that bordered the river. In the vineyard beyond, more than a hundred tents shimmered in the sun. When they came to a natural circle of trees, the forester pointed to an enormous trunk and whispered, "The woman lives in that one." The trunk was more than five meters wide.

Tadao asked everyone to move back and wait. He walked to the middle of the circle and faced the woman's tree. There he performed bows to each of the four directions, as he had seen Shinto priests do at religious events. Anything less, he thought, would be insolent. The ground was soft underfoot. The air was moist.

Without looking up, he went to her tree and placed his hands on the bark. He then lifted his eyes up the trunk and saw the dark-haired woman from the TV standing on the lowest branch. The way she crossed her arms made his confidence flee. He hadn't known many women, and he had never seen one place her arms quite like that.

He put his palms together at his heart. "My name is Tadao. Can you hear me?"

"Hello, Tadao-san," she called down.

Her knowing how to make the honorific of his name meant this meeting would go well.

"Call me Delicia." Because she said it slowly, he knew she was kind.

"Delicia-san," he repeated. "How are you?"

"I am ready to fight you."

"I hope to talk you . . . talk *with* you."

She did not answer, but turned suddenly toward the vineyard. Perhaps she did not want to talk with him today. He was not in a hurry. Nothing about his life and work required speed. In time, he would find a way to bring her down.

She threw him a withering look, and he heard the clanging chains and grinding gears of heavy equipment vehicles coming from the sunlit land across the river. When he looked up again, Delicia was gone.

Thirty-One

BRODIE'S NEWS OF Japan's preemptive offer for Beckett State Forest turned Minkleville upside down. Ishi called him to confirm the details, but Brodie admitted they were sketchy. He expected to work late, he said, on an article fleshing out the long-overdue blowback from Japan's defeat in 1945.

Within an hour, Delicia had posted a call to arms to her 628,000 Twitter followers.

Starting the next day, the Minkleville encampment began to swell. The far end of the vineyard became jammed with parked vehicles. The three portable toilets proved unable to handle the influx, and people were tromping into the brush wherever they could.

To those on the ground, the invasion from Japan had all the feel of a lightning strike. That sleazeball Murphy had kept the deal under wraps until his calendar was released, as required by law. It announced that Murphy was due to meet with the emperor's emissary two days later.

When the contingencies of the emperor's offer for Beckett were leaked, the residents of Minkleville knew the emissary would be coming north at some point with a mission to assess the "product." But they had no idea what that would entail.

Raul, the quickly chosen leader of the Provisional Beckett Circus—he was, after all, a ringmaster—organized his performers and any willing campers to become lookouts so the residents of Minkleville could prepare a definitive protest. Four people manned a post where the vineyard road met the highway, day and night. Another crew was placed at the entrance of Beckett State Forest. Both of these outfits had protest signs at the ready. Raul named them "Minutewomen" in deference to an earlier revolt against another heartless force. Like those colonial firebrands, the

Minutewomen were determined to make Japan's emissary uncomfortable from the moment he arrived.

Raul and the "mayor of Minkleville," a Pomo from Geyserville named Burt, planned how they would flood the area if it became clear a tree was to be harvested. They would risk arrest and fines for trespassing on state land. They talked about peaceful occupation of equipment. But they had had time for only one disorganized meeting when Ishi got a text from the Minutewomen at the Beckett entrance, saying forestry people had arrested them and taken them off-site. Cops had just that minute re-turned their phones.

Ishi spread the word by text and voice. He was on his way down to prepare his access line, in case someone needed to climb up or if it be-came obvious he'd be more valuable on the ground, when the emissary's group walked into the grove.

He parked himself where he could see and not be seen. He expected a delegation wearing suits. But only one man among them looked Ja-panese. He was small of stature, but seemed in command of everyone.

To Ishi's dismay, he was taken with the man from the first glimpse. The contrast between his comfort in workman's dress and his upright formality and innocence got his attention. His bowing to the four direc-tions reminded Ishi of Pomo ceremonies he'd attended as a boy. His skin prickled.

When Delicia confronted the visitor, Ishi saw her in a new light. Af-ter all the training and combat he'd been through, his instinct—unlike hers—was to hide. He was embarrassed. Delicia's defiance of the gentle man below her gave him a headline. His next piece had to be about her. All about her.

But diesel motors and the clanging of chains coming from Minkle's killed the exchange. Delicia disappeared into the limbs, and for a minute, the emissary looked like a boy at a county fair who'd lost his balloon.

Sure that a state takeover was in the works, Ishi climbed as if escap-ing enemy gunfire. He couldn't see the vehicles until he reached the limb that held the banner.

The gate to Minkle's land had been left wide open and a convoy like an armored division was halfway up the vineyard. A state police cruiser and two sheriff department vans led the way. A CALFIRE personnel truck came next. Two trucks carrying logging equipment followed them. Three special timber haulers with wider beds and reinforced uprights, a portable crane and a flatbed carrying a D9 Caterpillar dozer came last. No media were among them. This was a raid.

Ishi called Minkle, wondering if he'd been abducted. "Josh, are you okay? Do you know what's going on here?"

Minkle paused. "I'm *not* okay. And I *know*. You've got a logging crew coming your way and enough law enforcement to hold off the protesters."

"How? Did they—"

"Money," Minkle said. "*Money.* The state offered me a deal I couldn't refuse. Enough to pay my full mortgage for three months. Three months in exchange for access, so they could drop a tree—just one—and truck it out over my land. More time for me to figure out how to find another source of funds to keep my property from De Boulette."

"You've abandoned everything we've been working on. What about principles?"

"The deal was I had to keep my mouth shut until this Japanese guy showed up. Makes me feel like a worm, Ishi. The truth is saving the redwoods is bigger than me. Maybe bigger than all of us. But my apples? You know I'll fight for those."

"What about the Pomo? Have they bought you off for us, too?"

"That wasn't part of their deal. And I wouldn't have accepted it. They said they're not going to interfere with the protest 'cause it's on my land."

The equipment trucks stopped a good distance from the encampment, but the law enforcement vehicles kept rolling. They wove through a few tents and parked on the only open ground, which was on top of the Pomo pyre site. Ignoring the cry rolling through the crowd, half a dozen sheriff deputies exited and approached the Pomo section of the encampment en masse.

To Ishi, it seemed a battle was brewing. Burt went to meet them with that non-threatening stride that Indians perfected to survive confrontation with whites. A moment later though, he was thrusting his hands in exasperation when, like a grungy Tinker Bell, Raul glided to the rescue.

Delicia called Ishi's name. She was on the limb that held the other end of the banner. It was fitting they were both up there, like generals watching their troops move into place, which drove home the point that they weren't in command of anything. The motor noise made talk impossible. She pointed to her phone. They were texting when one from Raul appeared to both of them.

they're not here to take U down or drive us out

they just want 1 tree

Ishi texted back.

the word "just" always announces the beginning of the end

Raul waved to him, his other arm pointing to a beauty some seventy yards south of Atlas. It stood on a place where the bank protruded into the river, which allowed Ishi to see its base. It was smaller than Atlas, but still stood over 250 feet tall.

A logging crew appeared from behind the trucks carrying saws. They headed toward it.

Raul short-circuited Ishi's rising sense of betrayal. One at a time, he shook the hand of every sheriff and state trooper. He pointed to the south and, by God, the state police and sheriffs backed their vans off the pyre site and parked where he had suggested. Pomo in the area of that redwood began pulling up their tents with resignation, but not defiance. They marched their belongings closer to the kitchen area while the sawyers cleared brush around the base of the tree.

Next, the state police, sheriffs, and foresters—about twenty in number—formed a line and gestured to have the protesters move back.

It seemed a civil action until at the back of the tent area, a large group of brand new arrivals, maybe a hundred women and men, mustered as a unit and encircled the law enforcement and the sawyers. Walking with determination, they pushed toward the tree. Many held phones up, taking video. They made taunting gestures, as if daring the sawyers to drop the tree on them.

Ishi recognized the turnip-bodied older man as the logger Grayson, who had come there in the beginning with Baskin. Grayson assessed the forces arrayed against his men. His bellowing reached Ishi, though his words did not. He started up a chain saw with an enormous blade and ordered his men forward with their machines running.

Rather than make a show of drawing their sidearms, the law officers stood aside as the sawyers trotted forward. They went after the women first, gunning their engines and swinging the blades. Unfamiliar with how the saws moved and intimidated by the whining roar, the women scurried away. When the men followed them, the law enforcement re-formed their line. One officer made his point by waving a pair of hand-cuffs.

In less than two minutes, the action was over.

The man from Japan came forward. He bowed kindly to the crowd. Ishi wondered how much he knew about America and the problems that this piece of land held. The visitor donned a white hard hat a forester handed him. He walked along the river toward the chosen tree, crossed over, and stood to admire the trunk. Placing his hands together at his chin, he bowed. Something about his ease and simpatico with the sawyers helped settle the last of the jacked-up male campers. He inspect-ed the trunk, seemed to bless it with his hands. Then he took three steps backward and bowed again.

As if under his sway, some of the campers lowered their heads.

The foresters and state police kept herding the campers back until they stood below Atlas and Her Majesty. Mixed in with his frustration and horror, Ishi sensed a guilty excitement. He had never seen a tree this big come down.

The man from Japan recrossed the river. The sawyers nodded in his direction and marked the placement of their felling cut. They discussed the fall for a minute, then one started his saw. With consummate skill, he worked his six-foot blade along a level plane advancing in stages from the outside bark to the heartwood. To cut halfway through the trunk, he buried his blade to the hilt like a dagger into viscera. All the while, the saw rattled and snarled, blowing out a storm of red chips. At last, he inspected that his cut connected the gunning points he had marked on the sides of the trunk. He nodded in satisfaction to his partners.

Another sawyer took over, using his six-foot saw to make the snipe, a cut on an angled plane from above that met the felling cut along its inside line. When he was done, by prying on a long bar, they freed a huge wedge of redwood shaped like a section of orange from the trunk. That wood being removed would allow the trunk to rock forward into the cut. If all went well, the tree would fall straight across the river.

The sawyers moved to the grove side of the trunk where one started a level back cut, a few inches higher than the felling cut. To keep the tree from tipping backward and pinching the saw, the sawyer's partner drove thin wedges into the cut as it deepened. When the back cut was partially complete, Grayson used a smaller saw to cut out a cube-shaped notch under it, into which he slipped a huge hydraulic jack sitting upright. He pumped the piston until the ram was snug against the tree's end grain, eight inches inside the bark. The sawyer cut deeper still until all that was left uncut was a narrow hinge through the middle of the tree. He killed his saw.

In the quiet that followed, two sawyers pumped the jack's long bar to work the hinge to tip the tree into the felling cut. Everyone stood rapt, stoic in the face of the inevitable, as if watching a hangman slip the noose around a doomed man's neck. Women gnawed on their knuckles. Men pulled their partners next to their hips.

Though this whole show was for him, the man from Japan stood impassive near the police line. The sawyers groaned at their labor and the hydraulic pin rose imperceptibly. For a while, their teamwork and rhythm sucked up the crowd's attention. Then one after another, heads tipped to look at the top of the tree.

The crown shuddered. A single bump, like a heartbeat wished for, or as if the tree was responding to a minor earthquake. Its million needles quivered. The protesters rediscovered their passion. Their voices ached in equal measures of grief and awe. Some trotted forward only to have state police warn them back.

With the speed of a star moving in the night sky, those feathery tips on the crown began sweeping east toward the vineyard. The sawyers watched for microscopic changes in the back cut and eyed the trunk. The top jolted again, and now there was no going back. This jewel that had stood since before the Mayans built their temples was heading to ground, and a long-shielded piece of sky would be torn open. Even to eyes as experienced with death as Ishi's, the wonder of a tree being there, and the prospect of it not, seemed a passing more momentous than that of an animate being.

At an unseen signal, all four sawyers scampered into the grove and out of sight, running like boys from a disaster they hadn't meant to cause. Their flight raised agitation in the crowd. Ishi drew a long breath.

The top moved with more determination, traveling smoothly, becoming visibly out of plumb, perhaps three meters over its length. As it picked up speed, the foliage from top to bottom responded to air pressure. Branches on the near side scraped free of the neighboring tree. Like arms released, they bobbed in celebration. Sounds of tearing and cracking. Mid-fall, so much material was moving, Ishi's mind couldn't hold it.

A woman screamed. Several more joined her, all running toward the tree and then stopping, wailing, hopeless, as at the opening of a gallows trapdoor.

Like a mallet head, the top rocketed to the ground. Limbs thirty inches through dissolved in a cascade of snapping wood, as if an ocean liner under full throttle was shearing off pilings of a pier. The ground shook. Dust lifted in a shroud.

The whole eighty meters of trunk hit the ground across the river in one level unit. It rebounded fifteen feet into the air, all of its greenery shaking in chaos, before gravity won again. Then, as dramatically as it had hit, it came to rest.

Thirty-Two

WATCHING THAT GRACEFUL man bow down in her grove threw Delicia out of kilter. For a few minutes, his air of surrender and honor stroked a tiny sweet spot she'd felt when first reading about the mission of the Temple of Listening in the *Sacramento Bee*. It had taken her only a minute to see how the story neglected the grand irony: the emperor's remedy for climate change killing *his* Hinoki was to cut trees in *California*.

Hearing the trucks coming infuriated her. Kitamura's bowing had just been an act, a distraction. As an entertainer herself, she should have known better. The temple builder was her nemesis. Such a clever disguise.

To escape the humiliation of her gullibility, she flew up the limbs like a spider whose web had been bumped. Climbing hard and fast was the best alternative to screaming, a tool she wanted to hold in reserve until it became essential. She thought she was headed for her nest, but went past it to the branches that she found best to do her stretches. There she blocked out the world by throwing herself into her routine, chanting encouragement aloud. Almost growling.

But when the sound of the motors overwhelmed the environment, she climbed to where she could see the activity. It felt good to find Ishi there. Raul's texts eased her enough to watch the whole display of power and protest and loss, her emotions swinging: offense, disbelief, pride, disgust, and horror. She had never seen film of a beheading or a firing squad, but as the tree fell to the earth, that was what she compared it to. She'd been stupid to pin her hopes on Governor Murphy's fear of public opinion. Power was all men lived for.

She descended to her nest to grieve, but a newfound defiance overwhelmed the grief. She considered riding Her Majesty down to the ground, if it came to that. If Japan cut Beckett's trees, she would make a statement no one would ever forget. And because she could, why not make a spectacle as the tree fell, swinging limb to limb? That was her gift.

There were worse ways to die.

Articles and polls had been mostly in her favor, but power and money had crushed the forces of good. This foreigner was her enemy, but the governor was to blame. It was time to make this fight personal.

Without hesitating, she dialed the California State Capitol switchboard. The first live person she reached recognized her name. Before passing her call up the chain of power, the woman said, "God bless what you're doing, Ms. Fortunado. I've always been a fan."

Two handoffs later, while on hold for the governor's chief of staff, Delicia was rehearsing her speech when he picked up.

"I have a few minutes, Ms. Fortunado."

"Then I'll keep it short. I'm not coming down."

"I understand that you're upset. Believe me, our highest priority here is *your* safety."

It felt good to let him hear her cynical groan. "You must think women are dumb."

The chief of staff paused. "I assure you my wife is very smart."

To let him think he'd landed a blow, Delicia bit her tongue. "If so, she'll advise you how badly this is going to play in the news. The local Pomo reporter is going to rip you a new one."

"Ms. Fortunado, I can't run a state based on fear of what might happen in one little place. This offer from Japan presents a huge window of opportunity."

She felt vertiginous. "Opportunity? The word is *rape*. Taking sanctity that's not yours."

The last thing she expected from the chief of staff was chuckling. "Ms. Fortunado, you're overlooking who humans *are* in the world order. We see something we want, we take it, and we use it. It's hardwired. It's our nature . . . so, by definition, it *can't* be bad. And you're not going to change that by sitting in a tree, no matter how old or beautiful it is. Take our friends the Japanese, for instance. They have a great need for this wood, and I might add, a responsible use for it. You sound like the kind who knows we could help relations along if we offer them something."

The depth of his entrenchment was appalling. "*Last* week's rapist coming through the 'window of opportunity' was De Boulette," she said. "This week it's *Japan*."

"I beg to differ. I've met the young man the emperor sent over. He's not the pillager your supporters and some disgruntled local loggers are painting him to be."

Good. He'd heard about the loggers who opposed anyone taking the redwoods. "I've just *seen* his work. First and foremost, he's a shyster. Second, he watched the felling with glee."

"Whoa! I *don't* want to talk down to you, but you have to understand that trees die. The truth? Climate scientists say the redwoods are doomed. It's going to get too dry for them to survive. I'm sure you'll agree that letting them rot on the ground only compounds the tragedy."

"You mean, the crime. So, rape the land with the Stars and Stripes playing in the background, and then sell it because it's *spoiled*."

His slow response told her this punch had hit its mark.

"I am *trying* to be responsible here," he said at last. "In the future, there will be other uses for that land. For all of California. Humans are nothing if not adaptable. We've always found a way to go forward. Sure, we make mistakes, but we learn from them."

She wanted to spit. "We haven't learned squat. And until your governor wakes up and does his human duty, tell him there's nothing I won't do to ruin his reelection chances."

She heard a sharp inhalation. "Ms. Fortunado, this *is* Governor Murphy."

And he must have heard *her* inhalation. Her humanity almost pushed her to apologize but what came out was, "Governor, have you ever been to this 'little place'? Have you ever *seen* the trees you're dismissing as soon-to-be-dead and a 'window of opportunity'? I mean, have you ever walked among them?"

He paused and she prepared for a lie, but he said, "Cheryl and I very much wanted to get up there when we first heard about the sale—"

"Give it a break, Governor! *You* arranged the sale! That's why you're in hot water."

"—But running the world's fifth largest economy is a huge undertaking. We just haven't been able to get away."

She sat slack-jawed.

"As for Beckett, it's had a wonderful life as a forest. And in time, the land will find use again . . . for De Boulette or Japan or some other buyer. And *you* should be proud that your stand has brought attention to the wonders there. It will, no doubt, result in greater support for the other redwood parks we have that are more viable. So I very much hope we're going to be able to come to a reasonable—"

Her phone died. Her mind choked with missed comebacks and regret until she realized she'd made her points. More than three saws were running now, and several huge diesel motors had fired up, too. Fumes were enveloping her perch.

When she put in her fresh battery, she called Raul to see if her idea was even possible. "What are the chances you can get me an eighty-foot cable? Seven-eighths."

Raul, master of illusion, laughed. "If it can be imagined," he said, "it can be done. Are you thinking what I'm thinking?"

"I just had a bad call with the governor of California."

"Damn you, girl! You're walking another kind of high wire! What'd our boy Murphy say?"

"He says the trees are going to come down. And we should thank him for being so proactive."

"That figures. And is that why you want the cable?"

"It's just dawning on me. I've been looking for weeks at the circle of trees in this grove. It's like a perfect theater in the round. And now here we are with all of our out-of-work friends. Why waste our talent?"

"I like your thinking. I *love* your thinking."

"We don't have a lot of time. The only thing that will kill the sale of the trees is public opinion. Having people come here is one thing. But it's passive. Broadcasting the mission out, you know, with a splash, could really change everything. Whatever we can muster will help. But we'll want to do it before Japan signs the contract. How long do you think it'll take for us to get in shape to put on a show?"

Raul cleared his throat in consideration. "Some of us are already out to pasture. But between us we know lots of performers just craving a chance."

"Good," she said. "Let's have a meeting. Tonight if we can. The only entrance requirement is being able to haul your butt into Her Majesty."

"I'll put out the word," he said. "Say, can you smell the smoke?"

"The fumes? They're making me sick."

"No, I mean *smoke*."

She sniffed with greater attention. "I do. What's burning?"

"A fire erupted last night west of Willits. The wind is bad over there today."

"How far away is that?"

Raul weighed his answer. "I'm not an expert on fire, but it doesn't just depend on distance. It can really move through steep hills."

She looked. A light brown cloud hung in the distance over the hills east of the valley.

OVER THE NEXT hours, the sawyers cut the tree into logs and hauled them away. At the same time, more protesters arrived. The kitchen grew. Tents sprouted among all the old vines. A truckload of portable toilets came late in the day. No one knew who paid for them.

And all the while, Delicia mulled over the notion of a show. The more she conjured, the clearer it became. Images wouldn't leave her alone. The trees lent themselves to her passion for it. Not just the circle of them and their height, but their architecture. Their branches and crowns formed a green big top and enclosed a space in which anything could happen. *Anything*.

She was biased, but to her mind an important part of the reason people went to circuses was to see performers defy gravity, if only for a short time. Trapeze artists, rope acrobats, pole performers, and tightrope walkers. If her foot would allow it, she would get back on the wire.

She was the opposite of naïve. Putting on aerial acts in the trees would require skilled circus riggers. She wished she knew where Teeko was. Long before he became her catcher on the trapeze, he'd been a master rigger. And though it wasn't his job in Moscow, he'd quit the day after her fall, thinking he should have checked their work.

BEFORE DARK, FOURTEEN performers in colorful clothes hung in and around Delicia's nest, looking like Christmas tree ornaments. There was Shirley, the black-skinned fire eater who doubled as a stripper in the men's tent when local statutes allowed; the jugglers Octo and Becca, in matching outfits that made them look like Lego pieces; Botox, the lion tamer; Li'l Ambrosia, who'd taken over riding the elephants after Delicia went full time into aerial acts; Simón, the trapeze catcher; Divot, the gypsy pole climber; Suki, the rope wizard; Paloma, the knife thrower; Peter and Dieter, two of the best clowns in the business; Hector the contortionist; LeAnn, the gymnast; several women performers who were new to Delicia; and of course, Raul. All so different, but marked as a troupe by talent, joy, and the smell of sweat.

Ishi was an honored guest. Everyone cheered him as he walked hand over hand on the rope he and Delicia had hung between their trees that afternoon.

Noting their lounging behavior, Octo kicked things off. "I'd like to welcome you all to the first redwood chimpanzee symposium." Circus people knew how to laugh at themselves.

"You all are the best," Delicia said, sniffling with emotion. "What we're going to do has never been done before."

Shirley's grin was as wide as the Hoover Dam. "You're damn right. We specialize in *impossible*."

Raul played a drum roll on his chest. "I paced off the distance between the trees. The closest two are eighty-one feet apart. So a decent ring will fit nicely inside, along with a whole bunch of people."

"That's perfect," Simón said. "That allows us to run all the ground acts no problem. But in the end, I think what people are going to come for is the aerial stuff."

"Request to have that stricken, Your Honor," Shirley said to a hierarchy that wasn't there. "Simón is biased toward things happening in the air." Good-natured hoots and boos.

"It's not about me," Simón protested. "The real act here is Delicia. That's who the people will come for."

"Hear, hear!" Becca said without raising her head from Octo's shoulder.

"Can you be ready?" Botox asked.

Delicia felt determination working her face. "I'm strong and mostly pain free. But I'll need a couple weeks of wire time to find my footing. If it's going to be an eighty-footer, I'll need to figure how it moves."

"You'll go with a net, right?" Raul asked.

"I hate to, but I probably should."

"So," Dieter said, "we all need to get to work on finding materials."

Divot stood. "Unless we think 'going Podunk' is going to save this forest, we also need other acts, a lot of them."

Botox clapped hard, a holdover from how he demanded the attention of his lions. "I propose we divide into departments and get as much help here as we can. Pronto."

No one disagreed.

"Delicia," Botox continued, "you are the media person. The face to the world. LeAnn, you're the best organizer, and you've got a ready ground crew in tents across the river. All they need is orders."

"I'll do the carpentry," Hector said. "Build the ring. We'll have to rake away those needles to set up solid ground. So LeAnn, that's a first job for your crew."

Li'l Ambrosia waved her hand. "Botox and I should work together getting animal acts. My main goal? An elephant. Because with Ringling Brothers going under, this redwood circus will be a memorial to the old style. And don't give me any shit—"

"You mean, a requiem," Octo said.

"—about me saying this because I *ride* elephants. Of *course* that's why."

Everyone loved Li'l Ambrosia.

When the dust had cleared, their enthusiasm had sketched out a one-ring circus, a single matinee that would be a jewel in the woods. If things went the way Delicia wanted, it would never be forgotten. Among them they'd assigned tasks to eleven departments, including finance and legal, and had drawn up a list of performers to enrich the show. They made their best guess about when they would be ready.

Delicia's friends cheerfully dispersed with their agendas, scampering through branches. The way they slipped silently down her rope called to mind a battalion of winged monkeys. None of them suspected how much she had in common with the wicked witch.

Too excited to sleep, she headed to her high perch above the banner. Climbing Her Majesty transformed into ascending to the wire under the big top to close the show. She heard the music building. Moscow's wire being thirty-seven feet up seemed a piddling amount. After six weeks of living several hundred feet off the ground, height had lost its relevance. The challenge they had all set themselves demanded a steep climb. Which was her favorite kind. She had no time to lose. Until she had a wire to train on, she would use every move, every handhold and all her footwork in Her Majesty as a trigger for some past show.

Like most elite athletes, Delicia's body memory was so astute she could reel out most every performance she'd ever given, step by step. Even with the music. Her first thought for the redwood circus was to redo the show in Moscow. Announcing that would make good press. But four years later, she wasn't the same woman. She needed some unforgettable elements. Something that had never been done before, so that whoever saw it would link the show with the trees. With no luxury of time, she would need her subconscious to churn out ideas.

Her group had agreed on a date four weeks out, not because it gave ample time to prepare—quite the opposite; it would drive everyone impossibly hard—but because Delicia insisted the show happen long enough before the primary for voters to apply maximum pressure on

Murphy to do the right thing, meaning, aborting the sale to the Japanese, taking Beckett off the market, and saving it in perpetuity.

Before she fell asleep that night, she found words for her last banner.

Thirty-Three

JUST PAST DAWN, Ishi woke to voices ringing through the grove. Members of the Provisional Beckett Circus were calling out to each other. Some were on the ground. Others were scaling the seven trees that would create the container for the one-ring circus . . . if the governor didn't step in to crush it. The night before, they had discussed the risks. But they'd agreed to push ahead, thinking Murphy wouldn't dare to shut them down.

Delicia's celebrity, media savvy, and now her goodwill among her fellow circus people were proving to be effective assets. In every issue of the *Post Ethical Times*, Brodie swept off his hat to her contributions at warding off the assault on the valley.

Ishi had learned the day before that Brodie had taken to calling her directly, sometimes even before running things by him. Another hard blow. By helping a white woman suck the light from everything around her, Brodie was, in his own way, repeating history.

But quitting was not an option. That would end the Pomos' tenuous foothold. Ishi's gut told him that Beckett's trees would come down and be shipped to Japan for temples. And his depression visualized tracts of De Boulette vines rising and falling across Minkle's land.

Some people might have argued that Ishi was having his day in the sun. But he saw the attention as an aberration, not a sign that the future would repair crimes of the past. Delicia would move on to her next horizon, and he would return to the Rancheria, maybe marry Amber if she would have him.

Waiting for his tea to brew, he noticed a shift in the smoke. The air tasted more acidic. The brown-grey cloud rising behind the hills to the east was darker than it had been the previous sunset. It reminded him that he'd awakened in the night with a dream of things burning. But the skies hadn't been red, so he'd dropped back to sleep.

What he knew about forest fire was that if it looked like it was coming toward you, you were already in trouble. The valley had only two sensible exits, the main road north and south. Both routes ran parallel to the current fire line, so in reality, people would be tempting fate rather than fleeing it. The only other way out, the road to the coast that ran by Beckett's entrance gate, was windy, narrow, and steep. Traffic would jam it. And if you made it to the coast and the fire kept coming, there you would be, caught between the flames and the sea.

The morning news announced hundreds of firefighters arriving in Willits, with more on their way. Fortunately, it was early in the fire season and firefighters were available. They already had enough forces in the low ground to protect the town. New arrivals were building a line above the fire to keep it from cresting the hills to the west. If they were too late or if the wind turned wrong, it could charge through the twenty miles of rugged uncut timber terrain between Willits and Greenley before crews could scramble to catch up with it. The trip by road took most of a day. Escapees would be clogging the outbound lane. One car accident could precipitate the loss of hundreds of lives.

Beyond the danger, the media backdraft of the fire was taking over front pages and TV news. Burned humans, houses, and horses crushed every other story. Eccentric people choosing to camp in 1,500 year-old trees made a splash only on slow news days. And right on cue, the governor jumped at the chance to highlight the state's efforts to fight the fire.

Even without that threat, the media blitz to go after the governor had little time to intensify. As Delicia had promised her gathering, she and Li'l Ambrosia were hard at work on a new banner. She called over to tell Ishi she'd need help hanging it that afternoon. She'd run out of material for new letters, she said, so this one would be her last.

Raul seemed undeterred by the smoke. Later that morning, Ishi saw him and LeAnn walking through the vineyard encampment, forming a hand crew to prepare the ring in the grove. Those enthusiastic souls set to work, scraping away centuries of needle duff and making piles a good way back from the ring of trees. Others flattened out the soil underneath to make solid footing for the sprinting and dancing feet of horses, dogs, clowns, and whatever other acts they could seduce to the project.

At Delicia's meeting, they had all pushed to get big cats. Botox said he would call his friend who was caring for several recently retired circus elephants on a preserve in Oklahoma. Though public pressure against animal acts was mounting, most of these performers felt that every self-respecting circus needed pachyderms. And if the elephants came early, they could pack the performance soil hard as part of getting in shape.

In addition to her talents for raising men's libidos in the stripper tent, Shirley also happened to be gifted at raising money. Significant bills would come due fast and furious: lumber, staging, musical equipment— because music and fantasia went together—bleachers, electronics, generators, lights, toilets, and food. The most complex production would be ordering and securing I-beams, piping, cables, and staging overhead for the trapeze and high wire acts in ways that didn't require boring into the trees. Costumes? This would be a display of shows past.

THE RESIDENTS OF Minkleville watched rapt as Ishi and Delicia hung her new banner. As she had promised, she was getting personal.

"I ran out of red fabric," she called to Ishi, "so the green GOV is from two of my blouses. I hope it hooks his Irish blood."

And as they read her message down below, they laughed and cheered.

GOV, YOUR CIRCUS OR MINE!

DELICIA'S CLIMBING INTO Her Majesty had numbered Ishi's early days of idyllic ease. He looked back on them fondly as people swarmed below him and now even on his level in the other six trees. The only reminder of the village Charles Gervin had massacred was the 30 x 30 spot where the bodies had been burned, cordoned off again with flimsy crime tape. The rest of that history was being crushed underfoot by members of a well-meaning fringe of white society.

After they hung the banner, he watched the activity, wondering how he could extend his series to include this new village and its certain dissolution. Could it be that his time in Atlas was making him philosophical?

Villages come and are burned, he thought. *New ones arrive in the same location only to disappear for other reasons.*

As he saw it from his perch, the partying and carrying on late into the night among the Pomo and white campers—and the performers, too—spoke to a denial of death.

Thirty-Four

DELICIA WAS FURIOUS. Murphy took less than twenty-four hours to divert focus from the sale and rape of Beckett redwoods to the now-named Wolf Hollow Fire. In fact, he used the fire to bolster his position: the trees would be better cut now and sold than left to stand and burn in the new climate reality. She texted Brodie:

is anybody more skilled in talking out of both fucking sides of his mouth!!

As the fire danger heated up during that day and the next, she conferred with Ishi, Raul, and others about how to respond. How much effort should they expend, in case they needed to leave? They all agreed that if she and Ishi came down, they'd never get the opportunity back. The only good news was that she'd gotten a tentative agreement from *Takes On America*'s parent company, CBN, to film the redwood circus live.

"President Sherri Wallis came right out and said there's never been anything like this," she told them in a conference call. "She said my getting back on the wire for the first time since Moscow will draw a huge audience and that it has to be documented and enjoyed."

The wild card was Kitamura, the Japanese tree annihilator. No one knew anything about where he was, or where the emperor's offer stood. Kitamura had disappeared about the same time as the trucks that went to a mill in Oregon, one of the few places left in the country that could cut a log that big.

Of course he was going to like the wood. Raul said a forester told him the pieces he saw that day were extraordinary, even for old growth redwood. A perfect trunk section. But the nonsense about building a temple that would last 1,000 years was a Japanese fantasy. Or perhaps a mutual ego-stroking technique—Japanese wisdom complementing American resources. When would the shitstorm of hype around resources ever stop?

In late morning of the next day, Delicia saw spotter planes flying over the eastern side of the valley. The Wolf Hollow Fire had blown through the fire lines above Willits and was roaring west in terrain where it was virtually impossible to place personnel. CALFIRE had been shifting its forces into the Greenley Valley since dawn, reporters said.

By late afternoon, the rolling wave of fire had begun climbing the far side of Greenley's eastern hills. And before sunset, Delicia saw flames rising behind their crests. Occasionally, sunlight reflected off windows of firetrucks stationed on the fire road that ran along the high ground. Crews were prepping a furious fight to save the valley's high-end infrastructure. After dark, headlights from departing cars of protesters sprayed the high limbs of Her Majesty as they wheeled out to rumble down the access road. The highway hummed with vehicles escaping to and from the coast, which only showed the public's general confusion when faced with Nature's power. There were remarkably fewer tent lights in the vineyard.

Ishi and Raul called a meeting in Her Majesty. They all agreed that unless they were in extreme danger, Ishi and Delicia should try to stay. But to save their caravan's vehicles, the rest of the players decided to bail out immediately, drive out the southern route and hole up somewhere near Santa Rosa until the fire had been beaten.

As quickly as they had injected the protest with their infectious joy and promise, the Provisional Beckett Circus performers dropped down Delicia's rope, loaded their vans and cars with what they could easily gather, and headed out of the vineyard. Their departure triggered many of the last stalwart campers to pull up stakes.

At Delicia's request, Ishi had stayed with her to discuss the signs that would make them flee. She heard Ishi's side of the call from Burt, the Pomo spokesman on the ground. As a unit, the Pomo had committed to stay, even as everyone else was leaving. Because it was Pomo land.

"No," Ishi said. "Go! Losing people when you can escape would be stupid. It would play really badly for us. . . . I know," he said forcefully, "but the world won't end if you're gone for a few days. . . . No, the governor won't risk state people to drag you out. Not with the fire raging all around. That would be his Waterloo. . . . We'll be all right, and we'll come down if we have to. . . . Do me a favor on your way out, though. Let me know if my keys are still on my truck's console."

When the thirty Pomo were gone, Delicia said that she and Ishi were "alone, like in the old days."

He snorted. "The old days. Hard to believe it's only been ten weeks."

"Seems we've been here at least a year," she said. "For all we've accomplished."

The corners of his mouth flexed in dismissal. "Getting attention isn't really accomplishing anything."

"I think half of the world's population would disagree with you," she said.

"You mean whites?"

"No, Ishi. I mean women. There's never any change without attention coming first."

He looked away, looked at the reddening sky. "The guy approach to change is surprise. Take 'em down before they know what hits 'em."

"That's why I wanted to talk with you face-to-face," she said. "We seem like we're on opposite teams, lately. Texting isn't working for us."

"You wanna talk? Here's what I think: you brought your media talents, sure. And you stole the show."

When she wrinkled her brow, he asked, "Who was last to leave here? The Pomo. We're the ones who are most committed . . . and the most ignored! It's pissing me off that you've even got Brodie dancing to your tune. You need proof? Just look at his articles. Look at all the articles out there about you. I mean, I can't *blame* you, 'cause that's who you are." He looked to be making a decision about what to say. "It *looks* like you *emit* light, but to me it feels like you're *taking* it."

A bolt of horror ran through her. "This is why we need to talk. I'm not perfect. Actually I'm ruined. But I have thought that the trees and the Pomo village were the same issue."

"They're adjacent on the map. But two different worlds. One is backed by power."

"*I* see them as the *same—*"

"*Yeah, right!* A flat piece of massacre land next to trees that make human hearts soar." He was hot. He'd been holding a lot in.

"You don't get it," she said. "We're sitting in trees the Japanese want to 'massacre.' This place is a death site about to happen." She spread and shook her hands as if to hold the grove, the hillside. "You and I are fighting the same forces. Poachers that took my beautiful elephant matriarch, Maya, were driven by grinding poverty. Poverty created by rich people abusing them. They are rebels doing whatever they have to do to get weapons to fight the white *and* Black people who are running—make that, ruining—Africa. I'm in Her Majesty to cry out to the world to stop the insanity!" Voicing her defiance strengthened it.

They faced each other, standing on the two main limbs of her nest. She realized that when he'd come for the meeting, he'd chosen a seat distant from her. Even now he looked overhead to the rope that linked their trees. He'd be taking it back to Atlas in the dark. But she wasn't his mother. He was smart enough to have thought that through.

Thank God, he made ready to talk.

"You say we're in this together." He shook his head and pointed east. "I know better. Over there, everyone in my unit fought as a team . . . until the enemy was put down."

She didn't like where this was going. "Then what?"

"Then I went back to being 'one of *them*.' " He grabbed his ponytail. "To being an Indian. Sometimes a 'boy.' "

"Oh, Ishi." She beheld his beauty. He was manifesting an honorable acceptance of how things were, the lowly status brought on by his blood lineage. "You're not lesser. Not in my eyes. Not in the eyes of every—"

He interrupted her. "There was only one time I was even close to equal to them. The time they needed silence."

"Silence?" Not a notion she'd ever associated with combat or with men in general, except maybe when they were sneaking up on something.

He stuck his hands in his pockets, balancing there in the night. The low light from her solar-charged LED found a place to land on the upper surface of his high cheekbone, the trait that marked him as much as any other. His upright stillness in that moment seemed an inheritance from the trees. Perhaps his ancestors *had* lived in that village, had absorbed the nature of the redwoods, and had managed to escape the withering gun-fire.

In any case, these were Pomo trees. *She* was an interloper. She'd barged right in, not for him—if she was going to be honest—but to right a wrong about her part in Maya's death. As much as the trees spoke to her, as much as Ishi's cause needed her support—or so she imagined— she was using them to drown guilt from a bad night on a continent far away.

"Silence . . . about what we did." His jaw thrust forward. "My unit attacked a village in Bamiyan. At night. We knew the Taliban owned those people. We knew they lived with them. They had to have, because we chased them for three days after they took out four men from my unit. We were on their heels and, boom! they disappeared." His look had turned hard, far away. "The only place they could have gone was into that village. And Charlie Company had already emptied it the week be-fore.

"So we surrounded them and we . . . opened up on them. We *all* did." He paused. Was he hearing gunfire? "The silence was about the victims we found in the morning. Those warriors we saw fleeing into the night? Most of them were women and children."

She didn't ask him to go any further. The bridge between the two poles of his agony were clear. The seconds that passed were a long time. "Do you drink?"

His body jerked at the question.

"Raul left me some whiskey, is all. If you drink, I'd be happy to share it. You know, while we're deciding if we should make a run for it."

She hadn't considered that her invitation required him to sit by her.

"We *have* made a bit of a splash," he said, his voice rising from the depression it had sunk to. "And I couldn't have done this much without you. Murphy wouldn't have batted an eye about a Pomo in a tree. If he had, the foresters would have taken me down." He crossed to the trunk, walked out the limb that led to her hammock, and sat beside her. "Your jump stopped the world that day. It's the reason we're still here."

She leaned and pulled Raul's flask from the pocket of her day pack. A pint, half gone. She hadn't tasted it yet. Now Ishi was blocking the light. His profile was etched in white like the edge of the moon during a lunar eclipse.

"You go first," he said.

She did. It tasted better than the container let on. Or she was thirsty to change the air between them and the air from the fire, too. She held it in her mouth and swallowed little bits at a time. It was golden, like a single malt scotch. She passed it to him.

"To Raul," he said, raising the bottle, "And to all your friends."

"Have you talked to Amber?"

"Before I came over. I told her I was going to try to stay. Gave her the logic we all talked about."

"And?"

"She sent me a bunch of voicemails. There's only so many times I can listen to someone telling me I'm insane and selfish. I stopped opening them."

"Oh, shit," she said. "Look."

The fire had broken over the eastern hills in two places, a little farther north than the earlier flames had indicated it might.

He drank some while shaking his head. "Dammit. So often history turns on tiny details."

" 'For want of a nail?' "

He turned to her. She liked how he squinted approval.

Their phones beeped in unison. A joint text from Brodie, responding to one Ishi had sent, telling him he and Delicia were going to stick it out in the grove if they could.

They read his eloquent concern about getting to safety, couched as cutting losses for a protest well done.

Ishi's phone beeping a second time made him groan. "Burt couldn't find my keys anywhere." He leaned back to let the light, such as it was, splash her face so he could see her. "We're going to have to ride this thing out."

That was cause enough for her to take a second pull. The sting of it came with a thought of what she'd overlooked. "I'm going to call the local stations to let them know we're staying."

He gave her a thumbs-up. "You might as well reach out to *Takes On America* too. Leave a good message in case it's the last one we get to send."

A chill ran through her. If he was that steady in the face of death, he was out of her league. Or maybe he'd always viewed this protest as ending in death.

"But don't tell them we're in the same tree," Ishi said. "In case we *don't* burn. I don't want to hurt Amber unnecessarily."

His comments put her back on her heels.

They were quiet a while. Ishi took the bottle so she could use her phone and tipped it hard into his mouth. "Just so you know, no one else knows about what I did. I've never broken the oath we swore. Even our COs don't know. At least they didn't ask what we did."

He coughed. The smoke was thicker. Most of the residential lights in the valley had gone out. Headlights from fire vehicles swarmed up the slopes across the valley. But the quiet on this side confirmed they were alone.

She spoke for a minute with the Santa Rosa TV station manager, who let her record a statement.

The manager expressed her concern and mentioned getting a helicopter to swoop in. Ever the news person, she said, "It'd be great if we could film *that*. Take care, Delicia."

Ishi spoke to the darkness as Delicia scrolled for the *Takes On America* number. His tone was flat. "I suppose if they find our charred bodies up here . . . or down there, it won't matter too much if we're together or not."

She flashed on the image of two charred bodies holding each other. Her nerves jangled as she waited for the call to New York to go through. When the manager at CBN set her up for a short recorded interview, she was more eloquent than she had been with the local station, speaking about the resources of the earth and how those who professed that life would go on without interruption *after* "the taking" were plain wrong. She didn't mention Murphy, but she hoped he would hear it.

As she hung up, the idea that she might die up there that night struck her as more real. She looked at the fire working its way down the ridge.

"How far away is that, do you think?" She took the flask and swallowed some without being delicate.

"Three miles. Maybe a little more."

"How much time do we have?"

Perhaps fatalism was a good thing. He seemed amused, the first time she had seen him with any cheer in a while. "Depends on how the wind blows," he said.

"What did you mean when you said, 'It won't matter too much if we are together or not?' "

"I meant that if tonight's the night we're going die, maybe you'd consider letting me die with the memory of holding you."

She breathed. She took another drink. She wanted to say yes with the same confidence that it took to set out on the wire on any given night. But since she wasn't sure of how to die, let alone how to be with him without confessing her own secret, she said, "You probably shouldn't be walking hand over hand on a rope in the dark." She laid her hand on his thigh, felt him stroke her back.

She coughed, then giggled. "If we're going to do this in my hammock, there's a chance it could kill us."

Their first kiss started with half-smiles of irony.

Thirty-Five

I SHI WOKE TO smoke and first light. A little less smoke, it seemed. His throat was raw, but neither he nor Delicia had coughed in the last hours. He smelled the earthiness of her body—like his, unwashed for a long time. Flashed on her flexibility, balance, and strength, as they'd made love in her hammock.

He rolled his head to the east. Last seen, the flames were halfway down the hills. Remarkably, he saw no fire there now. Just smoke streaming straight up on hillsides of torched trees, like countless birthday candles just blown out. And below them, some blackened vineyards down to the valley floor.

Delicia coughed lightly as she slept through her last dreams, her lips resonating against his clavicle. He marveled that the great wall between them had crumbled. It had crushed his prediction that they were on the verge of a full rupture. Oh, how the press would have gobbled up any whiff of drama between them.

Instead, they had lived to fight alongside each other for another day. A long convoy of big trucks was moving north on the highway. He silently praised the women and men of the fire crews.

His being awake gradually roused Delicia. She kissed his neck, cradled his cock as if to say "later," and sat up. Even in the throes of passion, they had been meticulous about their clothes. She rose and handed his to him.

Unlike first-time lovers, as soon as they were dressed, they went immediately to their phones.

The valley's "good news" caused Ishi's chest to implode. Greenley had dodged a bullet, but not because the fire had been stopped. The wind had turned and driven it north. A little after midnight, it had broken the height of land at the end of the valley and poured down into the wasted woodland on the way to the Lost Coast.

Ishi's gut told him CALFIRE chiefs would see that turn of events as a blessing to let exhausted fire crews rest. There wasn't much to fight for in that stretch of land. No vineyards and few buildings. Maybe to avoid bad PR in an election year, they would send a skeleton force to make a show of defending the eyesore of humanity up there, the Dead Creek Rancheria, home of the Pomo.

Delicia listened and tried to comfort him. She said the Pomo would have fled and that he should remain hopeful at the lack of news. But she was distracted. Her sympathy couldn't mask her jubilation at being free to continue her vision of the circus. In contrast, Ishi's self-contempt made him a lone passenger on an asteroid hurtling through deep space.

His mailbox was jammed with texts and voicemails. He opened one from Amber in that string he'd ignored. She pleaded with him to leave Atlas, to not be the hero. She threatened to come there herself and drag him down.

The ones she'd sent after midnight worried him. He put in his earbud and listened to all six, a crescendo of her pleading with him to help the Pomo act in concert in the face of the fire turning. The last one had come in when he was asleep in Delicia arms.

we need you, dammit

Eli had sent one at 3:13 a.m.

amber says you're staying put

the old Pomo don't want to leave so I'm staying to fight

like father like son

looks bad

maybe we'll both ride over the moon tonight

A knife in the gut, and for good measure, a twist.

He remembered thinking of himself as valiant by choosing to stay at his post in the face of death. And later, as he was kissing Delicia, he'd justified himself as being authentically human when all the chips were down.

What a fraud.

Amber's last text had come in before dawn. She hoped he was alive somewhere to receive it. She was in the Willits hospital. Eli had second and third degree burns over half his body. He'd tried to save a grandmother. She begged Ishi to come if he could.

I don't know what will become of our band if both you and Eli die

Delicia was by him, rubbing his back. When he told her the news, she cried out—as *he* should have done. The knife twisted again.

"Are you going to go?"

"I need to think about it." He pointed to Atlas.

Her hand slid down his chest in a gesture of goodbye.

AS HE WALKED hand over hand to Atlas, he saw how he'd let his stand for his tribe disintegrate into opportunism. He was no longer the Marine who'd dashed down an open slope under enemy fire and carried his wounded lieutenant to safety.

Was nobility beyond his reach? Did duty to family outweigh duty to his tribe? And if the tribe was most important, would that mean staying in the grove to the bitter end? Or should he come down and do what he feared more: marching into Murphy's territory in Sacramento and taking a stand in the cloister of white power?

He felt wistful that Delicia was not part of those choices. She would not stay forever. She was too driven to conquer other high points. Their night together had been chemistry crossing with fate. Yes, he could work more closely with her in the short term, but his greater work lay with Amber. And he had just bombed their bridge. The pain he'd brought upon himself was that if he made efforts to repair it, he would have to come clean about ruining it in the first place.

Ash covered every surface in his nest. A few rays of light over his hammock told him some floating embers had burned holes in his tarp. It was done being his water collector. He walked back and forth on the limb to his porch, ginning up his nerve to call.

When he opened his phone again, Brodie was leaving a voicemail.

"I'm here."

"Thank God. How'd you get out of there?"

"Didn't. Delicia and I stayed. Is your property okay?"

"Never mind that. You know the Rancheria burned. It was directly in the path. There were some casualties. No IDs yet. Do you know if your father's okay?"

"I've just found out he's in Willits's ER. Badly burned."

"Damn. Damn. Well, don't blame yourself. Fire has no conscience."

In that instant, Ishi saw how much like fire he was.

"Are your lungs okay?" Brodie asked.

"A little rough. I've got some calls to make, and I'll get you something for tomorrow."

"Skip it. Aren't you coming down? I mean . . . your father."

"I've got triage to do, Efan. Combat teaches that disaster opens doors."

HE CALLED AMBER. She hooted at his voice and burst into tears.

"Are you burned?" he asked.

"A little. I helped get people out."

"Have you seen Eli? Can he talk?"

"They won't let me. But I'm going to hand my phone to the charge nurse. Maybe she'll fill you in."

After Ishi confirmed his identity, the nurse carried Amber's phone to Eli's bedside. "He's on medication for the pain," she said. "Coming in and out of consciousness. I'm sorry to say he's touch and go."

She clicked the phone to video. Eli's face was bandaged.

"He can't see," she said, "but maybe he'll respond to your voice. Try it."

"Pop, it's Ishi. Can you hear me? Pop?"

The mummy figure moved.

"He's giving you a thumbs-up."

"Pull through, Pop. We need you. *I* need you."

"He's pulling the phone to his mouth."

The video showed the ceiling. There was a hoarse rumble and then the words, "Stay strong, boy. Stay there. Plant your arrow."

"He's drifting off, I think. Any last words?"

"I'll carry the torch, Pop. I'll carry it."

FATE ALLOWED ISHI time to consider that his chance to set things right with Eli might slip away. Late that afternoon, the ER nurse supervisor broke protocol and called Ishi directly to tell him Eli had died at 4:32 p.m. Amber called ten minutes later and he spoke with humility and sorrow.

Because of its relationship with Ishi, the *San Francisco Chronicle* included a small article announcing that the Wolf Creek Fire had taken the Dead Creek Rancheria Pomos' homes, land, and chief. Later, the *New York Times* would pick up Ishi's article, "The Death of a Chief."

Condolence texts and voicemails jammed his inbox. There were too many to read, but Minkle's name caught his eye. Unlike most, Josh's began with an apology . . . for letting the state crew in to cut the tree. The message concluded:

unless you insist we're not done working on this

you must know Murphy's using this tragedy to protect his turf by kicking the destitute in the teeth

now the SOB's gotten the county to block the highway access to "our" vineyard

That word "our" was the best Ishi had seen since Eli died.

but he can't keep me from posting a sign on my land

so I'm inviting any people who want to return to our action to come in via my orchard

Ishi texted the news to the Dead Creek Pomo that if any of them wanted to camp in Minkleville, this would be the time. As if he were the mayor of the village, he proclaimed the section below Atlas and Her Majesty was reserved for Dead Creek Rancheria Pomo.

By sundown six cars had returned. All whites, all repeat offenders. One of them agreed to become the parking marshal.

Delicia called over on the jungle phone to say the Provisional Beck-ett Circus vans were on their way up from San Francisco, where they had shopped for more materials now that they knew what the show needed. They were bringing the cable and two new tarps for water collection. She was focusing on the importance of going through with the show, and more importantly getting good publicity about the protest back onto the front pages.

She waved a disgusted hand across the valley. "One mansion on the hill burned and, wouldn't you know, the *LA Times* did an article on every single thing and opportunity they and their three stellar children lost. Cry me a river of material things!"

She definitely was warmer to him since their hammock rock 'n roll —that's what she called it—but they were back in separation mode. With people returning and new scrutiny bound to come, he realized their night would not be repeated.

Amber let him know the Sebastopol Pomo were scrounging tents, not for themselves but for the Dead Creek Pomo who needed shelter in Min-kleville. He asked if she was going to join them. She confessed she was still a wreck about the choices he'd made.

"Let me put it this way," she said, "I can't be that close and not have you."

Thirty-Six

TADAO TRAVELED NORTH with the convoy of five tandem trailer logging trucks, each carrying two logs that were six meters long. On the California leg of the trip, a state forester chauffeured him in an official vehicle. It took hours to cross the rugged hills to the center of the state. Many of the roads were so narrow that traffic coming the other way often slowed down and sometimes pulled over to let the special trucks pass. The main highway north was wide, the signs were huge, the state went on and on. Drivers in automobiles passed them slowly while they and their passengers pointed at the cargo.

When they crossed out of California's jurisdiction into Oregon, Tadao climbed into the cab of the lead logging truck. He enjoyed riding high off the road, and the roar of the big diesel engine excited him. The next day, when they got to the mill in the town with the beautiful name, Roseburg, he stood in awe looking at the size of the machinery. Sensei was mistaken. Americans did not need to exaggerate the size of things. They were telling the truth.

The staff at the mill treated him as a special guest. They gave him a tour of the cutting sheds, the workshops, and the drying houses. That night, the head of the company hosted him and the company officers with a fine meal of sushi and warmed saké. Everyone was smiling. They leaned forward to understand his halting speech, and their amusement seemed kind.

For some reason Tadao didn't understand, they seemed interested in the people in the trees. They knew the name of the woman, Delicia, and they explained things he hadn't yet grasped: that she was a star in the circus, that she had fallen once, and that she was now rising again.

"She is using the trees for her career," Tadao's host, Mr. Calloni, said. With a glint in his eye, he added, "And she is leading all the men around on a string."

Tadao understood the words, but their meaning confused him. He didn't remember seeing any string near her tree.

In contrast, Mr. Calloni's face grew dark when he said something about another person in the grove. An Indian. Calloni said *he* was the dangerous one. When Tadao asked what an Indian was doing in America, Mr. Calloni first chuckled as if Tadao was teasing him. Then he seemed thrown by the question. At last, instead of using words, he modeled a man holding a bow and pulling back an arrow.

Because the art of *kyudo*, Zen archery, was revered in Japan, Tadao understood this as a powerful omen, though he didn't know *kyudo* was also a tradition for the people of India. His sense was that *kyudo* masters understood *kami* as well as priests. It was as powerful a path to awakening as the traditions of tea ceremony, Ikebana, and temple building, arts where the entire world was illuminated in presentations of harmony and generosity. Sometimes *kyudo* masters demonstrated their attainment on Japanese holy days and at consecrations of land and temples.

"Ah," he said. "Emperor Akihito will be pleased there is master in forest . . . in *the* forest."

Without saying so, it seemed many at the table found fault with a *kyudo* master in the sacred grove. But having seen how different Americans were about the elements of the natural world, he accepted that those core teachings in his country had not yet taken root in the culture here.

BECAUSE OF THE importance of this sale and, in the larger picture, the healing between America and Japan that would come from it, it made sense to Tadao that the mill arranged to offer its whole operation for a day, two days hence, in order to process the redwood. It showed that America honored the emperor and supported Japan's quest to pacify *kami* for the betterment of her people. For something this momentous, allowing Tadao ample time to properly assess the wood seemed in keeping with the priorities of humanity. So when he bowed upon meeting the workmen and their bosses, it was with immense gratitude.

Promptly at 7:00 a.m., they began processing one of the smaller logs that Tadao estimated to have been fifty meters off the ground, which was higher than Hinoki ever grew. This "stick," as the sawyers called it, was nearly as big as a subway train car.

First, they locked it into position on a carriage that rolled on a special track. A huge bandsaw lopped off one outside surface as if it was butter. The machinery flipped the log like a child's toy and in three more passes, made it square.

The aroma that filled the warehouse was sweet and earthy. The color of the wood was a deep red, a cousin in the spectrum to the blessed Hinoki. It wouldn't shock Japanese worshipers too much. These qualities gave Tadao ideas to include in the Temple of Listening's design to further please the sensibilities of the *kami*.

After cutting the log directly down the center, they transferred it to another carriage that took it through a circular saw six meters in diameter. Tadao inspected the heart wood. Its grain was perfectly straight, and after the tree had grown to twenty centimeters—about thirteen hundred years ago, the manager explained—the annual rings became so fine Tadao had to lean in close to see them from the stepladder they had set up for his inspection. Marveling at them, he saw them as a timeline of human history.

The main sawyer worked in a Plexiglas booth close to and above the saw. His fingertips flew across a computer's keyboard. His program converted the metric measurements Tadao gave him to US Customary. With the push of a button, the operation whirred and produced every kind of beam and board with each kind of grain Tadao asked for.

For the first time since he'd arrived in America, he had no translation problem.

THAT NIGHT, HE wrote separate emails to the emperor's representative and to Sensei via his son, Satoru, saying the quality of the wood was divine. He wrote that above the whir of the saws he sensed *kami* cheering. There *was* the matter of the people in the trees, a larger situation than he'd understood when he left Japan. He described to them as well as he could what he had seen. But he confessed to not understanding the situation. These partiers—it was the only word he could think if to describe them —seemed to be interested in only a few trees that bordered a shrunken river and an open field. He looked forward, he wrote, to the plane ride to San Francisco so he could think of what was to come and how to handle it as if he were Sensei.

To the emperor's representative, he included a special request.

In the morning, he was pleased to see his petition for two million yen had been granted. It wasn't until after taking tea that he learned about the fire. Unclear if it had taken some or all of Beckett State Forest, he waited a terrible hour wondering if America's *kami* were protesting human imbalance in concert with Japan's *kami*. On the way to the airport in Eugene, he received word from the Japanese consulate in San Francisco that the forest had been spared.

TADAO PASSED TWO nights in San Francisco waiting for the Consul General to have Governor Murphy unlock the gate to Beckett State Forest. When the deputy consul drove Tadao into Beckett's campground, four days had passed since the fire. Smoke still hung in the air while they walked among the public groves Tadao had seen on his first trip. When granted permission to be left alone, he walked north, taking pictures and estimating board feet in the trees. He imagined returning many times in the coming years to select trees for temples in Japan that the elements had weakened.

But his sights were set on retracing his steps from the week before. Armed with the consul general's report that all the "partiers" had fled to escape the fire, Tadao was expecting to tour their grove and to discover in the quiet what about it had drawn the partiers there. As he approached the grove along the river, he was surprised to find the ground under the trees raked mostly clean. He saw some construction on the edge of the seven trees that formed a huge circle. In the vineyard, a truck rattled along the farm road coming from the apple orchard. Most of the tents were gone, but a few people were setting up new ones.

His agitation rose. No police were there to protect him, as they had been the day the tree was cut. To spy on the grove, he first circled above it. While he watched, a scrawny man with a beard appeared on the lowest limb of the circus lady's tree. Using a rope hung on a pulley, the man put his foot in a loop, lowered himself down from the tree and walked away.

Temple craftsmen sometimes used this technique for raising materials. It gave Tadao a terrible choice.

Except for taking the bus to town on simple missions, he'd never gone anywhere without an invitation or announcing his intentions by calling ahead. If the circus lady was still there, he had to speak with her, but he was only beginning to learn about negotiation. Most disturbing to him was the realization that the little he knew about Japanese women would not help him here. He hadn't fully recovered from how she had dashed away the day they cut the tree. On top of it all, he worried he might forget his English just when he wanted Delicia to understand how her saving the trees had made her an important person for his people. She was a female samurai, protecting this source of redwood. Her fame and honor had led him to her.

At last, for the welfare of generations of Japanese people yet to come, he walked to the tree and called her name three times. "Delicia-San."

When she didn't reply, he placed his foot in the loop and hauled himself up.

Once on the landing limb, he climbed, placing his feet where the bark showed that others had walked before. High above him, he saw a hammock in the neighboring tree and remembered the words of his hosts at the lumber mill. A man from India was living in a neighboring tree. Was he a dangerous man, or a *kyudo* master? And how many people were in the trees? Did he need to thank them all? Sensei would insist he did. Perhaps the deputy ambassador could purchase gifts to honor them.

He heard heavy breathing in the limbs above him, punctuated by groans. Those were not the exhalations of a man. What would a woman be doing to breathe like that? He climbed with more attention, making no noise, until he saw a woman's body in a tight suit that did not cover her legs swinging from a rope that hung between limbs of her tree. It was definitely her, though she had her hair tied back. She was doing a hand-stand on the rope, and it was swaying back and forth. She was making it sway. As she swung, she let go of one hand and supported her whole body with the other.

He must have moved, because her eyes found him. She screamed, bent the arm she was standing on, and fell out of the pose. She escaped, sprinting hand over hand, and hid herself.

Thirty-Seven

THE JOY DELICIA took from aerial routines came from how total focus on the wire—or the rope, or the trapeze bar, or the swinging catcher's hand reaching across space to grab her flying body — narrowed her world to simple reference points: space, timing, breath, grip, connection. The Perfect Present of performing allowed no room for doubt, or grief, or love gone wrong, or regret for a slight mistake she'd ever made in the air or on the ground leading up to this moment.

Swinging gently on her slack rope in a one-handed handstand 170 feet off the ground, she had just acknowledged how close she was to getting back to peak conditioning when her eyes caught movement on a limb thirty feet below her. She flinched. Instinct took over. The next thing she knew, she was dashing along her slack rope and concealing herself in some of Her Majesty's young greenery on the far end of it.

"Jesus Christ! Who the hell are you?" She gasped for air. Her heart pulsed hard in her neck. "What are doing? Don't you know not to sneak up on me like that?"

"I sorry."

It was a man, looking up at her. Dark hair, dark eyes wide.

"I Tadao. I *am* Tadao. Your friend from Japan."

She shook her head violently. Murderous thoughts like these didn't arise for friends. She knew instantly who he was, and yet, his being there seemed an illusion. "I *know* your name. How did you get here?"

"Yes. Thank you for . . ." and he mimed hoisting himself up on the rope.

"Delicia, are you okay over there?" Ishi calling over meant she hadn't tele-transported to a parallel realm.

"The guy from Japan is in my foyer."

The man bowed. "Sorry?"

"What do you want?"

"I come back talk with you."

"We have nothing to say."

"I come back thank you." He bowed again.

For her, bowing the way Japanese did always seemed laced with hypocrisy or poison, but this Tadao fellow managed to turn it into a charming art. "What do you want to thank me for?"

"I come talk with you. May I?"

Feeling cornered by the surreal moment, she huffed. "I need to dress. Five minutes, then come up."

He nodded. "Thank you, Delicia-san."

There he was again with that honoring shit, that little technique he'd used to deceive her to cover the arrival of the loggers. She climbed into her nest, thinking to dress in a way to unnerve him. He was a Buddhist monk or something, no? The aquamarine glitter blouse with thin shoulder straps showed her cleavage. That should work. The hiking shorts with many pockets would give him a look at her thighs. She brushed her hair.

She texted Ishi that the Japanese tree killer wanted to talk and asked if he'd come over. Her phone beeped.

give me five

She called down. "If you are there, Mr. Tadao, I am ready."

The small man's agility impressed her. He moved better than Ishi up there. And she was dismayed at how he stood politely on the low limb in her nest, not making any move to find a solution for her awkwardness about where he should sit.

"Sit there," she said at last, pointing to an inconvenient spot out on that limb, hoping it would rattle him. But he complied and settled down as if it were solid earth. She leaned back against the trunk where she could splay her legs a little. In battle, every tool should be used.

"Thank you, Delicia-san." He raised a finger of correction. "I no . . . I am no Mr. Tadao." He pointed to his chest. "Kitamura family name. Little name Tadao. Thank you."

She knew this, of course, and also that his grace in sloughing off her instinct to badger him threatened her advantage. This man of perfect skin was an unfortunate enemy—down to the way he raked his bangs to the side like a young girl.

He bowed as if to be forgiven for what he was to say. "You go in trees like . . ." His face wrinkled in thought, his fingers miming something moving fast.

She nodded. "Like a cat."

"Yes. Cat. Sorry." Then he brightened. "Oh, like monkey." And he mimed a monkey's handiwork.

She wagged her finger. "Like a woman in the circus."

He nodded, showing he knew more words than he could come up with.

"You fall one time, yes?" He showed concern.

He kept coming up with things to throw off her balance, to weaken her resolve to defeat him. "Yes, but I'm fine. And you build temples."

He replied by offering his hands palm-up, as if that were proof of their capability. For all she knew, maybe that was how a carpenter in Japan interviewed for a job.

She heard Ishi's breathing as he came across on the rope that linked their trees. Kitamura heard it too. A look of apprehension crossed his face. *Good.* She wanted that. He kept glancing up the whole time Ishi was climbing down.

When he saw Ishi, he stood with great dignity and bowed. That stuff must be his cobra dance, she decided. Lull victims with humility before striking.

Ishi didn't bow in return. He didn't get close enough to extend his hand. He took a seat on the third nest limb, which placed him higher than both of them. Kitamura wouldn't be able to see them both without turning to look.

All good, she thought.

"I'm Ishi. Who are you, and what are you doing here?"

"I Tadao Kitamura. Watanabe and Son temple builder from Japan. And you do *kyudo*."

It wasn't a question, but it seemed as if he had researched Ishi. She wondered if Ishi did whatever *kyudo* was, and why she didn't know.

"I have no idea what you're talking about."

Kitamura mimed shooting an arrow with a bow.

Ishi laughed with a touch of bitterness and pointed to the vineyard below. "My ancestors did when they lived here. Before they were murdered like dogs."

"What is muhduhd?"

Ishi tipped his head, then slowly drew an imaginary knife across his neck.

"Oh, so sorry, Ishi-san. Your family from India."

"Yes. Indian. American Indian."

Kitamura nodded. Delicia wondered what about Ishi seemed to please him. Time to set him on edge.

"Mr. Tadao, let's get one thing straight." She gestured at the grove. "These trees are too special for temples. You understand? This tree here is very old. *Very* old. Seventeen hundred years. Maybe more. It's too important to cut. Too famous." She made the sound of chainsaws. "Very bad."

Kitamura nodded enthusiastically. "Trees beautiful."

It was an answer to her prayers.

"Very special." He put his hand on his heart. "They good for temples. Thank you for save the trees. *Tennō Heika* say thank you."

She wanted to kill this Tenno character. "Who is *Tennō*?"

"Japan Emperor."

"The Emperor?" She made an X with her forearms in front of her. "Tell him I'm not going to let him cut these trees. Hundreds of people are coming to sit in them."

His look turned sad. "*Tennō*'s temple very special. A place for Tohōku people."

Before she could tell him she'd never heard of Tohōku, he made a sweeping motion with his hand. "Ocean water. Big water. No good."

He kept hitting her from the side. "You mean a wave? Tsunami?"

"Yes. Tsunami." He brightened. "You know it! Japanese word. Big wave. Many people die. Emperor temple for tsunami people."

She looked at Ishi. His eyes were boring into Kitamura. "That was a tragedy," she said, immediately realizing she shouldn't be giving him any ground. "But these trees are *living beings*. They're more special than dead people. They deserve to be honored. Do you understand?" His lack of any response made her feel powerless. "It's absolutely stupid to kill trees for dead people. It's actually immoral."

Tadao turned his head to the side and breathed through his teeth, then said, "*Tennō* temple live one thousand years. Redwood," he paused and repeated the word, pointing to the limb he was sitting on, "best wood."

"It may be," Ishi said, and Kitamura's head jerked to look at him. "But it's also the oldest wood on earth, and we're not going to let you kill it. That would be a crime!"

Kitamura shook his head and made a half bow. "We agree. Sorry for sound against you. Yes, best wood. And *Tennō*'s temple very important. Home for *kami*. Japan people no listen to *kami*. *Kami* angry. Ground shake. Tsunami come. I build temple, say, 'Sorry, *kami*.' "

"*Kami*?" she asked. "What is *kami*?" She was pleased that the question seemed to throw him.

"Americans no have *kami*?" He opened his hands to the forest. "Yes, you have. *Kami* right here, very old." He made a tiny measurement between his thumb and index finger. He showed it to Ishi, too. "People." Then he spread his hands at arm's length. "*Kami*. Understand? *Kami* big, people no big. *Kami* important. Big hearts. Very powerful." He shook his head in disgust and curled his index finger into the crook of his thumb. "People hearts small. People hurry . . . no good. People hungry . . . sad. War bad. Bombs and tat-tat-tat." He'd run out of adjectives. "*Kami* no happy."

He'd hooked her a bit. She pointed up. "*Kami* is God?"

He nodded, then pointed down. "Ground *kami*, too. Water *kami*. Tsunami mean water *kami* angry. Redwoods very strong *kami* trees. I build Temple of Listening, *kami* come back. People happy again. People good again."

She kicked herself. For the two weeks since hearing of Japan's offer, she'd thought she'd be fighting an economic opportunist. Her haphazard knowledge of Japanese culture had missed this *kami* thing. He presented himself as passionate, as caring about things as *she* was. But his Stone Age superstition made him unreachable.

"He's talking nature religion," Ishi said. "Some kind of animism. Are you a priest or something?"

"No. I build temple."

"*Kami* is Buddha?" she asked.

Kitamura nodded, sat up straight, and slapped his hands together at his heart. "Buddha special man. *Kami* no man. *Kami* bigger. Everywhere. We can no see *kami*."

She looked at Ishi. He seemed to be paying too much attention to this drivel. "We don't have *kami* here," she said to Kitamura, though he'd already asserted they were everywhere. "And if we did, you'd kill them by cutting the trees down. You should use your own *kami* and your own trees to build your temples." She was losing track of any logic. Fury boiled behind her eyes. "These trees," she said, "these are ours. And they must stay. I will sit here forever if I have to."

"So will I," Ishi said. "And so will many people."

Kitamura moved his hands, as if he were working with wood.

"What are you doing?" she asked.

"Thinking. Sorry. Why you sit in tree? What Delicia-san and Ishi-san do?"

She was pleased with the question. "We are waking people up so they leave the trees here untouched forever."

"You sit and people no cut?"

"Will you cut this tree if I sit here?"

He shook his head matter-of-factly. "I no cut. First, I ask you go down."

"Don't you get it?" she said. "There's very little left in the world that tells us we are sacred."

He nodded vigorously. "Sacred. Temples sacred. *Tennō Heika* temple very special."

She looked to Ishi, hoping he could take the baton.

He obliged her. "Temples aren't living things," he said. "They're models. They're stiff. Dead." He pretended to be a statue. "But trees are the real thing. They are truly sacred. Trees are most powerful like this, standing alive. Only blind people want to take them down. When people wake up, they *stop* cutting."

"In Japan," Kitamura countered, "when people wake . . . they take a little."

She jumped in. "But your emperor wants to take the whole forest here. That's not a little. This is one of the last stands. How can you do this? How can you justify it?"

Kitamura did not respond. Perhaps he hadn't understood.

"How many trees does it take to build a temple? One tree? Two trees? Why cut all these trees?"

He nodded and held up one finger. "One tree, two, I build temple."

"Then you've already got your tree. Now go back to Japan."

"Yes, thank you. Japan have many temples. Always building. Always fixing. *Tennō Heika* buy your forest."

"Have you cut all your forests down? Ishi asked.

Kitamura's face darkened and he shook his head.

"Then cut your own."

Kitamura conferred with himself. "Trees sick and no seeds."

"So after you make your forests sick," she said, "your solution is to take ours? You kill our *kami* to make your *kami* happy? Your emperor is sick."

Kitamura blinked, almost as if trying to make her disappear. She'd caught him.

"Trees die." He pointed to trees in the grove. "Here trees old. Someday they die."

Governor Murphy had used the same line on her and had defeated her reply, but she tried again. "Then you can cut the ones that die."

On another face, his smile would have been patronizing. "Dead trees make too late to build."

Delicia's heart crashed. "I won't let you cut these trees. You say *kami* have feelings? I will make these *kami* angry. Angry with you. Angry at the Japanese people."

This seemed to crack his opaque cover. He couldn't help looking at her as she ranted. His eyes widened.

Turn the screws, she thought. "Over my dead body." She folded her arms to leave no mistake about her resolve. "I mean it. I will die for these trees."

Her peripheral vision picked up the intensity of the look Ishi gave her. It confirmed they were a real team now.

"So you have no problem cutting all the trees to build temples all over Japan," Ishi said. "You talk about a big heart, but you don't have one. Not at all."

Kitamura sat stunned for a long while, then placed his hand over his heart. "Sorry, Ishi-san, Delicia-san. My heart no small." He sucked his lips. "My heart broken."

She froze. Ishi sat up.

Seeing he had their attention, Kitamura said, "*Tennō* ask Kitamura . . . sorry, ask Watanabe and Son build Temple of Listening. Very special temple. You know Nagasaki?" His eyes became clear, and for the first time they bored into her.

"The war?" she asked.

"Yes, America bomb Nagasaki." He waited for her to acknowledge that she knew this. Ishi was nodding. "Many Japan people still sick."

Though images and thoughts blazed in her head, she had no reply.

Tadao pointed to the flesh in his arm. "I one. I sick man."

He didn't seem the least bit ill. "You?"

"My family. Mother, father, mother parents, father parents. All die with nuclear. Nuclear in me. I not live long. I can no have family."

And like that, the little man had them both on their backs.

Kitamura went on. "Now we have Fukushima problem."

"The nuclear plant?" Ishi said.

"Yes." Kitamura made the sound of an explosion. "More bad nuclear. *Kami* no happy. *Kami* angry."

"I'm sorry for you, Tadao-san." Delicia's voice came out softer than she intended. She gritted her teeth. "I know the Japanese have suffered. But why are you telling us this?"

"Japan people need wake up, too. *Tennō Heika* temple is help. My heart not small."

Thirty-Eight

ISHI FOUND HIMSELF pulled by opposing forces.

One current was the excitement and throbbing presence of veteran protestors returning to the massacre land. Newcomers were arriving, too. In a matter of days, their tents half-filled the vineyard. More portable toilets were delivered. And everyone arriving knew that the culmination of their action was going to be a circus in the redwoods to shift the way America treated her resources.

The number of Beckett Provisional Circus personnel tripled with the arrival of many performers who had prime years left but had been shunted aside in the circus's 21st century paradigm shifts, warped by heightened reliance on bottom lines and the new kind of high pyrotechnic, animal-free shows.

Minkle had returned to the fold and was being true to his word. Traffic drove through his orchard day and night. One flatbed delivered full equipment for the aerial acts: cable and stabilizing gear for Delicia's high wire act, and supplies for the trapeze acts. Delicia's trapeze friends streamed in from San Francisco. Among them were experienced riggers.

The next morning, Ishi watched three men in temporary rigging across the grove swinging from one tree to another, calling measurements back and forth and to people on the ground. The terms they used sounded like a secret code.

Their progress was turning Delicia's words into reality. But it took seeing the cable laid across the ground a hundred feet below where they would hang it for Ishi to believe she was going to get on wire again.

Across the redwood space, a pert young gymnast caught Ishi looking. She waved cheerfully before loping after a man who was trotting backward while juggling a stone, two sticks and his hat. She interrupted her course—for Ishi's benefit, he presumed—to perform a forward flip, landing with no bobble and then striding away with an exaggerated swagger. As much as anyone, she embodied the joy of circus.

Hector and his squad of carpenters built boxes to create the performance ring inside the grove. Electricians designed and built systems for lighting and audio. Animal trainers and staff built a temporary causeway across the river. They constructed quarters among trees in the next grove downstream to house the animals as they arrived. Horses, big cats, an emu. Word was that elephants were on their way. Whenever Ishi perched on his landing limb, he saw clowns polishing their routines.

Shirley took on two assistants to manage finances. Their first order of business was to gather donors. To her delight, corporations came forward with donations to burnish new reputations with the public. Octo oversaw a group of digital wizards, some from across the river, some whom he gathered online, who managed media for publicity, tickets, and transportation.

The great coup was that CBN signed the contract to carry the show live. Ishi could feel the crowd's confidence swelling. Their numbers and sheer joy were silencing Governor Murphy's agenda to shut them down. People spoke about this being the leading edge of renewed environmental responsibility. They would force Murphy to take Beckett off the market and send Japan's emperor packing.

Knowing Murphy could send in the highway patrol, California Bureau of Investigation, and even the state National Guard at any time, they were cheered that his staff chose to work overtime on distractions, to have voters not pay attention to what was going on in Greenley.

The contrasting current that plagued Ishi, the dark cloud that hung over his days, was remorse, rekindled from having told Delicia of his unit's crime in Afghanistan, combined with hearing Kitamura's eloquence on the suffering of his people due to America's treatment of Japan in another war.

In the middle of the week, those Dead Creek Rancheria Pomo who had lost their homes and set up their tent compound around the pyre site demanded a four-hour halt to all the circus activities to properly inter Eli in that sacred ground beside Amber's brother, Marco.

Ishi attended from his highest station in Atlas. Armed with a microphone, he gave the eulogy for his father. He spoke of the old man's commitment to the Pomo mission of being seen as a whole people, deserving of a rightful home on the land. From that day forward, a sense of reverence balanced the wild circus energy.

ELEVEN DAYS AFTER the fire, Shirley blasted out news that cheered and unsettled everyone in equal amounts. The Japanese fellow Tadao Kitamura had sent a donation of two million yen with a letter of good wishes for the redwood circus to go well. Shirley said the $25,000 would bring them close to breaking even. But that day's meeting in Her Majesty grew heated. Some argued that the money amounted to a bribe and that they shouldn't take it. Ishi was impressed with how skillfully Delicia argued for the opposite position. In the end, she got them all to agree to thank Kitamura properly and to send him a formal invitation to the show.

Since their night together, Delicia had shifted into what Ishi took as a pre-performance regimen. She was singularly focused on every detail. Their texts rarely dealt with things other than logistics. She divided her time between rigorous training and meetings with riggers and planners.

From the beginning, she had insisted that the wire be hung very high. Early on, the crew saw Ishi's landing limb as the safest point to set it for her entrance and exit. As soon as it and the safety net went up, she began rehearsing, having workers clear the grove so her show would have the element of surprise.

Though Ishi attended the staff meetings, all agreed he was a third wheel in circus matters. With Minkle's support, he spent his days writing articles and speaking with lawyers and state legislators, trying to convince the state to purchase Minkle's vineyard as the future home for the Dead Creek Rancheria. The beauty of it was that if the state gave Minkle a fair price for the land, Minkle could pay off his orchard's mortgage and De Boulette would have to find another piece of land on which to place their flagship vineyard.

Late into the evenings, a group of the Pomo began designing a village for the land. To Ishi's dismay, one design included a plan to build a
casino some years down the road. But the numbers were clear. Casinos
were about the only way Tribal nations were able to pull themselves out
of poverty. There was subversive irony in stripping white gamblers of
their money as a long-delayed revenge for their campaign of genocide.

Thirty-Nine

UPON TOUCHING DOWN in Narita International Airport, Tadao received a text that Sensei's son, Satoru, had sent a few hours earlier. Sensei was in the hospital and he, Satoru, was staying with him. He should look for Kumezo to pick him up.

Tadao stopped in a concourse lavatory and splashed cold water on his face. In the mirror, he looked ashen. From a distance he saw Kumezo standing in the baggage area as if enveloped in a sphere of sadness. Like a fly caught in amber. He remained bowed longer than Tadao.

"Is it all right, Tadao-san, if we go directly to the hospital?"

Tadao's quick bow communicated *yes*.

Sensei's driver had found Sensei on the floor that morning, chilled and incoherent. "He must have gotten up in the middle of the night and fallen."

"Does he have broken bones?"

"Only a bump on his head. That could be enough to cause his condition. But they are scanning him now to see if it was a stroke."

"I thought his heart was the problem."

In the middle of nodding, Kumezo shook his head. "Age is the problem."

After a silence, Tadao said he had much to share about America and the Temple of Listening. Realizing that he most wanted to share it with Sensei, he became flustered. "Have doctors said if Sensei will be able to come home soon?"

"They have not."

"So there is a chance?"

"Sensei would say there is always a chance."

Kumezo honked at a car for turning in a normal way, then bowed twice in apology when the driver's face showed surprise.

THOMAS HENRY POPE

234

Entering the hospital, Tadao regretted wearing the fancy traveling robes Sensei had ordered for him. Staff and patients' families were paying him extraordinary deference. He was relieved to slip into Sensei's room.

Satoru sat in a chair next to the bed, hands on knees, gazing at the floor.

A smaller, paler version of Sensei lay in a bed with the head raised. It placed his slackened face in an amphitheater of machines. His eyes were open, though Tadao and Kumezo's arrival did not get their attention.

Strangely for a man raised in a legacy of death, Tadao had no training for events in hospitals. He stood quietly, looking at and reflecting on his teacher, his surrogate father, lying there alive—according to the instruments—but beyond reach. It was glances from Kumezo—never one to push others—that helped Tadao remember he was Sensei's heir, and with that responsibility came etiquette and bold decision-making.

He wanted to learn what Satoru had been told, but to speak about Sensei as if he wasn't there seemed like something only a child would do.

So he spoke. "Sensei, it is Tadao. I am back from America."

Did Sensei's head jerk slightly at the sound of his voice?

"You were right. The robes protected me, and people there are . . . not like Japanese." He waited until he realized he had nothing to wait for.

"The redwood is extraordinary. It is worth ten times what *Tennō* has offered. And I believe if anything will pacify *kami*, it will be a temple made with this wood. So I have come for your blessing to buy the forest."

The beep of a machine showed how ghastly quiet the room was.

Satoru did not move as he spoke. "Sensei cannot hear you. Doctors say he has suffered a stroke. They have prepared us for the worst outcome."

Tadao had returned to confer with Sensei about this momentous decision, and how to properly convey it to *Tennō*. "I would really value his advice. Do you think he will wake up in the next few days?"

Satoru looked up. His face was gray.

"They told me Sensei's brain has all but shut down. And that the brain guides the heart. Those numbers on that machine are measuring the performance of Sensei's heart. They have been dropping since he returned from the brain scan."

Satoru looked at his old friend and colleague Kumezo, but for some reason he did not look at Tadao.

At length, he said, "We will soon be on our own."

Forty

AS THE DAY for the redwood circus approached, Delicia had Becca ramp up Delicia's posts to Governor Murphy, alternately daring and enticing him to attend the circus in person.

@GovernorThaddeusJMurphy

@DeliciaFortunado *promises to come down if you attend the circus in the redwoods*

Otherwise status quo

Is it a deal?

Perhaps like Delicia and her supporters, Murphy was waiting to learn if Japan was going to make good on its offer to buy Beckett. When they still had no word two days before the contract deadline, Delicia allowed herself to get excited.

The next day, the governor's chief of staff called after her midday rehearsal on the wire. He asked her to hold for the governor. Her heart hammered in her chest.

"Ms. Fortunado, Governor Murphy here. Are you well?"

"Better than ever," she said, impressed with her poise. "And practicing for the show."

"How wonderful that you're proving wrong all the doctors who said you'd never get back on the wire. I'm calling to give you the news first, out of respect. Japan has followed through on buying Beckett State Forest. The papers were exchanged an hour ago."

Delicia focused on making her voice strong. "And?"

"It isn't really a contest between you and me anymore. I spoke with the Japanese consul general this morning. He was clear that the purchase doesn't change Japan's support for your group presenting the circus there. The emperor and Mr. Kitamura see this as a celebratory way for ending your protest. I agree. You have been successful. You've got too many people and parties invested for anyone to create disharmony now. And as a sign of state support, I've asked the county to arrange with Mr. Minkle to station ambulances on the site.

"So we're in our last chapter on this. You have been a worthy opponent. For both our sakes, let's avoid the spectacle of having to chase you through the trees. Now that a foreign country owns the land, the federal government would probably support me sending in the National Guard. They have a number of people trained to climb anything."

Delicia gritted her teeth to keep from saying anything that would make him change his mind about the circus. "I'm sorry, sir. There's just no way to spin the trees coming down as *successful."* *She took a long slow breath.* "Can you at least have the trespassing and resisting arrest charges against me dropped?"

"My hands are tied by the rule of law. I'll go easy on you in the press, but I can't let you get away with it. Everybody else would want similar treatment."

Delicia's presence in Her Majesty ensured that high drama would always be part of saving the redwoods. But she'd never quite known what form it would take. "Don't you think a picture of officers handcuffing me in my satin outfit might turn off voters?"

Murphy exhaled in exasperation. "I wish we weren't having this conversation."

"Dammit, Governor. You've never responded to my invitation. Will you come see the show?"

"You mean, *Gov, My Circus or Yours*? That's a threat."

"No, the Twitter invitations, saying I'll come down if you show up to see me perform."

"If it was just a matter of me believing my presence would bring you down, I'd do it. No question. But my schedule in the run-up to the primary is packed."

"Be creative. Set up an event nearby. Show up and I'll come down. How hard is that?"

"The problem is, Ackerman County has a tiny voter registration. My opponent will hammer me for standing in front of a tiny crowd."

"Thanks for calling," she said, her sarcasm thinly disguised. "Here are my terms, which allow you a graceful way out. Let us be. Let us practice. And let the show go on. *And* if you and Mr. Kitamura *both* come to the circus, I'll come down willingly. Otherwise, you'll have to catch me."

THE NEXT DAYS became a blur. Delicia relied on the professionalism of her core group to carry out the functions of creating a circus. The eighty-four-foot wire crossing high in the grove unified the space.

Underfoot, the wire was solid, but in the middle of the span it had a spring in it and a slight side-to-side motion. Her friends pleaded with her to rig it with a pair of stabilizing lines to the ground. But for the drama of it and to raise the stakes, she fought the idea. Her slack rope work had helped her prepare for those characteristics, she said. The movement of the wire was inspiring new ideas for jumps and tricks. She told no one of the two shows she was designing: one for if the governor came, and one for if he didn't.

To inspire local attendance, the finance group placed 2,200 tickets for sale at Greenley's ice cream shop and the Mexican restaurant. They sold out in the first day. Performers and stagehands would share equally in any profit. As a way of thanking everyone, Delicia announced she wouldn't take any of the money.

For the well-to-do, three hundred tickets were available online at the cost of five hundred dollars each. Those buyers were told that revenue would constitute a legal defense fund for any mishaps or court filings regarding the protest and the show.

Delicia gave a phone interview with *Takes on America* to build viewership for the live broadcast. The interviewer saved her best question for last. "Ms. Fortunado, months ago you said you would never surrender those trees. But coming down is breaking that commitment, isn't it? How can you let the Japanese cut Her Majesty?"

She admitted making that promise, but added, "At heart, I'm a realist. There's only so much one person can do. But if I execute my performance the way I intend, it will answer your question. I hope all of your viewers watch."

THREE HOURS BEFORE the show, Delicia crossed over to Atlas as she had many times in the last weeks to access the wire. She met Ishi in his nest. Their hug was easy, and she gave him a lingering kiss with lips closed. It was their first since their night out on a limb.

"Have you heard?" he said. "A weather front's coming from the north. There's a twenty percent chance of rain."

She settled in the crotch of limbs where they could sit next to each other, and patted the bark for him to sit. "I've heard. But it won't rain. If it does, the trees will cover us. If they don't, the show will be even more memorable."

"Are you always this cool before a performance?"

"I'm thoroughly ready." The skip of her heart in that instant told a different story. She laid her head on his shoulder.

He adjusted himself to make her comfortable. "Mr. Brodie's jealous you didn't invite him up. He said he'd die for the chance."

"Some people have to stay down," she said, "or it's not a circus." She straightened up and looked him dead on. "Ishi, my only regret is how—"

"Forget it." He touched her cheek. "I'm going to miss you."

Her stomach lurched. Words failed her.

"It's okay," he said. "I know it's going to be anticlimactic after tonight. But if your foot holds up, offers from circuses will pour in. Whatever happens, I'm sure you won't be lacking for opportunities."

She laid her head back down. "I haven't been focusing on that at all."

"You've taught me a lot," he said. "But I can't keep up with you. I'm just a Pomo Nation man living in the country. And there's—"

She popped up again, unwilling to stand for that. Most men she'd been with hid their sense of inadequacy unlawfully. Ishi was in a class above. "You're right. There's no future for us. But as a man, you're a jewel. It's just that our stars are crossed. I'm on a path that makes our future impossible."

He squinted at her. His self-deprecatory smile peered out like the sun from behind clouds. "I'll bet no one else can say their whole relationship has happened two hundred feet off the ground."

"It makes a good story," she said. "Tell it someday, okay?"

"So you're really going to come down if the governor appears?"

She sighed. "Every show has to end. Better too short than too long. It's a maxim performers live by."

The loneliness of success surrounded her, loneliness engendered from tossing everything else aside so she could confront, boil, and consume every useful element of confidence and doubt. Her best coaches had led, berated, cajoled, and driven her along that razor edge that separated the struggle of never feeling good enough from the bliss of standing on her marks, knowing perfection was at hand.

When Governor Murphy had spouted his skewed positions on their first phone call—saying climate change was a runaway train that couldn't be stopped, and the redwoods were doomed and shouldn't be wasted—she had seized upon it as her launching point to seal her commitment to the trees. Just like that, the familiar wave of faith in herself had coursed through her body. She would demonstrate the Perfect Present on the wire. She could not bring Maya back, but by saving the trees, she would finally settle accounts, finally mend the disgrace that so troubled her.

With Ishi beside her, images of another life roused her doubt. But if she surrendered to it, if she gave any ground at all, the goal of her performance would be lost. Fighting temptation, she stiffened. In a matter of hours, she would step onto that wire with unwavering focus.

"Confession," she said. "I'm terrified about what I'll do if he doesn't show."

"Murphy? I don't get why he matters. You're going to be live on national TV."

She groaned. "Life is all about where we commit our bodies. What we do with them, the sacrifices we make. Talk is useless. It has no roots in the earth. If I do this right, after I come down, I will be linked with Murphy forever, and others will hold his feet to the fire when he defiles the environment." She made a guttural sound laced with cynicism and defeat. "But he was in Palm Springs this morning, so he's not coming." She took a deep breath to go where she hadn't been planning. "Can I come clean with you?"

She felt him nodding.

"I've as good as dared him. If he doesn't show, my coming down won't mean much. They'll say I was depressed, that I quit." She pushed her fingertips into his sternum. "I have never quit."

"But Japan owns the trees now," he said. "So how is it in his hands at all?"

She chewed on the notion of telling him everything. "Maybe Murphy is right. Maybe these trees won't be saved, much as that kills me to say. But the loss here has to sting enough to make everyone think before they continue to plow ahead like they've been doing. I want to be Murphy's albatross, so he'll never forget. We need him so badly to start doing the right thing."

She wasn't prepared for the trembling that took over her body. Then Maya's torso and the pool of her blood loomed in front of her.

"What is it?" he said.

He smoothed tears she didn't know were running down her cheeks. He held her and rocked her. But the macabre image wouldn't budge.

"You can't go out there, Delicia. Not if he is making you this vulnerable."

"Damn it." She buried her nose in his shirt, rubbed her face back and forth. She looked up at him and held his eyes firmly in hers. "Promise me what I tell you will never find its way into a story."

He took long enough to reply that she worried about his answer. "I promise."

"I *have* to save these trees."

"I know."

"No, you *don't* understand. I've failed already once."

"Failed? How?" He indicated the grove below. "Look what *you've* done."

Her chest felt encased in steel. Her lungs could neither expand nor contract. The world went fuzzy, grey, and then dark. Her head hit his chest. A minute later the spell passed. She revived with a huge gasp. "It's about Maya."

"The elephant in Africa?"

She nodded.

He shook his head, incredulous. "What about her?"

"I was responsible for her death."

"You were *not*. You told me it was your boss's duty to turn on the alarms."

She whipped her head violently back and forth. "No, no, no. That's just it. I lied. I lied to protect myself. To live with myself. It wasn't *his* duty that night. It was *mine*."

Even in her distraction she sensed Ishi pulling away, like a man in a canoe paddling backward. His brows hooked, his lower jaw thrust to the side.

Before leaving Africa, she'd vowed never to tell a soul. And perhaps out of guilt for his part in the drama and to avoid bad publicity, Joseph Wassama had agreed to make no issue of it.

Now that she'd broken her word to herself, something drove her to finish. "It was *my* duty that night. My duty that *whole week*. But when I caught that sonofabitch sleeping with Jamaica, I decided to defy him. I said, 'Fuck him.' And I never made the trip across the compound to turn on the alarm. A stupid five-minute walk. At the time, I berated myself for showing revenge with such a weak statement. Feckless. I even thought we might all laugh about it later. But so much was lost. Do you understand? I killed her."

The bones of her ribcage broke, shattered finally like the walls of an old clay vessel that had been dropped too many times. The boiling pain she had been carrying for those months flowed onto cool ground. And Ishi knew what to do. He held her on all sides so she wouldn't slip away.

They remained without moving until the bark against her skin began to cut like blades.

"So now, you see, why this grove is so important to me. Tonight is my chance to correct what I did in Africa." She didn't expect him to see.

"I do see," he said, taking her cheeks in his hands, nodding, then holding her close. "You *have* set your sights high, but I have no doubt you'll succeed. If not perfectly tonight, certainly over the coming years." His words were comforting, but they didn't alter the root of her solitude.

In the silence of being held, relief from having confessed came in waves. *Yes,* she said to herself, *he would make a fine partner, if I were going to stay. But this redwood circus is a one-night stand. One show and then in the morning disbanding, performers and audience alike going their separate ways, each carrying the lessons they've learned.*

Finally, she pulled away. "It's time for my warmup."

He proved his integrity by rising without protest and climbing to the top of Atlas to let her prepare alone. She went over her two speeches— for if Murphy came, and for if he didn't—and, flooded with the deep calm of resolution, she called down to her circus friends, asking them to clear the grove one last time.

LATER, SHE AND Ishi sat on Atlas's landing limb, surveying the crowd, pointing out people the other wouldn't know. The Minkleville supporters had become family. A few deputy sheriffs there to provide the presence of law enforcement had brought their wives and children. They saw county supervisors, vintners, and Mexican laborers with kids in tow. Loggers came too, garrulous men built like bulldogs or lanky shrubs, clustered in groups depending on their position, for or against cutting the trees. Efan and Dori Brodie had front row seats.

A group of five people carried animal rights signs, but the sheer joy and anticipation in the gathering willed them outside the grove.

Wearing all white, Aunt Stephanie blew Delicia a set of three kisses, each more dramatic than the last.

Kitamura stood in his Japanese robes beside the tech booth. They had heard he was coming, in spite of having recently buried his teacher. Seeing him, confirmed her work was almost complete. He bowed to her twice. His presence, his grace touched her. She dropped the last of the odium she had nursed for him and met his bows with one of her own.

Just before Raul strode into the space to blow his whistle, Amber led a silent procession of more than a hundred of her tribe in full Pomo Nation regalia. Standing like gods from a bygone era, they encircled the crowd. Amber did not look up. Delicia wondered if she and Ishi would ever have a life together.

The show progressed with tremendous heart. Raul directed the teams of jugglers, the dog handlers, the contortionists, the pole climbers, the ladder, rope, and hoop acrobats, the tumblers, and a fabulous array of clowns making the absurd seem real, and vice versa. During Li'l Ambrosia's ceremonial ride on a young elephant, Ishi brought Delicia's hand to his lips, which melted her. Three creatures in huge, headless, five-limbed costumes distorted the sense of what a body was. Sheila ate flaming wands that men on stilts produced out of thin air. A local woman came dressed as a lion tamer and brought the house down with her three tabby cats, which she got to follow her around with a catnip mouse dangling from a fishing pole. Twice, children ran out and gave the clowns a run for their money.

But Governor Murphy wasn't there. He had as good as said he wouldn't come. Still, she had hoped for a miracle. During the intermission, she stood and shook her limbs to ward off depression. Her concentration wavered.

She sat again. "I'm nervous."

"Thank God you're human," Ishi said. She hadn't seen him this cheerful in a long time. "My money's on you being flawless."

She wished his words would be true.

Right in the middle of the pony acts, the crowd on the south side of the ring stirred. Several men in suits helped clear a place for two chairs, and there he was, Governor Thaddeus J. Murphy, with a stylish woman.

Everyone saw him. Even Colleen, Queen of the Garranos, noticed. Her distraction led to a misstep, and she fell off her galloping mare. Professional that she was, she turned it into a practiced tumble, and a contingent of clowns ran out and copied her in every possible sloppy way to make it seem the dismount she'd intended.

One of the men in suits directed the governor's eyes to where Delicia sat. Murphy waved in a graceful manner that would leave onlookers assuming they were dear friends. How could he pull that off?

She waved back. Then, against all her instincts, she blew him a kiss. The woman with him grabbed his arm and tilted her head in amazement.

From there on, it was going to be an easy downhill run. She prepared by tuning her mind into her favorite image of tenacity: an osprey swooping down on a fish.

Forty-One

AS THE SHOW unfolded below them, Ishi felt Delicia's tension rise and fall. When the governor appeared, instead of celebrating that her wish had been answered, she drew in tight.

If that was how she showed she was nervous, she had a right to be. Facing a return performance doctors said would never happen and doing it live for viewers across the country would leave her open to endless analysis. Still, it was Delicia who had raised the stakes that high. It was consistent with what he knew of her. Pressure ramped up her belief in herself.

Between these considerations and watching the show, checking the condition of the sky fell from his priorities. Below them, 2,500 people rapt in a theater in the redwoods cheered Simón and his three partners. Each pair climbed to a platform on opposite sides of the grove. During Raul's rousing introduction, they put chalk on their hands and checked their equipment and each other. In a moment of natural silence, Simón looked up at Delicia and saluted.

Then, as if it were timed as part of the show, it began to rain.

The drops—there weren't many—flared like meteors burning in the atmosphere as they traveled through the lights below Atlas's landing limb. Raul, his hand raised to cue the music, stood still, looking overhead, waiting for a sign. From Simón? From the god of weather? As the moment expanded, a groan of disappointment passed through the crowd.

Delicia didn't move for a full minute. Then she laid her hand on Ishi's and locked him in her gaze. She said nothing. He didn't push, just looked at her, struck that he was the sole beneficiary of the care she'd taken with her makeup. He tried to etch her beauty in his mind.

Her hand relaxed. He presumed she'd decided the rain had gotten her off the hook.

She was lit from below, and her jaw cut a clear line, reminding him of his first glimpse of her in the cab of her Aunt Stephanie's truck. He remembered the tension, her distress, but not the specifics of what they'd said. Four months later, he was beside her at a peak moment in her life.

He rolled his hand over and laced his fingers into hers. "Rain of any kind this late in a drought year has got to be a huge sign of something."

She answered with a squeeze.

"You'll get another chance. Without even taking a step on that wire, you've proven the doctors wrong."

She squared her shoulders, looked at the wire, and extended her free hand to catch some drops. "Are you kidding? This rain blesses me. The higher the risk, the more memorable the show."

The rain stopped as quickly as it started, but in the light, stretching from Her Majesty's low limb across the grove, Delicia's wire glistened with moisture. With a breath of determination, she stood, slipped off her warm-up jacket, and took three dancer's strides to Her Majesty's trunk. He tracked her, his eyes trying to convince her to change her mind. With pursed lips she smiled at him, moving her head slowly side to side. Amused. A trifle condescending. With one hand for balance, she bent, twisted, and folded her torso and limbs. By turns, standing on one foot, she extended her legs in every direction. Lastly, she raised each heel to the sky, that posture that placed her outside the human realm.

Nor did the rain intimidate Simón and his three trapeze partners. As if nothing had changed, they wiped their bars dry and powdered them again. Stunned and searching for a corollary for such mettle, Ishi remembered volunteering many times to walk point as his squad moved through enemy ground at night, convinced he wouldn't die. How his mates had loved Indians then!

To his right, Delicia had let go of the trunk. She bent backward until her hands found the limb behind her, and raised herself into a handstand. She gracefully scissored her legs in the four directions while lifting one hand at a time. Her core was still as stone. As she stretched her groin, he marveled at how her teal suit revealed her quadriceps and the muscles across her back and shoulders. They rippled like creatures in their own right.

Music announced the start of the trapeze act.

Instead of normal trapezes—a steel bar suspended from two cables— these had two bars, set parallel, one three feet above the other. To the casual eye, when mounted it seemed each male on the lower bar had a woman sitting on his shoulders. For a few moments the two teams swung uneventfully through the space—left and right from where Ishi sat, toward each other and away—each artist sitting on a bar, pumping his or her legs. At a musical cue, the woman above Simón arched her back and rolled backward as if to dismount, but grabbed Simón's bar next to his hips, so she was hanging below him.

At the same time, the other woman bent forward and slid along her partner's chest and legs until she came to rest head down, her shoulders caught in his hooked feet and her feet locked over his shoulders. From then on, the show became a tumult of bodies grabbing, pulling, lifting, rolling, curling, entwining each other and the bars. Two shows at once, swinging.

It seemed all part of the exquisite slither when Simón hung from his knees on the bottom bar. But no one was prepared when the woman in the other pair flew through the space between them and caught Simón's wrists as he caught hers. Then the three artists wound over and under each other and the two bars until Simón's partner let go with a double spin into the waiting hands of the lone male.

Seeing them from above was like a dream sequence. Following them swinging over the sea of faces, Ishi became aware that many in the crowd were straining to see Delicia warming up in the shadows high above. And it was then he became aware of the detail that had escaped him because of all the pageantry and tension. They were performing with no net.

The next thing Ishi knew, Delicia threw both hands near his right hip. With a grunt her body flew over his head, landing on the limb to his left where she laid out in a forward split. She rose, poked in the needle foliage beyond her, and returned with a folded parasol and a balance bar.

She slid the bar across his thighs and squatted beside him. Her breathing was slightly elevated.

"I'm ready to go," she whispered. Her voice hadn't the slightest waver in it.

"Where's the net?"

"We changed it . . . to make sure everyone pays attention."

Simón's crew slid down ropes to the ground. They celebrated with pats and casual arms around each other. They bowed to the crowd. Then as if they'd done it in cities around the world, they turned as a unit and extended their left hands toward Delicia. She merely bobbed her head in acknowledgement. The band stopped playing.

After honoring Simón's team one last time, Raul let silence take hold. He shoved his top hat under his arm and held the mic in both hands like a preacher gathering his words. Finally, he raised the mic to his lips. "These trees and their ancestors have lived here longer than any society on earth. For a moment, let's become still like them and hear what they have to say."

Even the children raised their heads in awe of the space. The hair on the back of Ishi's neck rose. His field of vision expanded, almost as if it had no limit.

The lights faded and went dark. In the twilight, the trunks of trees swelled to announce not just their size and venerability, but something that defied a name. Ishi felt as if he were part of the duff under them or a castoff particle circling in the universe.

If he had any standing at all, it was simply as an observer of this vast emptiness. Yet every cell in his body tingled. For a rare moment the humiliation at his core vanished. There was no future, no past. Only this vividly colorful and never-ending present moment that, with few exceptions, he'd failed to notice in his time on the planet.

Delicia rose in the darkness and took her stand on the wire. A single spotlight found her there. For perhaps fifteen seconds, she stood without a muscle twitching. At last, she extended her upright thumb over her head so all could see. A hum of concern emanated from below, but she kept her thumb aloft, turning, showing it to everyone until gradually every throat encouraged her to go.

With her free arm held out for balance, she touched the tip of her parasol to the wire and shoved it ahead of her like a clown working a push broom on a lonely street. In vaudevillian form, she made her way across the grove and leaned against the far tree as if it were a lamppost, and she were watching traffic. Nervous laughter wafted up.

The sound of clearing her throat boomed from speakers around the ring, and she adjusted a headset microphone she must have donned in that period of darkness. She righted her parasol, and from the tip of it ripped the rag she'd used to dry the wire. It floated to the ground. She'd been prepared for rain all along. "No smattering of drops should stop a show. Don't you agree?" she told the crowd.

Applause, and cries of *Yes, yes*. For a passing instant, the tenor of belief wafting up convinced Ishi even he could walk on the wire.

"I'm sure you know this virgin redwood grove is one of the last on earth. Some of you probably think I came here to perform right from the start. Others may think I came here to save the trees. Neither view is right. The *trees* called *me*. Tonight, my work here is done, and to say goodbye, I will prove the doctors wrong."

She swept her hand to the crowd. "We have people here who want to save the trees, and others who plan to take them down. We have a man from Japan, Mr. Kitamura, who wants to use them to build a temple for his people who have suffered so much. He wants to transport their grace and power to Japan to awaken his people to grace and power." She sighed and paused.

"Perhaps I'm different. I see holes where beautiful things used to be. Imagine the hole that will sit there," she said pointing to Her Majesty, "after she is taken. It is my sincerest hope that the Japanese honor her corpse for a thousand years."

The music started. With the pizzazz of a Broadway dancer, she pushed herself from the tree and, elbows jutted dramatically out, opened the parasol. Waving it overhead, she danced to the middle of the wire, where without any preparation, she slid her front foot forward. The musicians mirrored her movement with a glissando, their notes bottoming out into silence as she laid out in a full split.

Her balance seemed so true to Ishi's eyes that if she needed the parasol to stay steady, she had cast an illusion over the night. "At this point, you may be wondering if I'm stuck and . . . oh, my god. Yes, I am. I am truly stuck. And there is only one way out." She pretended to be losing her balance and groaned into the microphone. Then, as if lifted from above by wires hooked to her shoulders, she drew her feet together until she was standing. It was an act of sheer will, sheer power.

When the cheers died down, she said, "They told me coming out of a split that way was impossible anywhere, let alone on a wire. Ahh! A woman loves a challenge."

She sashayed to Ishi, collapsed her parasol, and extended it daintily. "Please."

When he reached out to take it, she pulled it away and then thrust it, back and forth pretending to battle him with a fencer's foil. In a flash, she opened it and threw it over her shoulder. It flew a ragged course to the ground. "Too bad," she said, with a boisterous laugh that was too rich to be just performance.

Ishi realized he had never heard her fully laugh.

Her body struck a pose of making a big deal of glaring at him. "Nothing in life quite goes the way we plan, does it?"

The band played again and without any transition to gather herself, Delicia began moonwalking on the wire, strutting and sliding away from him, with some part of her body hitting every beat.

From his vantage point, he saw how she made a two-footed step work on a single line, each leg moving like a bird's wing, and how the snapping foot that took the weight behind her caught the wire in an instant, making it look as if it had never left it.

The crowd leapt to its feet.

She returned to him in a series of cartwheels. This time she stooped, pulled the bar from his lap, and while turning, tottered a little. Ishi sensed it wasn't part of her act, but she chortled, and skipped to the center of the grove. There she went up on one foot and hopped along the wire, putting her free leg through various positions she had practiced by the trunk, including the straightened leg over her head. Clowning again, she jounced her weight like a boy on a diving board and got the wire to sag and lift her back. "Oooh, I liiiiike that. It gives me a new idea. How high can I go?"

Before letting the wire become still, she took a few steps, pulled the bar into her abdomen, tucked her head, and, in a flash, did a forward roll that left her straddling the wire. She brought one calf on top of the opposite thigh, let go of the bar—which moved not an inch in her lap—and mimed being an old man on a park bench reading a newspaper until the crowd's amusement died down.

She stood. "May we have music, maestro?"

The musicians struck up a funky pop piece, to which Delicia danced, in steps both forward and backward.

Ishi sought out Kitamura. His eyes were glued to her. The governor, too, was captivated. He scanned the faces of the Pomo. Amber was smiling. All the Pomo were smiling. The loggers were loosening up. Several were trying to copy Delicia's dance moves.

On the far side of the grove, she turned with the bar, sighed once loudly, and veritably pranced to the center of the wire. Raising her right thigh to help hold the bar at her waist and drew her freed hand across her throat to kill the music. "Oh, how I've missed this!

"We know metal on metal is really slippery, right? Here's a secret. There's a groove cut into the midpoint of the bar." Hands about three feet apart, she leaned forward and laid it crossways on the wire. She kicked up her rear foot into what looked like would become a handstand, but the bar tilted out of level. She grunted, fought, finally got a knee down, and hooked that foot over the top of the wire. She breathed hard twice and stood again. Laughing.

In her struggle, the wire had taken on a slight side-to-side motion. Ishi wondered if he was the only person who could see it. She waited for it to become still, stood, and bent again. This time her hands were perfectly spaced, and she went into a glorious handstand, with only the slightest tremor in her body.

By unlocking her elbows and pumping her arms in handstand pushups, she got the wire flexing up and down. After about ten repetitions, in the trough of the cycle, with arms bent, she touched her nose to the wire and pushed off from the bar as if spearing the sky with her toes. Released from her grip, the bar clanged on the wire as it fell.

She rose, twisted in the air, and coming down, caught the wire behind her knees, and hung upside down as Ishi had seen her do on her slack rope. The bar pierced the ground in the center of the ring like a thrown spear. Cries of distress gave way to cheers.

Upside down, she laughed. "In the twenty times I've practiced that, this is the first time it has ever stuck into the ground. This must be my lucky night."

Righting herself to a sitting position, she turned to catch Ishi's eye. "Action and inaction *both* have consequences."

Then she stood, spread her arms like a platform diver, and moonwalked away from him all the way to the far tree. She leaned her back against it. The crowd seemed relieved to use its voice again.

When she'd caught her breath, she promenaded to the middle.

"We have our governor here. So glad you accepted my invitation, sir." She turned crosswise to her steel highway and bowed, extending one hand to him, balancing her weight with one leg behind her, making a full curtsey. She rose, beaming, and the governor smiled back. "The state forest has been sold—legally—and *that* part is good, I guess."

She turned with a finger on her chin and ambled like a poet waiting for words to come. Occasionally, her other hand fluttered beside her hip.

"I promised you, Governor, if you came tonight, I would come down. I keep *my* promises." She stopped and bounced the wire as if it were a slack line—the taut, elastic cousin of the slack rope usually strung four feet from the ground—going higher with each push. Finally with a grunt, she lifted off, flipped over backward, and landed with both feet, arms flailing a little until the wire settled. "Let the slack line heroes try that!"

Raul was transfixed. Simón and the other aerialists were gathered by him on the edge of the ring. "My goal in coming here," she said, "was to give voice to the trees. Thinking that if they could, they would call attention to what humans are doing to the earth. You know, stripping every-thing from it. Soiling the air, the water, and the land. But Her Majesty has taught me there's no better agent to make the case for the planet than these trees themselves."

The microphone was picking up sounds of her being winded. "These trees model Earth as it used to be. If we look beyond them, beyond the grove, it's easy to see we're coming to the end." She shaped her hands into claws and shook them to make her point. "But . . . *We. Don't. Look.* Instead, we fantasize that our suffering will go away on its own, and we bury ourselves in entertainment, because deep down, we know it won't."

She stopped squarely in front of the governor and looked at him over her left shoulder. "So while I have your attention, sir, I ask you, I ask you all, to spend part of every day reflecting on what we've been *given* and how fragile it is. The trees don't need us to save them."

She eased into a full split, arms out to each side. "We need *them* to save *us*."

This time, she was unable to draw her feet together in order to stand. As she put a hand on the wire to rise again, she chuckled. A kind chuckle. She stood and looked at the crowd below.

"We're a forgetful species. Not only do we forget what we've done, we forget to ask questions." Her voice was lovely, loving. It held no chastisement, as if she was stating clearly the truth and nothing more.

She paused a long time, by degrees becoming filled with a smile. Even from the side, her face was luminous. Beatific.

In that expansive moment, Ishi saw the wire as a bowstring and Deli-cia as an arrow nocked onto it. He imagined an archer the size of Atlas drawing the wire down, imagined him releasing it, and Delicia flying up into the greenery and disappearing.

Hooked by the idea, he scanned above her, expecting to see a wire or a hoop, or perhaps the fellow Teeko she'd talked about on a platform ready to catch her. His eye, though, was pulled back when she turned her shoulders and hips parallel to the wire. Without lateral vectors, it wob-bled slightly side to side under her feet. To his surprise she balanced as easily as she had on the slack rope. Of the people there, probably only her circus mates knew what a feat this was.

"I dedicate this last trick to the memory of the young Pomo man, Marco, who died here . . . and to the blessed elephant, Maya.

"Please don't forget," she said.

Three times she bent and straightened her legs. With each repetition the wire plunged a little deeper. In awe, Ishi watched her generating momentum for her next jump. Bending her knees one more time, she thrust up hard and launched herself—her body straight, arms stretched like wings, carving a glorious arc in the direction of the governor, her head gradually tipping down, like Saint Peter on the cross. And she held that position all the way to the ground.

Forty-Two

ON THE DAY *Tennō* received Tadao, the sounds of Tokyo traffic did not penetrate the outer walls of the Imperial Palace. How wonderful that past rulers had thought to create a sanctuary in the midst of their determined chaos.

Just returned from spending three days at the Temple of Listening site, Tadao absorbed the details of the grounds as *Tennō*'s attendant led him to a manicured garden. In spite of all the care that had been taken, Tadao did not sense one strong *kami* breath.

Tennō seemed older. He didn't rise from the marble table in the shade or shake Tadao's hand. On these points, of course, Tadao was a poor replacement for Sensei.

He laid his offering gift on the table next to the book that *Tennō* had been reading.

"I am very sorry about your sensei," *Tennō* said. "I wish I could have come to the funeral."

Remembering he was only to answer questions, Tadao merely bowed, while images of Sensei's funeral broke loose in his head: the wake, the pyre, the clouds of incense, the endless bowing, and people offering stock phrases of regret. And he remembered, too, that day in the hospital when he broke protocol by holding Sensei's hand. Sensei had squeezed three times at the sound of Tadao's voice. Satoru remained stoic until the end of all the celebrations of his father's life. Now he was taking time off, though Kumezo wondered out loud if he would ever return to work.

"Your letter says a tragedy occurred in California and that it may affect the wood we purchased for the Temple of Listening."

Tadao answered with a bow.

Tennō gently scratched the underside of the air as if it were a cat's chin. "Please tell me."

Tadao told *Tennō* about Beckett State Forest's *kami*. "They are unlike our *kami*, which come and go," he said. "Redwood *kami* stay. Their loyalty is overwhelming. That forest was the kindest space I have ever entered. I beg your pardon for saying so, Your Excellency, but it outshines all the temples I know. The power there rivals the ocean off the Omoe Peninsula."

"So why is that a tragedy?"

Tadao had dreaded this moment. "It's about the woman in the tree."

At this, *Tennō*'s face became wider, his expression ever so slightly more complicated. "Yes, you went back to see her. Did you speak with her?"

"I was not able to meet with her personally a second time. She put herself in the tree to ask Your Excellency if your offer to purchase the forest could be changed in a way to protect it."

Tadao's face burned under *Tennō*'s inspection.

At last the emperor said, "And you love her."

Since *Tennō* had not asked a question, Tadao merely laid his hand on his chest.

"You can tell me, Tadao-san."

"It was impossible not to. She was *kami* in the flesh."

"Was?"

"She begged me to help save the trees. When she learned I would not, she surrendered her life."

Tennō closed his eyes as if learning about the death of a family member. "I understand."

Tadao felt sure only people who had been there could understand. "In doing so, I believe she upset the redwood *kami*. Now I fear that if we bring the wood here, they will not come with it. I also worry I have angered our own *kami*."

This remark penetrated *Tennō*'s grace. "What makes you say so? Your intentions are worthy."

Tadao explained that since returning from America, he had in quick succession traveled twice to Omoe. "The second time was last week over the longest days of the year. I brought no ruler, paper, or phone. For long hours I sat still in the middle of where the temple is designed to go, looking toward the sea." He thought of the fishermen who were now back on the water. How he wished his life would let him join them.

"When *kami* of wind, water, and land did not show themselves, I called them by clapping. At last, they appeared with escorts of lesser protectors. Wind *kami* perched in the trees, while water *kami* were so numerous they blocked my view to the east."

Tennō looked with great attention over the top of his glasses. "Go on, Tadao-san."

"They did not open their mouths, but they spoke to me."

To Tadao's relief, *Tennō* seemed to understand. "What did they say?"

"They said they are not slaves to human ambitions. They said we Japanese are pompous about tradition, and we shouldn't expect to sway them with the temple. After I confessed my weak understanding of what life is, they commanded me to listen. And I did listen. I listened as if I had torn my ribs apart to expose my heart."

He explained to *Tennō* that, at times, they ranted about what humans had wrought. And their anxiety about the future riled them to such a state that he feared for his life.

"They repeated much of what the woman said," he continued, "what she said that night on the wire when she offered herself."

"On the wire?"

"Yes, *Tennō*. She balanced on a wire between two massive redwoods. She walked on it, danced on it, and jumped like an angel. But then she dove and hit the ground."

Tadao could not read *Tennō*'s response. But at least the words that had tormented him for weeks were out. "The water *kami* at Omoe said they are not upset about human suffering. But they grieve that we seem dedicated to taking all beauty down with us.

"Their last words stung. *So, Wounded Pretender, build your little temple. We cannot stop you. But don't expect much in return.*"

Forty-Three

IN THE DAYS after Delicia made her point, Governor Murphy worked to reestablish his credentials as a nature enthusiast. Even Brodie acknowledged his masterful balance of championing the need for better stewardship of Mother Earth with a perfect amount of regret and self-chastisement over "mistakes of the past." His reenergized campaign slipped past his primary challenger, and charged forward with a head of steam toward the general election.

Delicia had barely hit the ground when Ishi rocketed down his access line. There was, of course, nothing that he or anyone could do. But her choice ended his action in the trees. Drama was like that. To confirm that reality, tabloids spun crap about the modern twist on Romeo and Juliet he and Delicia had lived. Which hurt the prospects for the Pomo, and in particular Ishi's prospects with Amber.

Effectively homeless, the Dead Creek Rancheria Pomo divided along old fault lines of depression about their future. It showed in the numbers that chose to stay in Minkleville. Some, including Amber, expected their fate would remain unchanged since 1856—the government would make weak promises that they would soon find reason to forget. Expecting to literally have to rise from the ashes, they salvaged what they could on the Rancheria and began creating cover for the coming summer months with many fewer trees to help them.

Slightly less than half of the Dead Creek Pomo stayed on at Minkle's. They kept a block of toilets, moved the kitchen facility closer to the water and made it sturdier. Hearing about their exposure, a wedding banquet company gave them a worn festival tent. The Pomo rolled up the sides and pitched their tents underneath its grand shade. It seemed like a cousin to outdoor bazaars Ishi had seen in Kabul. He assumed that Murphy had pushed the county to lift its blockade of the highway access. The

Pomo pooled their income and government stipends and made do to feed themselves. The future was uncertain, but that condition was familiar to them.

Ishi mostly stayed in his trailer in town, but he pitched a tent on the land and enjoyed the times he slept within a stone's throw of Atlas and Her Majesty. For a while he visited the grove often. In the first weeks, it looked like any place after a circus had moved on. The ring in the duff that had been scraped flat and hammered hard for the performances now lay like a sore in a sacred world. Perhaps in a ritual connected with grieving, the Provisional Beckett Circus performers removed Delicia's wire and the larger infrastructure. Some of Delicia's supporters had made a half-hearted attempt to pile up the trash abandoned in the chaos of that night—jackets, coffee cups, and shoes.

Someone had driven a two-foot cross into the spot where Delicia had come to earth, which, given her nonbeliever status, seemed inappropriate. But it served as a rack to hold temporary offerings: a baseball cap, several cheap necklaces, a pair of ballerina shoes, the parasol she had used that night, and some paraphernalia that could only have come from some of the performers. Around that were the requisite candles, all burned to nubs, and cards that, as time passed, sagged with condensation dripping from redwood needles.

If, in those weeks, Ishi had had a dime for every thought that began with, *If only I had . . .* he could have taken a month off. In fact, Brodie told him to do just that, saying he was miserable to be around.

But though the passions of many of the faithful had faltered after Delicia's offering, Ishi's had not. He wrote several pieces with the intent of keeping alive the promise she'd demanded of him, of everyone. To never forget.

Ever the media realist, Brodie informed him that one memorial piece was about all the public could stand. "We do news, after all. Things that are rumbling today or that may split open tomorrow."

So as much as Ishi could, he did his thinking away from the office. The bulk of that was looking for clues in Delicia's railing and gestures that might have foretold what she was going to do. Had she planned it from the beginning? Had she fulfilled a death wish? If not, when did she seize upon jumping? And might he have been able to say or do something at that point to keep her alive? Many times, he revisited the night they had spent together, devastated that he had missed what must have been coursing through her heart.

A petition to the California legislature for granting the massacre land status as an historic site never got out of committee. As far as the lawyer Ishi had hired knew, it was never even debated.

On Independence Day, an unsubstantiated rumor started making the rounds: a joint task force of California and Japanese foresters had taken a tally of the Beckett's standing timber. This was not devastating to the Pomo who lived on-site, as they expected every day that they might hear huge trucks rumbling into Beckett to begin the final desecration that would render Delicia's life worthless.

Fortunately, though, the trees did not come down right away. Signals from Japan seemed few and weak. Ishi regularly ran searches for the Temple of Listening and still found only the original announcements of the Beckett purchase in the Japanese media.

Then in August, the emperor of Japan signaled, via emissaries, his resolve to take a few of the best redwoods in Beckett State Forest. They were to be used to build the Temple of Listening on the easternmost point of the island of Honshu, some twenty kilometers distant as the crow flies from the coastal city of Miyako.

But in a providential stroke, the emperor also resolved to guard in perpetuity the rest of the trees in Beckett as a sanctuary for the trees themselves. The land was to be known as the *Delicia Fortunado Listening Forest*. The emperor requested that funds to keep it open to the public come from the overage of Japan's preemptive bid and purchase of the land. This was to be understood as a gift to America to help her understand her duty to the earth.

"Without every country and community in the world making a statement," the emperor wrote, "humans will be hard-pressed to change their ways on the planet." Between the lines was a Japanese apology for their egregious action against the US in the 1940s.

This inspired the on-site Pomo to solicit and receive enough donations for two dumpsters and a towing service to clean up what the weekend warriors of the environmental movement had left behind. In their early optimism that events might finally turn their way, the on-site Pomo had carefully collected all the jettisoned crap that the protest and circus had created. At last, it was on its way to a landfill. Two beater cars that no one had come back to claim were hauled off, and the Pomo donated the money involved in their junking to the local radio station.

Delicia's jump had been the deciding factor in Minkle's willingness to let the Pomo buy the vineyard. But he needed a figure north of a million dollars for the 371 acres. Together with Burt from the Sebastopol band, Ishi inquired about getting loans or grants from indigenous tribes that had working casinos. From what they heard back, their financial situations were not quite as rosy as the public and their websites boasted.

Brodie toyed with the idea of shaming the casinos, but Ishi told him to back off.

"Then what's your plan?"

"You mean *after* I ream the governor's ass? I'm going to force him to push the legislature to buy the land for us."

Brodie's look carried admiration. "I have a reamer, if you want to borrow it. Size eleven. Should do the trick on most every politician."

Ishi loaded tools in his truck and drove to the Dead Creek Rancheria land. Having no trees nearby to pass flames to it, the Grandma Oak had survived the fire. It was no surprise that he found a group of Pomo resting in her shade.

He'd made fewer visits there than he had intended since coming down. But the cool mood that greeted him quickly passed when he explained that if they worked together, they had several months before the election to pressure Governor Murphy to do one right thing.

"In my father's name," he said, "let's call all the West Coast tribal nations to see if together we can mobilize one last, meaningful action against this government. Our tribe needs a home. The trees our ancestors prized are still there. Japan's payment for Beckett far exceeded what the state was expecting. There is surely a million dollars with our name on it.

And if we demonstrate decently in Sacramento for the next ninety days, I think we can finally go home."

He left them there and, on foot, went to find Amber.

Sources:

An American Genocide: *The United States and the California Indian Catastrophe:* Benjamin Madley - Yale University Press

Killing for Land in Early California: *Indian Blood at Round Valley 1856 - 1863:* Frank H. Baumgardner III - Algora Publishing

Timber Wars: Judi Bari - Common Courage Press

The Legacy of Luna: Julia Butterfly Hill - Harper Collins Press

The Last Stand: *The War Between Wall Street and Main Street over California's Ancient Redwoods:* - David Harris - Times Books

Facing the Wave: *A Journey in the Wake of the Tsunami:* Gretel Ehrlich - Pantheon Books

Grand Avenue: Greg Sarris - Hyperion

Where the Dead Sit Talking: Brandon Hobson - Soho Press, Inc.

The Removed: Brandon Hobson - Ecco

Indian Killer: Sherman Alexie - Atlantic Monthly Press

Skins: Adrian C. Louis - Ellis Press

There There: Tommy Orange - Alfred A. Knopf

Discussion Guide

1) This story brings together three distinct protagonists from different cultures. What are the roots of each one's troubles? Is embedded cultural grief different from other kinds of obstacles? Who has the most to overcome? Who makes progress?

2) Which traits held by the main characters are unique to them? Which traits do they share?

3) At what point in the story did you grasp Tadao's place and goal in the narrative? Which of the fifteen secondary characters—Brodie, Baskin etc.—stick with you? How do they contribute to the story?

4) What themes does this story explore?

5) Does Tadao's view of taking redwoods to honor Japan's victims of the earthquake, tsunami and subsequent nuclear accident have merit, or is he part of the problem Ishi and Delicia are combating? Is Tadao a sympathetic character or an antagonist? Which character(s) were you rooting for?

6) Do warfare, racism, and resource extraction have a common thread? Are awe, reverence, and magic related? How far should sacrifice go?

7) Do Indigenous peoples deserve compensation? Even if you think not, would there be justice in the Dead Creek Pomo getting their village land back?

8) Discuss the various kinds of bravery in the book. A number of characters break laws. Should all illegality be treated the same? Is morality ever black and white?

9) Is it sound logic to cut and use the redwood trees before they die and rot from climate change? What are the problems of this approach? What makes sense about it?

10) Does any character in the book embody pure evil? Is De Boulette's conduct typical of corporations? What is responsible corporate behavior?

11) Each character makes bold decisions. With which of their decisions did you disagree? Which turns of events caught you by surprise? Is Delicia at fault in Marco's death?

12) By exposing the Pomo massacre, is Brodie to blame for what happens to the characters? Is journalism to blame for consequences that flow from presenting the facts?

13) Discuss each character's view of death. Does Delicia have a death wish? Is her final choice in the story selfish? What might have become of her had she made a different decision?

14) How do you see Tadao evolving into his role in Japanese society?

15) Were you angry with Ishi for spending the night with Delicia? Will he and Amber heal their relationship? Should Amber bother? Will Ishi make a good chief?

16) Would you be tempted to attend a circus in the redwoods?

Ingram Content Group UK Ltd.
Milton Keynes UK
UKHW012012260523
422432UK00012B/102/J